FORGET
me
NOT

FORGET
me
NOT

ALYSON DERRICK

SIMON & SCHUSTER

First published in Great Britain in 2023 by Simon & Schuster UK Ltd

First published in the USA in 2023 by Simon & Schuster Books for
Young Readers, an imprint of Simon & Schuster Children's Publishing Division,
1230 Avenue of the Americas, New York, New York 10020

Text copyright © 2023 Alyson Derrick

1 3 5 7 9 10 8 6 4 2

Simon & Schuster UK Ltd
1st Floor, 222 Gray's Inn Road
London WC1X 8HB

www.simonandschuster.co.uk
www.simonandschuster.com.au
www.simonandschuster.co.in

Simon & Schuster Australia, Sydney
Simon & Schuster India, New Delhi

A CIP catalogue record for this book is available from the British Library.

PB ISBN 978-1-3985-2434-7
eBook ISBN 978-1-3985-2435-4
eAudio ISBN 978-1-3985-2436-1

For the queer kids living in a place like Wyatt.
Hang in there. It gets so much better.

FORGET
me
NOT

CHAPTER 1

I'VE SPENT MORE HOURS THAN I CAN COUNT LYING awake, finding hidden pictures in the random patterns of my popcorn ceiling.

A rack of antlers with asymmetrical drop tines. A bundle of tulips gripped tight by spindly fingers.

Most of them I've found before. After all, there's only so much to discover on a ten-by-twelve ceiling. But sometimes I see something new. Like Mom's old schoolmate Mrs. Lassam's thick-rimmed glasses, which I've been staring at for the past hour. I haven't been able to stop thinking about her since she walked out of Sunday Mass with us this morning.

The question she asked me was simple enough. *What are your plans now that you've graduated?* It should've been an easy answer, the same bullshit story I tell everyone, but I've been spending so much time thinking about my *real* plans that I almost told her the actual truth. I covered it, of course, but I could've ruined this whole thing. I need to be more careful the closer it gets.

One wrong word to the wrong person in the wrong place, and our plan will be blown to hell.

The truth is I hate keeping secrets. I always have. All they really do is tear people apart.

But this . . .

This is different.

Because this particular secret is the only thing keeping me whole.

She is the only thing keeping me whole.

I know it might sound a little extreme, but sometimes it feels like she's the only one I can be myself around, like she's the only thing holding my feet to the ground and without her, I might just forget who I really am and float away.

She's so much more than *just* a secret. She's everything to me.

For my own eye health, I force my attention away from Mrs. Lassam's glasses and flip over onto my stomach to snag my phone off the corner of my bed. *3:17 a.m.* The screen lights up with a photo of me, which I'm sure looks slightly egotistical or at least super weird from the outside. But when I look at this photo, I don't see myself. I see what I'm smiling at: the photographer.

I see Nora.

Instead of my long, dark-chocolate hair, I see her dirty-blond, chin-length cut, which she's forever regathering into a mini-ponytail at the back of her head. Instead of my sharp jaw-line and bony shoulders, I see her two dimples, set deep into the freckled cheeks of her round face, and her strong arms.

Even though every part of her is forever carved into my mind, tonight, after what almost happened after Mass, it's not enough to just imagine her. I need more.

I slide out from underneath my blue-and-white-striped comforter and tiptoe silently across the carpet to my desk. Somewhere along the top shelf is a thin orange granite rock, lodged in the gap between two sections of wood. Slipping it out, I crouch down on the floor and stick an edge into one of the screws holding the metal vent over the air duct. They take longer to unscrew than they used to. After being taken out about a million times, the little crosses are almost stripped down to perfect circles. Honestly, I should probably replace them with fresh ones soon so they don't draw any attention.

Quietly, I set the vent cover on the floor beside me, then carefully reach inside the duct to remove an orange shoe box. Without fail, the familiar worn corners and peeling Scotch tape send my heart pounding. I glance back at my closed bedroom door before turning on my flashlight and removing the lid. Inside is a mess of handwritten letters and photographs but also things that wouldn't mean anything to anyone other than the two of us.

The blue-and-yellow tassel off Nora's graduation cap from Wyatt High, the local public school that's about ten minutes from the Catholic school I attended. An empty movie theater popcorn bag from when we drove into the city to go on our first *real* date. The stretched-out yellow hair tie she gave me off her wrist the first time we had sex, all arms and legs in the backseat of my Volvo, tucked deep into the woods on her family farm. A winning lottery ticket we found in a deserted parking lot the other night and vowed to cash in once we finally get out of here at the end of summer, when we can be together.

This box. It's the only physical evidence I have of our two-year relationship, everything precious to me. If someone found this, they'd know *everything*, which is exactly why it needs to stay hidden for the next two months.

At the very bottom of the pile, I find what I've really been looking for: my favorite photo of Nora. It's a small rectangular Polaroid, shot in black-and-white so it seems fifty years older than it actually is. We decided when we first started dating almost two years ago that it would be safer for us to only capture memories via Polaroids. No digital evidence for someone to find on either of our phones.

In the photo Nora's treading water, shoulder-deep in the crick when it flooded last spring. Her wet hair is hanging down around her face in messy tangles, and her mouth is open just enough to see the teeny-tiny gap in her front teeth. She looks sexy. You'd never guess her mouth is open because she's about to announce the gnarly wedgie she has.

I hear the creak of my parents' bed and jerk my head up to the wall we share. I freeze for a second, listening, but no other sounds escape their room, so it's probably just one of them rolling over. Even so, time to put this stuff away. I drop the photo hastily into the box and place it back in the duct behind the vent, then wiggle the rock back into my desk, like nothing is there, nothing happened at all.

I hurry back to my bed, my heart beating in my ears. What if that wasn't just one of them rolling over in bed? What if one of them had walked in here and seen me? I just keep replaying different scenarios in my head and the longer I lie here, the worse the reactions become.

I can't do this anymore tonight. I need sleep if I'm going to make it through another long day of holding this all in. And I know there's only one thing that's going to calm me down enough to get there. I just hope she doesn't mind. This'll be the second time in the past week that I'll be calling and waking her up.

I dial Nora's number, my fingers automatically gliding over the screen as if I'm entering my passcode. I burrow deep under my covers, then stick my phone between my ear and the mattress.

"Hey, babe." Her voice sounds after a few rings, extra raspy from being woken up, and extra cute. "Can't sleep, huh?" she asks, even though she knows I can't answer, not with my parents on the other side of my paper-thin walls. Luckily, she doesn't have to worry about that, because her bedroom is all the way up in the attic of her oversized farmhouse. Not that I've ever actually seen it.

"You know how I've been on that environmental documentary kick?" she asks rhetorically.

I nod to myself, feeling slightly guilty for not having watched the two she sent me . . . but not guilty enough to actually watch them.

"Okay, well, I just watched this one about meat and it was *so* mind-boggling . . ." She goes on, telling me all she's learned about the meat industry's effect on the environment. "Anyway, I'm thinking about going vegan," she finishes, and I can't help but let out the quietest laugh at that.

"I know. I know." She giggles. "Says the girl whose mom runs the biggest beef farm in the county. That'd probably be more of a blow to her than . . ." She laughs again, but this one sounds different, forced.

She goes back to the documentary, telling me all the little details about it. She talks and I just listen.

One thing I love about Nora is that she oozes passion. Pure unfiltered passion, for *all* kinds of things. It's easy to get excited when you're around her, even about stuff you never cared about before.

Sometimes if I really can't sleep, she'll talk to me like this for hours on end, and somehow, she always manages to find things that are worth saying.

Despite how much I like listening, her soothing voice manages to melt the tension I've been holding in my muscles all night, and after half an hour or so, my eyelids finally begin to grow heavy. And even though Nora would never admit it, I'm sure she wouldn't mind being able to go back to sleep right now.

"And don't get me started on deforestation. That's a whole other—" She stops midsentence when I softly clear my throat into the phone.

"Okay. Good night, Stevie. I'll see you tomorrow." She pauses; then, ever so softly, she whispers, "I *love* you," as if she's saying it into my ear. She doesn't just sling it around like she's said it as many times as she actually has. She says it like she means it, each word encased in her whole heart.

I want to say it back to her. I want to say it so badly my throat aches, but I know I can't.

Not even in a whisper.

Not here.

CHAPTER 2

—————

THE FIRST THING I DO WHEN I WAKE UP IN THE morning is check my Instagram message requests, and sure enough, I have a new one from an account with no followers, no posts, and no profile picture. FarmGirl8217, aka Nora. Not the world's most clever handle, but she was barely sixteen when she came up with it, and I'm the only one who ever sees it.

Can you meet me any earlier this morning? I have news!

My heart leaps, but then immediately deflates when I remember that I already promised Savannah and Rory I'd meet them for breakfast. Even though I could cancel, even though I *want to* cancel, I need to keep up some semblance of normalcy with other people in my life or they might get suspicious. And considering I already ghosted them on Friday . . .

Noon is the earliest I can come today :/ News!? Tell me! I type back.

I'll tell you when I see you.

Nora! Tell me now! It's about the apartment isn't it? Did we get it???

We missed out on our first choice, but the next one we applied for isn't *so* bad.

I'll see you at noon ;) she replies after a minute.

I roll my eyes and let out a grumble as I delete the conversation. Nora *loves* surprises, and I . . . can't stand them.

The moment I step out of my bedroom door, my mood is instantly killed further by the voices of a couch full of Fox News anchors carrying up the stairs. I thought my dad would be at work by now. Normally I'd give it a few minutes until the TV clicks off, but I have to get down there and get going or I'll be late for breakfast and that'll make me late for Nora. So I take a deep breath, grit my teeth, and descend the stairs into the living room.

"This guy." The brown leather couch creaks as my dad turns around to face me, dressed in a semiclean set of coveralls with GREEN'S AUTO REPAIR printed across the back in cracked vinyl lettering. "This guy ain't nobody's fool. Not like those idiots on CNN," he finishes, his thumb pointed over his broad shoulders.

I tense my jaw, biting back a snide comment. It feels like I have to do that more and more these days, and I'm not sure if he's getting more intolerant or I'm just becoming less tolerant of him.

"Morning," I force out instead, but he's already leaning back in toward the TV, which is mounted on the wall between two deer heads. He's not even listening.

Good talk.

It wasn't like this when I was growing up. Back then we actually enjoyed each other's company. He'd let me run the switch on the car lift at the garage all day, or rent a small aluminum boat and take me out fishing on the reservoir, just the two of us. He listened. But that was before Nora, before I understood just how toxic some of his beliefs are. And before he became so obsessed with these talking heads that nothing I said could ever change his mind.

When I set our plan in motion, I didn't foresee that I'd have much trouble at all leaving him behind, considering I can barely stand to be around him now. But somehow I still feel sad about that.

I shake off the thought as I grab my car keys off the hook and head out the front door.

But just as it swings open—*Oof.*

I almost run smack into my mom on the front porch. She's clutching a green plastic watering can in one small hand and in the other is the WORLD'S BEST MOM mug that I got her a million years ago.

"Whoa, careful, sweetie." Her dark brown eyes widen over sun-spotted cheeks as she holds her mug out to steady the sloshing coffee.

"Sorry. I uh . . . didn't think you'd be here," I say, surprised to see her. It would normally take a plague of locusts to keep that lady from her Monday-morning prayer group.

"I decided to play hooky today. I was hoping you and I could hang out for breakfast."

"I actually have to go," I reply before I let myself even think about it, slipping past her off the porch, eyes locked on my black car parked in the driveway.

"I thought you didn't start work until noon today. Where are you headed?" she asks from behind me.

"I'm meeting Savannah and Rory at the Dinor," I tell her,

continuing to walk toward my car. The misspelling is so common around this part of Pennsylvania that it didn't even strike me as wrong until my sophomore year.

"Well, wait. What time do you get off?" she asks, making me turn around, but I keep my eyes on the stained mug in her hand, focusing on a white chip in the green paint. "The summer farmers' market opens today—I was thinking . . . maybe you could help me pick out a few flowers for the front step?" She motions with the mug to the bare concrete step I just walked down. There's a big part of me that wishes we *could* do that together. Before I can stop myself, I meet her eyes and they absolutely light up as she misinterprets it as an opening. "And then after, maybe we could take a drive out to that bistro we used to go to all the time! Or head over to Dairy Qu–"

"Yeah, probably not." I cut her off, trying not to think about that killer chicken sandwich and laughing at our old booth in the corner. She physically deflates before I can look away. *Shit.* Why does she have to make this so hard? "I have to stay a little later today, we're training a new barista," I lie . . . again.

"Oh. Of course." She shakes her head like it's nothing, like she believes me. "You're busy."

"You have a ton of flowers anyways." I try to change the subject, looking around at the slew of potted plants lining the edge of the porch.

She pulls her cheeks up, the straight line of her lips forming a small smile, but all she says is "Have a nice time with your friends," then turns her back to me.

I hesitate there for a second, my feet feeling like concrete blocks. It would be so easy to slip back into the past, to go to the farmers' market and Lola's Bistro and Dairy Queen, pretend like I'm still the girl she wants me to be, someone she would be proud of.

But things are different now. *She* made them different, I remind myself. I've spent the past year building up this space between the two of us, but she's the one who started it. I'm just making everything easier for when the time comes. Easier for her *and* me. Because come August, we won't be a part of each other's lives any longer. So I pick up my feet and continue toward my car.

Still, the guilt bubbles up inside me more and more with every step, so I try to picture Nora and me in California. And when the visual forms, it reminds me that it'll be worth it. That my real life begins when we get out of here. Together.

The moment I open the heavy metal door into the Dinor, I'm hit with a wave of voices, each one desperately trying to be heard over the next. The warm yellow lights illuminate the white tables and red booths, all filled with customers. I love coming here for breakfast because it's packed to the gills every single morning, a reminder that this town still has some life left in it. It's a sharp contrast to the storefronts on either side, both plastered with sun-faded pages from the *Wyatt Argus*, a newspaper that doesn't even exist anymore.

I pause in front of the ancient gumball machine, where you can win a free cup of coffee if you can manage to snag the color of the week, but ultimately, I decide to pass. Last time I got one, it was so old and hard that it honestly might've been a jawbreaker. The jury is still out. Besides, I do technically work at a coffee shop, so free coffee isn't that much of a prize.

I scan the busy dining room and finally spot Savannah's fiery ginger hair at a booth next to one of the large windows. It was easier when she had an absolute mane of curls, but right before senior year, she decided they weren't *in*. So she's been flat-ironing them every day since, which must take forever.

"I don't remember, it's honestly a blur," Rory is saying as I approach. She throws herself back up against the booth in laughter, her messy bun bobbing around on top of her head. "Stevie!" she says as I slide in opposite them. "Oh my God. You missed the greatest party of all time."

"What happened?" I ask, though I highly doubt I missed much of anything at Jake Mackey's graduation party on Friday. I really don't see why Savannah is with him.

Rory sighs, shaking her head. "You couldn't even . . ." She laughs into Savannah, who clutches her arm, giggling and nodding so hard that I worry her head might fall off. "*Right?*" Rory says to her.

"You kind of had to be there," Savannah finishes, trying to get herself under control, wiping tears away with a paper towel off the roll at the end of the table. "Speaking of which, I can't believe they made you stay so late you couldn't even celebrate your own graduation with your best friends. That job is practically slave labor," she says.

Savannah. I bite the inside of my cheek until I taste metal. It's like she doesn't think at all about what things mean before she says them.

"It isn't so bad," I tell her, remembering that night. Nora

and me lying in my car with the seats reclined, watching stars dot the sky through the moonroof, Phoebe Bridgers's ghostly voice singing softly through the speakers while we continued planning our future.

"Well, I'm just saying we miss you. I mean, I remember when we used to spend every single weekend together."

We did, back when we were young enough to want to build forts in the woods behind Rory's house. Before Savannah started dating the lovely Jake Mackey, who once jingled around a handful of coins in front of my face and told me that's how they name kids in China, and all the two of them did was *laugh*.

Savannah continues as if it's all still the same. "It's been the three of us since preschool, and this is our last summer before college. It's already June, and I know *you're* not getting out of Wyatt, but I'm going to be all the way across the state in Philly come August, and Rory's heading to some school in North Carolina," she says, tucking her hair behind her ear to reveal a big hoop earring.

"UNC." Rory karate-chops her hand against the table with each letter. "They have a great biomedical research program. How many times do I have to tell you that?"

Savannah knows that Rory is attending UNC. She just likes to get under her skin. And despite Rory's sky-high SAT scores, she still hasn't figured that out yet. It's always been that way, even when we were kids.

Savannah ignores Rory's fuming and speaks directly to me. "My point is that even though *you're* not leaving town, *we* are, and things won't be the same. I just want to make sure we get to spend some of this time together."

Maybe a year ago, that would've made me feel some pang of guilt or remorse, but not now.

You have no idea, I want to tell her. I want to tell her that *nothing* could keep me in this town. That in a few months I'm going to be farther away than either of them, so far out of Wyatt they'll never see me again. I want to tell them both they don't even know the real me, not anymore.

But I would never do anything to jeopardize our plans. I can almost hear Nora telling me, *Hang in there. This is all temporary*. I just have to keep this up for two more months.

"Look, I'll really try to make more time. That's my bad," I say, glancing between the two of them, trying to seem sorry.

The server comes from behind me and breaks up our conversation as he sets down a short stack of pancakes in front of each of them.

"Hope you don't mind that we ordered, but we were *starving*," Rory explains as they both drench their pancakes in maple syrup.

"What can I get for you?" the server asks. Ryan. I recognize his voice immediately, much different than Pat's ten-packs-a-day rasp. I look up to see him smiling down at me, his silky black hair swooping down over his forehead, just above his light-brown eyes.

I open my mouth to order, but he stops me. "Wait, wait." He looks up into his head, tapping his pen against his temple a couple of times. "Two eggs over medium, bacon, hash browns, and . . . rye, no butter?" he asks, scrunching his face up.

"Close. Wheat," I correct him, grinning.

"Gah! Next time," he assures me, scribbling my order down

in a messy shorthand. "I'll have that out for you stat so you don't fall behind." He motions subtly to my friends' plates and then disappears into the kitchen.

When I look back at Savannah and Rory, they're both smirking coyly at me. "What?" I ask, looking between them.

"I've tried so hard to stay out of it, but *girl*." Savannah rolls her eyes, shoving a bite of pancake into her mouth. "You're killing me."

"What?" I repeat, slightly irritated now.

"He's totally into you!" Rory practically shouts across the entire restaurant.

"Oh, shut up," I scoff, waving them both away, my face turning red.

"What, you're not into him? I think he's cute, for . . ." Savannah shrugs without finishing that thought. But when I don't say anything back, she leans over her pancakes, her hair almost dragging through a puddle of melted butter and maple syrup, and completes it. "Is it because he's . . . *Asian*? Is that why you're not interested?" she stage-whispers. I glance over my shoulder to make sure he didn't hear, but thank God this place is filled with the sound of so many forks hitting plates it seems to have drowned her out.

"Savannah, *I'm* Asian."

I look over at Rory, hoping for some backup, but all I get is an apathetic shrug. "I mean, yeah, but like . . . not really. He's like *Asian*, Asian," she says, peeking over my shoulder.

I guess they only consider me half Korean when there's an opportunity for them to laugh at someone's racist joke. Maybe that's the reason I've felt so comfortable around Ryan ever since he started working here a year ago. He didn't go to our school, so I don't really know him, like . . . at all. But he's the only other Asian kid in the whole town, and we've exchanged the kinds of looks over the off-color things customers say here that tell me he gets it.

The thing is that he *is* really cute. If Wyatt wasn't the kind of place where there's a distinction between "cute" and "cute for being Asian," he'd probably have girls lined up at the door to go out with him.

Just not me . . . obviously.

The two of them finally take the hint that I don't want to talk about this anymore and move back to the previous topics of discussion: the party, Savannah's boyfriend, and . . . some other things that I don't even hear because I've stopped listening.

When my food comes, I start to shovel it down. The sooner I finish, the sooner I can get out of here to go see Nora and hear her news. But then I force myself to take a deep breath between bites so it isn't obvious.

"Stevie? Yes or no?" Rory asks.

"Huh?" I look up at her, confused.

"You want to go to the outlets with us today, or not?" she repeats, clearly annoyed this time.

I shake my head, pulling twelve bucks out of my wallet. "No, sorry, guys, I have—"

"—to work," Savannah says with me. Of course I don't have to today, but that's the reason I got a job at a coffee shop two towns away. I knew no one would ever venture over there, and so they'd never find out that I'm only there for about ten of the twenty hours I say I am.

"Stevie. Work, *again*? Are you serious?" Rory asks, drooping her shoulders.

"Tomorrow. Let's do something tomorrow, okay? I'll text you," I assure them.

"You better! Or I'll come to that coffee shop myself and tell your boss you're stealing . . . I don't know, Splenda or some shit. Then we'll have you all to ourselves," Savannah says, pointing her fork threateningly in my direction.

"I promise." I hold my hands up in surrender as I slide out of the booth to leave, but I'm already thinking about how to get out of that, too.

CHAPTER 3

TEN MINUTES LATER MY VOLVO BOUNCES DOWN THE overgrown dirt roads that run along the farthest edge of the Martin farm, where the hundreds of acres of sprawling fields start to give way to the thick, green forest. You can tell no one ever really comes back here other than me, because the weeds crawl so far over the road that they skim the sides of my car, a constant reminder to me that we're safe here.

I pull off into a small nook, where Mother Nature finally got used to my visits and stopped growing. The moment I step out of my car into the fresh air and hear the rushing of the crick in the distance, I feel lighter.

The sound gets louder as I weave my way through the massive trees, gnarled branches and vines twisting together above my head. I walk for a hundred yards, until the forest opens up to a grassy bank. The wildflowers we planted are finally starting to sprout up, all long leafy blades and green buds waiting for their moment to bloom.

And there, sitting among them . . . is Nora.

The moment I see her, the muscles running up the back of my neck finally relax, through no conscious act of my own, and the layer of anxiety that usually sits underneath every one of my thoughts seems to completely melt away.

I notice a thin purple bra strap hanging out of her white tank top as I walk around a cluster of white birch trees with thin bark peeling away like old paint. I crouch down behind her and slip it up onto her shoulder, my thumb dipping into the hollow of her collarbone.

With one touch, finally, I can breathe again.

I kiss her neck.

Her soft jaw.

Her cheek.

And finally, I trace my lips up to her ear.

"I love you, too," I whisper, the words I've desperately wanted to say back to her since our phone call last night, the ones that have been circling through every thought since.

The corner of her mouth pulls up into a smirk as she turns her head toward me, her lips finding mine.

"Shouldn't you be crafting nonfat caramel macchiatos?" she teases into my smile. I wrap my arms around her, twisting her tiny ponytail around in my fingers.

"Shouldn't you be baling hay?" I prod, slipping into our usual routine.

"We don't even grow hay, genius. And for your information, I'm supposed to be pulling fence," she replies, but when I lean back I see that she's serious this time.

"Wait, really?" I ask, the muscles in my body tensing up again. "Nora, I thought you were off today!"

She shakes her head. "Stevie, it's *fine*. Relax. I didn't want to wait, so I got something worked out with Albert. He's gonna do it today," she says.

"What do you mean? What'd you tell him?" I ask, picturing nineteen-year-old Amish Albert blurting our secrets as we speak.

"I just asked him to switch shifts. It's really not a big deal. Trust me." She laughs to try to lighten the mood as she reaches out for my arm, but I push her hand away.

"You promised me you wouldn't do something like this. It's too risky. What if he followed you? What if he figures it out or says something to someone? Or God, Nora, what if your *mom* finds out? What if she sees him doing your work? She . . . she'd . . ." I fall back onto my butt, my hands dropping between us.

"Stevie, stop. Please." She scoops my shaking hands up in hers, firm, solid. "I just really wanted to see you today, okay? I'm sorry. I won't do it ever again. I'm sorry. I'm sorry. I'm sorry," she says, kissing my hands between each *sorry*. She places them up over her shoulders and I lock my fingers behind her neck.

"We're just . . . we're *so* close. I don't want to mess it all up now." We lock eyes and I find myself wishing I could just keep my arms around her, keep her safe forever.

"I know. I'll be more careful, okay? Please don't cry." She tucks my long hair behind my ears and pulls my face toward her. "I'm sorry," she whispers again, catching the tip of my nose with hers.

Then she kisses me hard, her fingers sliding into my hair.

I close my eyes and breathe deep, taking in the familiar smell of the mud and the grass, her skin in the hot summer air as we kiss. It would be an understatement to say I haven't been too crazy about this town the past couple of years, but this particular place, these woods, with the sun shining perfectly through the canopy . . .

I love it here.

"You think you'll miss this?" I ask after a while, pulling my lips away from hers.

"I don't know." She pauses, rolling her forehead back and forth against mine as the crickets chirp all around us. "Yeah. Maybe a little. Will you?"

I feel a push and pull on my heart. Even with all the things I don't love about it, I've never known any place *but* Wyatt. Yes, Nora and I can't stay here, hiding away in this perfect patch of forest forever, pretending the rest of the town doesn't exist. We both know that, but it doesn't make it any less scary to leave it all behind. When most people leave town after high school, they do it knowing they'll always be welcomed back. But the fact is that in a few months, Nora and I will be leaving our families and the only place we've ever called home. For good.

"Maybe a little," I repeat back to her. We sit there for a minute, heads pressed together, but then another thought occurs to me. "You remember that first night we met? We were lying on the floor of the basketball court at my school and all the lights were off, and you reached over and took my hand, laced your fingers in mine."

"I remember," she says, sliding her fingertips over my palm.

"Before that, I had never had feelings for anyone. Not even a little. I thought maybe I was just broken or something. It didn't seem like there was any other answer. And then you, this girl who I had just met, took my hand. So simple. And something just switched on inside me that I didn't know *could* switch on, and everything finally made sense. But when I think about it now it almost wasn't even about being gay or whatever, it was about *you*."

Nora smiles at the memory but raises an eyebrow. "Why are you telling me this?"

"I guess because I just wanted to say even if there *are* things I'll miss, I'm not scared to leave Wyatt. As long as I can leave with you. It sounds corny, but I'm realizing that Wyatt doesn't feel like my home anymore. You do."

"My little *cheeseball*." She smirks for just a second before her mouth falls into a straight, serious line, her growing pupils looking directly into mine. "I love you," she says, kissing me again. "If we do miss it, babe, we'll miss it together. Okay?" She shuffles up onto her worn boots and holds her hands out for me to take, lifting me up too.

We start walking down our path. The same path we always take out here, the only one carved out in the thickness of the brush. I follow her along the crick, over rocks, and around the areas where the dirt has eroded away. Sticks crackle under our feet, and shadows slide across them as birds swoop overhead.

"Wow. She isn't even remotely interested in my big news," Nora says innocently.

I let out an audible gasp and she smirks over her shoulder at me.

"I completely forgot! Spill!" I yell, jogging a couple of steps to catch up to her as she stops and turns to face me. She's grinning from ear to ear, which has me doing the same even though I don't know if I'm right about what she's planning to tell me.

"We got the studio!"

Her smile widens as she watches me process.

"Wait . . . you mean, our first choice? The one with the green walls and tiny bathroom?" I ask, guarding my excitement until she nods. "Nuh-uh! I thought they went with someone else!"

"I guess it fell through." She shrugs. "If we can pay first month's rent and a security deposit by Friday, it's all ours, babe."

"Oh my *God*, we're gonna have an apartment!" I throw my arms around her and she lifts me off the ground like I weigh nothing, even though I have almost two inches on her. This is everything we've been waiting for. The last thing we had to figure out. "So when's our move-in date?" I ask as I loosen my grip around her and my feet touch back down to the dirt.

"September tenth."

"Yikes. That's cutting it pretty close with the start of the semester."

"I know, but at least it means we can keep working and saving up a little longer. Maybe we'll even have enough to splurge on that wooden Ikea island that you're always—"

"Ooo! Can we!? Can we get it?" I ask, grabbing pleadingly onto the front of her shirt.

"I already have it added to my cart," she replies.

I let out an excited squeal as I wrap my arm around her waist and walk beside her along the path again.

"I love this feeling," Nora says as we step over a tree branch together.

"What feeling?" I ask as she smiles up to the sky.

"Like . . . my life is finally about to start after being on pause for the last eighteen years. I never thought I could look forward to my future so much. I guess I never really thought I'd even have one. But now, moving across the country. A new apartment. Maybe someday a house on a farm. A wedding. Having kids! I mean . . . it's *so* cool that it's not just possible, but beginning. And I get to do it all with . . ." She shakes her head and smiles. "I get to do it all with *you*. I mean, are you fucking kidding me? It feels like a dream. Doesn't it?"

I make her stop on the trail long enough to kiss her. "You're cute. Now who's being a cheeseball?"

"I'm serious."

"I know. And I love hearing you talk about our future." I walk into her, making her step back until she's pinned up against a tree, and then I dip my lips down to hers for a longer kiss. Her hands wrap around my back as I pull away. "You really think we can have kids someday?"

"Well, yeah . . . ," she says as I go in for another kiss, but her lips are pulled into a mischievous smile instead. "But slow down, because we can't make them like this."

I laugh at that and pull her away from the tree, back onto the path.

"So should I pay the money for the apartment tonight?" I ask.

"Considering all my money is in cash in a cigar box under my bed . . ."

"Yeah, I'll pay it tonight." I shake my head at her. "You know, you're going to have to open a bank account eventually, Nora," I tell her *again*. She refuses to, because her mom has been paying her under the table in cash for so long that she thinks the IRS is going to come after her or something . . . I don't know.

"So, I've really been thinking a lot about that last documentary I watched . . . ," she starts, ignoring my comment and enthusiastically swinging around a skinny tree to face me. "I think I'm going to do it, babe, I'm really going to try the veganism thing. Did you know it takes over six hundred gallons of water to produce *one* hamburger? The way we eat is killing the planet, and I probably eat more meat than most people out there. I mean, I know beef is like water to us Martins, and it's basically the only thing I survive on, but pretty soon we'll be out of here and it just seems like such a small sacrifice that does so much good and . . ." I catch her face in my hands before she can doubt herself any more, and her hazel eyes meet mine.

"I believe in you," I tell her, and I do. "Plus, you'll have us looking like we actually belong in California." I tickle her in the stomach, and she jumps out of reach but almost trips on a rotting stump in the process.

The path grows more uneven the farther we walk and the bank gradually lifts higher from the surface of the crick, but the water gets deeper and wider as we near the reservoir.

"Whoa," Nora says. "This is new." Soon we're standing about fifteen feet above the crick, looking at a fallen oak tree stretching the whole way across the ravine. I walk over to inspect the woven maze of roots that was unearthed when it fell, leaving behind a six-foot-wide crater, but Nora is eyeing the trunk.

"Come on. Don't." I reach for the bottom of her shorts, but she has already leapt onto it and taken a few steps out so that she's hovering over the ravine.

"It's sturdy. See." She jumps up and down, but her boots

knock pieces of bark through the air and into the coursing water down below in a way that's not that convincing.

"Nora, please?" I plead, holding my palms out toward her as if I can will her to come back . . . like that's ever worked before.

I watch in silence, my stomach doing flips as she takes another ten confident steps, putting her halfway across. She makes it look as simple as walking down the sidewalk, but I still hold my breath until she makes it safely to the far bank.

"Your turn!" she shouts, her voice echoing with the rush of the water between us. I peek over the edge and quickly step backward to a safe distance. Nora cups her hands around her mouth. "You want to live your life playing it safe or take a little risk once in a while?"

"Playing it safe!" I yell back without hesitation.

She grins. "Come on! We can walk back on this side, maybe try to find a new path while we still can!"

"Sometimes I hate that can-do spirit of yours!" I shout, forcing myself to step out onto the thick trunk. Obviously she's not going to budge on this one.

"You'll thank me someday." She laughs and watches as I move across, one three-inch step at a time. I want to say *I doubt that*, but each step uses all my concentration.

I try to focus only on the tree under my feet, but my eyes keep refocusing on the water a full story below.

The tree.

The water.

The tree.

The water.

My breath hitches in my lungs as a gust of wind blows

through the ravine. I crouch down to steady myself, digging my fingers into the shallow grooves of the bark. A splinter jabs under my fingernail, but I barely feel it at all.

"Stevie," Nora calls from somewhere too far away. "You're okay."

You're okay. You're okay, I repeat over and over in my head, and then quietly under my breath.

"Hey, Stevie, look at me," she says. Slowly, I pick my head up to find her crouched down on the other end of the tree, just a couple of yards away. "Good." She smiles. "Just keep your eyes on me, babe." Her voice is even, but tense.

"Okay," I croak.

I stand up again on my jelly legs, then remind myself to breathe with each step. As much as my eyes want to look down, I force them to stay glued to Nora.

My legs turn to jelly again for a different reason as I take her in.

The way the sun illuminates the strands of hair that have broken loose from her ponytail.

The light smattering of summer freckles that are just beginning to show themselves.

The way she grins at me, making me feel invincible. Like I could do anything, go anywhere, as long as I have her by my side.

And before I know it, I'm stepping down off the tree.

"What did I tell you?" Nora smirks. "Cake."

Before I can celebrate my triumph, though, the atmosphere around me changes.

Something's not right.

I watch as Nora's entire face completely transforms.

Her eyes go wide. Her nostrils flare. Her jaw hangs open.

The ground under my feet shifts, and I look down to see that I'm standing on a big rock now only partially lodged in the wall of dirt.

And just as I take this in, it tilts under me even more and starts to slide down the steep bank.

My center of gravity shifts. It feels as if the oxygen has been sucked clean out of the air between us. Everything moves in slow motion.

Nora's hand shoots toward me, veins pulsing under her tan skin.

I desperately reach for her, but my fingertips barely graze hers.

And then I'm free-falling backward, my whole body in thin air.

I squeeze my eyes shut as the blue sky blurs into the trees, into a wall of mud.

The very last sound I hear over the rushing water is the one that's usually my favorite, Nora saying my name. But this time she's screaming it and there's pure terror filling up every part of her voice, turning it all wrong.

June 18

Dear Stevie,

I don't know if this journal is going to make me feel any better, but I have to talk to someone and the only person I can talk to is you, even if you can't hear me. I just got back from the hospital. It's been six days since the accident and they still have you in an induced coma. I met your parents. It was weird. It is weird. That they know I even exist at all. But even more that they don't know that you're everything to me. Your mom seems really nice. I see why it'd be hard to think about letting her go. Despite everything, I can tell she really loves you.

Sometimes when they both leave, I sneak into your room for a couple of minutes to hold your hand. I know you'd probably give me shit for being too risky, but you don't know what it's like to be here with you . . . without you.

I so wish it was me in that bed, because it should be. This is all my fault. You didn't want to do it. You told me you didn't want to do it. I am so fucking sorry. I'm sorry, Stevie. Please wake up.

I love you,
Nora

June 23

Dear Stevie,

It's been eleven days. I overheard the doctor today and she said they're waiting for you to wake up now. I really need you to wake up. I need you to be okay. I can't do this without you now that I know everything life could be. I miss the sound of your laugh. I miss the way you twist your fingers around in my ponytail. I miss being woken up by your middle-of-the-night phone calls when you can't even say anything.

Please wake up. Please. I love you. I want to hear you say it back to me.

Nora

CHAPTER 4

*B*EEP. BEEP. BEEP. BEEP. BEEP. BEEP.

My alarm blares right next to my head. I reach out, swatting at it, trying to get that god-awful sound to stop, but my hand keeps cutting straight through the air where my nightstand should be.

"Sweetie." I hear my mom's soft voice from beside me.

Five more minutes, I try to say, but it comes out all garbled, complete nonsense.

She runs her fingers gently down the side of my face. I try to lift my other hand to bat her away, but my arm gets all tangled up in my bedsheets.

"Stevie, can you hear me?" she asks, her hand still pressed against my face.

"Mom. *Five more minutes,*" I say again, and this time it's audible, but it sounds like my throat is filled with gravel.

And *jeez,* that alarm. I start to rip free from the sheets to shut it off, but two strong hands clamp down on me, pinning my arms firmly to the bed. I try to open my eyes, but they just *won't.*

"Get off me!" I grunt, tossing and turning my whole body around the bed. "What are you doing?" My throat is on fire, and I can't breathe.

I need to get up.

I need to get these hands *off* me.

"Stevie, stop!" my dad's voice yells as the grip on my forearms readjusts. His grip, I realize.

"Mr. Green, please," says a woman's voice I don't recognize. Calm, collected. "Stevie, you need to stop fighting." I can feel her hovering over me now. Right in front of my face. "You're in the hospital. You're okay."

Hospital?

I feel my chest heaving, then everything constricts around my lungs, making me panic more. The sound of my mom's crying fills the room.

I try to open my eyes and this time they respond. But everything on the other side is too bright when I even take a peek and I have to clamp them shut again.

I try again to pull my arms free, but it's no use. I don't have any strength left in me, and soon darkness pulls me back under.

When I come to again, I hear my dad's muffled voice on the phone. I can only pick up every few words . . . *upset . . . sedated . . . waiting . . .*

Behind my eyelids my eyes are burning. I spend a few minutes forcing the lids open a sliver at a time. Eventually, the light seems to dim and everything starts coming into focus.

Finally, I register that there's a soft hand resting over mine, familiar, comforting. *Mom.* I turn my own over, grabbing onto her with as much force as I can muster.

All of a sudden she pops up from where she must have been resting her head on the side of my bed and looks at me like I've never seen her look at me before, tears pouring over her cheeks.

Mom? I try to say, but nothing comes out. I open my mouth to speak again, and she shushes me.

"Don't talk, baby," she whispers in a shaky voice, then turns away from me. "John. John! Get the doctor." She looks back at me, taking my hand and holding it up to her mouth. I notice a thin clear tube sticking out of my skin. I follow it up to a bag of clear liquid hanging on a metal rack.

My lungs start to heave again, up and down, as my eyes wander around the room: electrical knobs on white walls, a stainless-steel sink set into a teal countertop, a vinyl recliner tucked into the corner.

I look down at myself as much as I'm able to, lying flat on my back. Enough to see the sea-green gown covering my body and the pink fuzzy socks on my feet.

Hospital, I remember hearing.

"Mom?" I cry, barely more than a whisper. *What's wrong with me?* I want to ask, but I can't get it out.

A strong sterile smell hits me in a wave all at once, just as a middle-aged lady in a white coat enters the room. She hurries over to my bed, and I try to scooch away to the other side as I clutch my mom's hand for dear life.

The lady takes a step back from me. "It's okay, Stevie," she says, holding her empty palms out to me. "My name is Maggie." My eyes drop down onto the dark-blue monogrammed lettering on her pocket. MARGARET REICHER, MD.

My mom runs her hand up my arm and onto my shoulder, keeping me in place.

"Stevie." The doctor pulls my attention back to her face.

"You've been in a bad accident . . ." is all I hear her say, before the sound goes out.

An accident?

I look to the side at my mom, then notice my dad next to her, one big hand clamped onto her shoulder, the other one covering his mouth. *How could I have been in a car accident?* I inspect my parents again. They look fine.

"Stevie. Stevie, can you hear me? Do you remember my name?" a voice says from my left.

I blink hard, looking up again at the lady in a white coat next to me.

"Mary. Margie . . . MarrrrrrRRRR," I groan as a searing pain cuts through the back of my head.

"Is she okay?" my dad asks, worry filling his deep voice. I turn my head into the pillow, squeezing my eyes shut until the fog of pain clears enough for me to open them.

"Stevie. Can you hear me?" the woman asks again. I look up at her, and she continues. "My name is Maggie," she says in the same calm tone of voice.

Maggie. Right. "You've been in an accident. Do you know what happened to you?" she asks. I just squint at her in reply, my eyelids feeling heavy. "You fell, and you hit your head. You've been in an induced coma for the past two weeks, healing."

What the hell? A coma? No. That doesn't make any sense. I was just with Savannah and Rory—

"Stevie, I'm going to do a few tests. Is that okay?" She takes a pen-shaped tool out of her pocket and holds it up for me to see. When I don't answer, she moves closer, leaning over me.

She drags it over my arms, my stomach, and down my legs,

across the bottoms of my feet, asking me again and again, "Can you feel this?"

I nod, tracking a light pressure running up and down my body.

"What about this?" She runs her fingers down my cheeks, across my forehead. I nod again, feeling frozen in place, like a slab of meat on a cutting board, being poked and prodded. I just want her to take her hands off me.

She sits down beside me on the bed and clicks the end of her pen. A bright white light moves in front of my eyes, making me squeeze them shut.

"Can you tell me your name?" she asks. *Of course I know my name.* I clear my hoarse throat and suck my lips into my mouth, trying to get everything to work right as my head aches.

"Stevie," I finally get out. I lick my lips. "Stevie Green."

"What's your address?"

"Two fifty-four Fairfield Road."

She looks over at my parents, who both nod.

"Good. How old are you?" she asks.

"Uh—uh . . . ," I stutter. The ache in my head grows and what should be an easy answer eludes me.

"Stevie?" She looks at me expectantly, her eyebrows arched. I trace the outline of her gold-framed glasses, the sharp, downward turn of her nose, just like my grandma's.

"I'm . . ." I rack my brain for the answer, but all I can pull up are flashes of yellow brick and rows of maroon lockers. *Central Catholic.* "High school . . . ," I mutter more to myself than to her, everything feeling foggy.

"What's that?" She leans closer to me.

"I don't know," I reply. "I can't think right now."

Worry flickers across her face, but it's gone as fast as it came. "Okay." She clicks her pen off and slips it back into her jacket pocket.

"Okay?" my dad shouts, upset. I try to turn my head to look up at him, but I'm so tired. *"How is that okay?"*

"Her brain has undergone a major trauma. This isn't abnormal. Sometimes it just takes some time. We need to be patient with her."

Why is he acting like that? What does she mean? I just need a second . . .

I try to think harder, try to remember more, but every fiber of my being is getting pulled back to sleep and eventually, I have to give in.

CHAPTER 5

W HEN I WAKE FOR THE THIRD TIME, THE ROOM comes into focus much faster. The haze that was hanging around the edges of my vision has cleared, and the pain in my head has settled into more of a dull ache. I finally feel like myself, or in control of my own body at least.

My mom is asleep, curled up on a tiny couch under the window, the night sky pitch-black on the other side of the glass. My dad is passed out in the recliner, his work boots dangling off the end and onto the floor.

I breathe in, remembering where I am, and why I'm here.

There was an accident. I was in a coma . . . I was in a coma for . . . two weeks? TWO weeks?

There's a creak in the doorway and I jump when I see a girl standing just outside the threshold, in the hallway. Her dirty-blond hair is pulled half up into a ponytail. She's got on purple flip-flops and jean shorts, but not the kind you buy from the store. More like an old pair of jeans that have been ripped off at the thigh.

Why is she here?

She doesn't move, doesn't come closer or back away. She just stands there, looking at me. I watch her eyes light up and a smile spread across her face as her chest expands and contracts under the fluorescent lights.

"I heard . . ." Her voice quivers but still cuts through the silence, the random beeping of my heart rate monitor. My dad stirs awake in his chair with one loud snort as she steps through the doorframe, her flip-flops dragging against the linoleum.

"Oh, hi," he says, looking from me to her, suddenly alert. Her smile drops into a straight line. "Umm . . . now's maybe not the best time." He sits up, pushing the footrest back into place under him.

She doesn't look over at him, and I can't figure out why, but neither do I. We just hold each other's gaze as she takes a step toward me.

"Hey, I'm sorry. Could you come back?" my dad tries again, scooting to the edge of his recliner.

Still she doesn't acknowledge him. There's something about the way she's looking at me, refusing to let her attention stray anywhere else, that makes me want to let her stay.

"It's okay, Dad," I say, and she takes a couple more steps until she's standing at the foot of my bed. I look over at my dad, and he glances over at my mom, who is still fast asleep.

"Okay, well, umm . . . God, where do I even start?" He pauses, motioning to the girl like she's some kind of trifold foam board at a science fair. I look down at her hands, now clutched around the foot of the bed. "Stevie, this young lady here. She . . ." He stops to clear his throat. "Well, she saved your life."

Holy shit.

He continues, "I know you don't remember much about

what happened, but you fell. You fell a long way down into a ravine. And she heard you scream."

I *fell* into a *ravine*? What?

As he explains, she doesn't look away from me. Not once. She barely even blinks. I don't even think she's listening. Instead, it feels like she wants to tell me something else entirely.

"I don't know how she did it . . ." He shakes his head at her in disbelief. "But she got you out of there. Carried you *over a mile* on her back, through the woods and out to the main road."

The woods? What woods? Why the hell would I be in any sort of woods? And how did this five-foot-nothing girl carry me for that long? I stutter around my thoughts for a few seconds, but then I realize the magnitude of what he's saying. She's responsible for me being alive. I don't know what to say, but I look up at her face, see her hazel eyes looking back at me, and realize I have to say something. "Thank you," I tell her with as much meaning as I can.

She nods and leans toward me, just an inch or so, barely enough to even notice. Her eyes are scanning my face like she can't believe I'm here but also like she's . . . searching for something.

I clear my throat and glance at my dad as he stares down at his clenched hands.

"I don't . . . I don't know what else to say," I tell her, feeling slightly uncomfortable. "I'm sorry. What . . . What's your name?"

She sucks in a quick, sharp breath, her eyebrows knitting together over wide eyes.

"It's Nora. You don't . . ." She clamps both hands over her

mouth, quiet sobs escaping through the cracks between her fingers. Her breathing gets so big and heavy that it racks her entire body.

I don't know what to do. I open my mouth to say something, *anything*, but before I can figure it out, she turns her back to me and quickly disappears out into the hallway.

We sit there, my dad and I, both of us watching the door.

"That was kinda"—I shrug—"weird."

"I'm sure it was traumatic, finding you like that," he tells me. "You know, she's been here every single day that you have."

"She *has*?" I look over at him.

"Stevie." He comes over to sit on my bed, the whole mattress tilting under his weight as he scratches at his five o'clock shadow, which I rarely see. "What the hell were you doing at the Martins'?"

"Martin, as in . . . Martin's Meats?" I picture the oversized warehouses and the herds of cattle off Route 58, which I pass on the bus ride to school every morning. But I've never seen them up close. Right?

I shrug. "I have no idea."

"You were supposed to be at the coffee shop that day."

"What? What coffee shop?" I ask, squinting at him.

He cocks his head and furrows his brow. "The one you've been working at over in Endover for like two years now?"

A chill crawls up my spine even as I huff out a confused laugh. "Dad, I've never worked at a coffee shop. And I've never been to the Martin farm. And I have no idea who that girl was at all."

CHAPTER 6

S TEVIE, YOU'VE SUFFERED A CRANIAL FRACTURE AND significant bruising to the brain." Dr. Reicher holds her tablet out to me the next morning. She points to a crack on the back left side of the 3-D image of my skull. "This type of cranial fracture, while serious, should continue to heal on its own with time. However, we did perform a ventriculostomy, which is a big word for saying that we inserted a temporary catheter into your skull to drain some of the fluid buildup and relieve some of the pressure on your brain. You'll find a very small incision on your scalp, but the stitches should dissolve in about two weeks."

My stomach turns as I picture a gaping hole in my head and fight the urge to touch my scalp, too scared of what I might feel up there.

She continues, "Unfortunately, with these injuries, we sometimes see cognitive effects in the form of retrograde amnesia, which is the loss of ability to recall events that happened prior to the onset of injury, like you seem to be experiencing now. Sometimes these memories can come back in the days or weeks following the injury, but I do want you to know that it is also possible the memory loss could be permanent."

The room is starting to spin, but I squeeze my eyes shut for a few seconds and then force myself to focus on her voice.

"Now, *usually*, we see the loss of more recent memories, weeks, sometimes up to a few months prior. In your case, Stevie . . . it is so rare, but based on what your parents have gathered, you seem to be missing close to . . . two years."

Two years.

It's all I hear Dr. Reicher say before her voice is drowned out by a ringing in my ears. I just stare, watching her mouth form around words I can't comprehend. My mom's hand is on top of mine, but I can't feel it, not really, because my whole body has gone numb.

It's not possible.

Dr. Reicher crouches in front of me. I try to force myself back into the room. I think she's asking me if I understand.

I nod my head up and down.

Understand? No, I don't fucking understand, but I'll do anything to get her to stop saying things I don't want to hear.

Mom squeezes my hand until my fingertips turn purple, and Dad thanks the doctor before she leaves us alone in the room.

Nobody moves. Nobody speaks.

There's a pressure building in my sinuses that makes me feel like my head is going to explode, which would probably be the very last thing it needs right now.

I have to get out of here. I can feel it all the way to my bones, this need to run. I throw my legs over the bed and push myself up onto them, but they're too weak. My body gives out underneath me and I end up on my hands and knees, crawling.

Through the black spots strobing across my field of vision,

I see a door ajar, yellow light escaping through the crack.

The bathroom.

Hands brush against my back, gently pull at my shoulders, but I shake them off and keep moving until I can close the door, leaving my parents on the other side.

I scooch into the corner and hug my knees into my chest, closing my eyes.

Remember. Remember.

A scene forms behind my eyelids. I'm standing at the sinks in the girls' bathroom. Savannah's on my left. I watch her gather her thick red curls into a bun as the warm water rinses the pink soap off my hands. Rory busts out of the stall, demanding we ditch lunch period so she can drive us to Taco Bell with her brand-new driver's license. That *couldn't* have been two years ago. It was yesterday. Wasn't it?

There's a knock on the door that makes me jump. My eyes jolt open and suddenly I'm back in the hospital bathroom by myself. "Stevie, honey? It's me," my mom's voice says from the other side of the heavy wooden door. "Can we come in?"

"No," I reply, my voice shaking. I hold my breath and reach my hand up to search for the tangible evidence that this is all real. I slide my hand from the front of my hairline back until my fingers run into something short and prickly. I gently graze over a line of stitches, about an inch and a half long, the area surrounding it shaved down to my skin. Bile rises in the back of my throat.

"Dad and I are coming in," my mom says firmly as I suck in a deep breath, my brain aching for fresh oxygen. I close my eyes as I hear the door open.

Memories don't just disappear. Two years can't just be gone.

Maybe if I just take a second, if I can just really concentrate, I'm sure I'll . . . I'll remember everything. I'll wake up from this nightmare and be able to fill in this giant gaping hole in—

"Don't touch me!" I smack my dad's hand away from my shoulder.

"I'm just trying to help." He rocks back on his heels. "Don't get *mad* at me."

"I'M NOT MAD AT YOU!" I yell, looking up just long enough to see my six-foot, two-hundred-pound dad shrink back into nothing. The guy who has always just wanted to protect me. I don't think I've ever yelled at him in my life, at least not the life I can remember, and immediately I regret it. I press my hands against my forehead and force two breaths in and out of my lungs before I even attempt to speak again. "I'm *scared*," I croak out almost silently, looking between the two of them, my vision blurry. "I'm scared."

I pull my knees farther into my chest, trying to hold myself together, but instead I just crumble apart, tears falling uncontrollably as the pressure releases.

"I'm . . . I'm fifteen, but you're telling me I just turned eighteen." I keep my eyes trained on the floor. "I don't understand how all that time is just . . . gone. I didn't live it. I don't . . ." I wipe my hands down my face, but the tears don't let up at all. My mom locks eyes with me as she gets down onto the floor between my dad and me.

"Baby," she whispers, placing her hands firmly around my forearms, not caring at all that they're covered in snot.

"I don't know who I'm supposed to be." Senior year and

high school graduation. Prom. Varsity soccer and college applications. All the things Savannah and Rory and I have looked forward to forever. I've just missed them? "I don't remember growing up, but you're telling me that I did. You expect me to just *be* an adult now, but . . ."

Without hesitation, my mom crawls into the tiny space next to me, catching me in her lap and brushing her thumb down my cheek in a rhythmic motion like she's done all my life when I'm upset. We sit like that for a long time, until I can breathe again, until the tears run dry.

"Hey, we don't expect anything, okay?" she finally replies. "I don't know what's going to happen, but your dad and I, we know you better than anyone. And we are here to help you figure this out." She leans down and buries her face in my cheek, her dark-brown hair creating a safe barrier between me and the rest of the world. "We're here."

I reach out and take my dad's hand, feeling his calluses rough but familiar against my skin. I remind myself that my mom is right. They know me better than anyone and they're here.

Finally, it feels like maybe . . . possibly . . . the world might eventually make sense again.

Even if just for this moment.

CHAPTER 7

LATER THAT AFTERNOON, DR. REICHER PEEKS HER head into my room while I dig the last bite out of an orange Jell-O cup that I saved from breakfast.

"Hi, Stevie. How are you doing now?" she asks, stepping into the room and nodding hello to my mom and dad.

"Okay, I guess." I shrug, dropping my empty plastic cup onto the mobile table beside me.

"Any change to your memory?" she asks, and I shake my head. "Okay, well, don't give up hope. Like I said, it could just take some time. These things manifest differently in each individual, but it never hurts to ask questions or talk about things. You never know what might trigger a memory." She flicks her head to my parents.

"Okay. I'll try," I reply, perking up a bit at that. I guess in the commotion of earlier, I got so stuck on her saying it could be permanent that I forgot she said this could all be temporary, too. *Everything* could come back to me. It's hard to imagine, because it doesn't actually *feel* like any memories are missing, but if I can do anything to make them come back, I'll do it.

"I heard you tried to make a run for it earlier," she says.

"Uh, yeah," I reply, looking away, embarrassed, until she pulls a gray walker into the room from the hallway.

"Let's give this a shot. You might get a little farther," she says, winking from behind her glasses.

"Oh, I don't think I need that," I say, automatically associating it with my ancient great-grandma down in Florida.

"It's just temporary. Two weeks is a long time to have not used any of your muscles. Everything is going to feel weak . . . as you found out earlier. I'd like your parents to take you to the cafeteria to get lunch. The sooner you can get back to using those muscles, the better, plus I'm sure you wouldn't mind getting out of this room."

"Getting out of here sounds really nice, actually," I reply, even though all I can think about is how much better it would be to just be able to go home.

A little later the three of us sit on the outdoor terrace of the hospital cafeteria with trays of food. I close my eyes and raise my chin to the sun, so warm against my skin. It should be comforting, a natural boost in serotonin, but instead it unsettles me, because it feels to me that just yesterday we had snow, half a foot deep, icicles hanging from the roof on the other side of my classroom windows.

Shade moves over me, blocking the warmth from my face, and I open my eyes to find my mom standing above me, adjusting the shade of the umbrella over our table. My dad takes a bite of his cheeseburger.

They haven't said much of anything since this morning. I can tell they don't want to push me too hard out of fear of a second mental breakdown. So I guess they're waiting for *me* to talk. I have a million questions, but I really have no idea where to begin.

I set my fork down on the plastic tray, doing some simple math in my head. Knitting my eyebrows together, I look at my mom, nervous to ask what I want to ask, because if I'm eighteen and it's summer, I'm pretty sure I already know the answer.

"What is it?" She leans toward me over the table. My dad sets his fountain drink down to listen.

"I um . . . I graduated high school, didn't I?"

My mom's jaw drops open in surprise, then pulls into a smile. "You remember?" she asks, but her smile immediately disappears when I shake my head.

"No. But I want to jog my memory. I want to know every-thing."

"Right. I'm sorry," she replies, composing herself. "Yes. You did. Shortly before everything happened, actually."

I try to remember myself in a yellow cap and gown, walk-ing down the aisle to get my diploma, but . . . imagining is the best I can do. I try for something else.

"Did I make varsity? Did Savannah and Rory? Did we make it to the championships ever?" I ask.

"You made varsity. Lettered your junior *and* senior year," she says proudly. "You guys never made it to the champion-ships, though . . . and Savannah and Rory, well, they quit . . . when was it, John?" my mom asks, looking to my dad.

"I'd say about halfway through the season junior year."

"You're kidding me!" I stare between the two of them.

"We've been playing soccer together since we could walk. Why did they quit?" I ask.

"Um . . ." My dad looks at my mom, who looks back at him.

"We're not really sure," she says.

"I literally tell you everything." I draw my eyebrows together. "What do you mean, you're not sure?"

"Stevie, I don't remember. You'll have to ask them. What other questions do you have?" Mom asks, bringing a plastic forkful of salad to her mouth. Her tone is closed off, almost sharp.

Okay? Weird.

I sink back into my chair, poking around at the pork chop on my tray. I'm missing two whole years of my high school experience. How am I supposed to even know what to dig for? I can't even begin to imagine how much is missing. Inside jokes and school drama. All the parties I must've gone to and exams I passed or flunked. Summer sleepovers, SATs and college applic—

"Wait. So then where am I going to college?" I ask, nervous because I'm not sure I'm ready for this or that I could even still go, but also excited to see where the future is taking me. I've lived in this bubble my whole life. In the back of my mind, I've started to wonder recently what it might be like to actually get out of Wyatt. To explore other parts of the country. To go to college somewhere warmer, with a beach. Somewhere with a few people who maybe look kinda like me. Did I still feel that way?

"Oh!" My mom lights up and then I do too. *Wow. It must be something really exciting!*

She finishes chewing and swallows. "You got into Bower!"

I feel every muscle in my face drop. "What?" I must have misheard her. She can't possibly mean I'm attending the community college that is literally within walking distance of my house.

"You wanted to live at home to save yourself some money and keep your job at the coffee shop," she says, as if that's going to make this news any better. As if my mind is at all focused on some stupid part-time job right now. I don't even *like* coffee. Why the hell would I want to spend all day making it?

"Bower?" I ask again, incredulous.

"My old stompin' grounds," my dad says, proudly patting his chest a couple of times. "Actually, it'll be *really* good now for you to be around home after all of this, so close to us, you know?" he says, digging his big hand into a tiny bag of Doritos.

"Yeah. I guess so." I try to fake a smile for them, but my face feels too heavy to mask my disappointment.

There's a lot of room for change in two years, but I cannot imagine a single version of myself that would have wanted this.

"And you don't *have* to live at home if you don't want to down the line," my mom offers, but it doesn't make me feel much better. Whether I'm in a dorm room or at home, I'll still be stuck in Wyatt.

I wonder what else has changed, what else there is to know about how my life ended up, but right now I think I'm too afraid to ask more questions I might not like the answers to.

Later that evening my mom and I watch TV in my hospital room after my dad leaves to catch up on some work at the garage. Judging from the bags under his eyes, these past couple of weeks haven't been too easy on him.

On either of them, really.

I look over at my mom, all scrunched up on that tiny couch she slept on last night. She hides her exhaustion better than my dad, but I can still see it. It's in the way she carries herself. The way she sighs when she sits down and the way she drags the heel of her sandals when she walks.

"Did you sleep there a lot?" I ask, pulling her attention away from the muted commercials on the TV in the corner of the ceiling.

"I don't like to leave you here alone," she says with a shrug. "Beats that." She flicks her eyes to the pink recliner beside my heart rate monitor and the IV drip that they took out of my arm this morning. "Plus, if all goes well with your recovery, we should be getting out of here by the end of the week," she adds, and I can hear relief in her voice. I know I should tell her to go home, but the truth is I really want her to stay. I don't want to spend a night in this place without her.

I look down at my bed, scooting my body all the way onto one half.

"At least come sleep here."

She pushes herself up onto her elbow. "With you?" she asks hesitantly. "Are you sure?"

"Yeah?" I squint my eyes at her for a second, letting out a confused laugh. "Why wouldn't I be?" We spend half of our evenings sprawled out on her bed anyway, among hot cups of tea and a selection of snacks, watching movies until my dad comes up to bed.

She smiles up at me, then her feet pad across the floor as I throw the blanket back for her to climb in. We wiggle around a little to get comfortable until she ends up on her side, her arm stretched out above my head. I stare at the reality baking show on the TV, reading the tiny captions at the bottom of the screen. A couple of minutes later I feel her fingers combing gently through my hair, careful to stay far away from my stitches. My eyelids start to droop as I lose my battle with sleep, but they snap awake again when I hear a quiet sniffle from above.

I crane my neck to find her slightly glassy brown eyes looking back at me.

"What's wrong?" I ask, and the question elicits a sad sort of smile.

"It's just been a long time since . . ." Her other hand comes to rest on my cheek as she tries to find the words, but whatever they are, she doesn't say them out loud. "I missed you," she whispers instead, a tear spilling across the bridge of her small nose. I scoot up to lay my head down on her shoulder and she slides her arm around me, pulling me closer.

I guess I haven't given much thought to how hard this must've been for her. To watch me lie unconscious for weeks, not knowing if it would all be okay.

As I fall asleep that night to the faint smell of her familiar perfume and the feeling of her hand, warm on my back, I realize that maybe I'm actually just lucky to be here, lying in a hospital bed with my mom. Sure I'm in a town that I'll probably never escape from, with no idea if I'll ever remember the missing two years of my life, and that's definitely not the best-case scenario, but it's certainly not the worst, either.

Because I'm still here. I still have my family, the people who mean the world to me.

And I'm still alive.

CHAPTER 8

I'M DISCHARGED FROM THE HOSPITAL A FEW DAYS later. Per Dr. Reicher's recommendation, the very first thing I do when I get home is head into the bathroom and take a long, hot shower. It feels *incredible*. It's the first real shower I've taken in over two weeks and I'm not going to lie . . . it freaking feels like it.

When I step out onto the mat, I keep my eyes away from the mirror, just like I've done since I woke up four days ago. I don't know what I think it is I'll see, but . . . I'm just not sure I'm ready.

When I'm all dried off, I wrap the towel around me and cross the hallway, *so* looking forward to stepping into my room, *my* space. My evergreen-painted walls plastered with posters from floor to ceiling: *Outer Banks* and *Stranger Things*, Taylor Swift and the US Women's National Team. The old wooden desk in the corner, family photos lining the top shelf. Plants that my mom and I started from seeds sitting along the windowsill in mismatched pots hanging over my pink bedspread.

I swing the door open ready to breathe a sigh of relief, but as I step inside it's . . .

. . . It's not *my* room at all.

Across from me, all of my posters are gone, replaced by tons of little white spots, where the paint was ripped off the drywall. I drag my bare feet across a new beige area rug and over to my desk, which is now painted white. A line of books has replaced all but one of my framed family photos. The one with me as a baby being held by my dad, my mom standing beside us looking like the happiest person to ever walk the earth. It's always been my favorite. I slide my hand across the spine of each book, but my fingers catch on something hard and rough after the last one. Leaning in closer, I pull out a gray-and-orange-striped rock tucked between two sections of wood. I have no idea what it's doing there, but I place it back on the shelf next to the photo. Then I rest my hand on the cool metal of a silver MacBook, running my eyes across the completely empty windowsill, not a single one of our plants in sight.

The drive home today proved that not a single thing about Wyatt has changed. It's still full of the same empty storefronts. The same front yards littered with brightly colored plastic toys and turned-over bicycles. Even the same old man sitting on his front porch in a tank top watching the traffic go by. So I never expected my room would be so different. Have I really changed this much in two years?

I walk over to my door again, my hand clamped around the edge. I know I'll see my own reflection when I close it. I know the mirror at least has to still be there, because when I was ten, I had the genius idea to Gorilla Glue it there. I still don't know if I'm ready, but at this point I might as well rip off the Band-Aid.

I close the door and drop my towel, staring at my naked

reflection in the full-length mirror. Turning to the side, I run my hands over my chest, fingers dragging down each rib, across my flat stomach and onto my hips, taking in all the changes to my body, big and small. I flip my hair over my shoulders, and it actually might be the most noticeable difference. I have *always* wanted really long hair, but I could never stand that awkward midlength like an overgrown bob and I'd cut it before it could pass that point. I guess I finally found the drive, because it's hanging almost down to my belly button.

I lean in closer, examining my face, turning my chin to the left and right, up and down. Different, but not in a bad way. My cheeks aren't as full and my jaw is a bit more pronounced. I guess I look . . . *older*.

I turn my back to the mirror before I get too weirded out and make my way over to the closet, pulling the handle to reveal a line of hanging T-shirts, both plain and graphic in mostly muted tones. The girly tank tops and bright colors I remember are nowhere in sight. I reach into the top drawer for a pair of undies but pull out pajama pants instead. So I make my way down each one, until in the bottom drawer I find a pair, along with a bra that looks too big but isn't. I get dressed, picking out some blue jean shorts and a faded yellow T-shirt with a bundle of wildflowers embroidered onto the chest pocket. Cute.

Behind me, where my desk used to be, now sits my bed, a blue-and-white-striped comforter taking the place of the pink set I grew up with. Spread all across it is a mess of printouts, pamphlets, and books that my mom must've brought up while I was in the shower. It makes my palms feel sweaty. It's all the information I was given upon discharge from the hospital this morning. Dr. Reicher went over my recovery and upcoming appointments pretty thoroughly, but I know I should probably read it for myself. I just don't think I'm up for it right now. It all feels like too much. Especially when this room, my bedroom, *my* space, doesn't even feel like it belongs to me.

There's a knock at my door and as if on cue, my mom pops her head in.

"Feel better?" she asks.

"Uh, a little." I run my hand carefully through my freshly shampooed hair, inhaling the familiar smell of my cucumber-melon conditioner, one thing that hasn't changed.

My mom smiles. "You know what would make you feel better? Getting out of here. They said the best thing for you to do is to get back to your routine, your normal life."

I laugh pathetically, shaking my head. "What does that even mean? I don't remember my *normal* life."

"Well, right now, it could mean hanging out with your old ma?" She gives me a hopeful smile.

"Lola's is still open, right?" I ask, my stomach growling at the thought of our favorite little lunch place.

"Lola's?" She knits her eyebrows together.

"Yeah," I reply, squinting at her. "Best sandwiches in the county? We basically live there?"

Am I the one with amnesia, or is she?

"Uh, sure." She gives me a weird look but shakes it off into a smile. "I'd love to."

"I guess I'll drive." I step forward and pluck the carabiner with a car key attached off my desk. "These *are* mine, aren't they? For *my* car?" I ask, a smirk spreading across my face. I'm not going to lie, having my license *and* my own car *does* bring me a genuine rush of joy.

"Uh, no." She grabs for them, but I move fast enough that her hand cuts straight through the air.

"Come on," I plead. "Dad taught me how to drive when I was like eleven." I may not remember getting my license, but I do remember how to drive.

"Dr. Reicher said no driving until she clears you," Mom replies, extending her hand and wiggling her fingers until I hand over the keys.

"Fine," I grumble, following her out to her car, feeling like I'm still being treated like a fifteen-year-old, even though all traces of her seem to be gone.

CHAPTER 9

LOLA'S BISTRO IS RIGHT ON THE OUTSKIRTS OF Wyatt, and I'm hoping their chicken Caesar sandwich hasn't changed, because it's straight-up perfection. Just like at every other restaurant around here, you seat yourself, and without discussing it we both head to our corner booth beside a window that overlooks the tree line. Neither of us bothers to open the menu, because I'm pretty sure we know it by heart at this point. I might not remember my eighteenth birthday, but at least I can remember that.

As we're waiting for the waitress to come over, I recognize a group of old ladies from St. Joe's, shuffling in through the door.

"Hey, Mom, how are things at the church? Are you still duking it out with Mrs. O'Doyle?" I ask, a grin spreading across my face. Mom's been angling to run the church fundraisers for years, but Mrs. O'Doyle absolutely refuses to share her post. Even if her Lenten fish fry *is* more burnt beer batter than actual cod.

"Actually!" Mom sits up real straight in her seat, looking very proud. "You're looking at the new head of the Seventy-Sixth Annual Spaghetti Dinner."

"No way!" I say, shocked.

"It's August tenth! So I've got a little under two months to perfect my meatball recipe, and I want to get started sooner rather than later. You and your dad are going to be meatballed out by the time it actually rolls around."

"I'll *totally* help you with that," I say. I love a good mother-daughter summer project.

"You will? Really?" she asks.

"Wait, did Mrs. O'Doyle die or something?" I narrow my eyes at her.

"No." She snickers. "Why?"

"You're telling me she *actually* gave up her post?" I ask.

"Well . . . not exactly willingly," she says, cringing. "You remember her daughter, Sarah?" I nod, picturing her, a senior at Central Catholic. Or . . . no. I guess *I'm* not even a senior there anymore. Sarah would've graduated two years ago.

"She got pregnant about six months ago, and word got around that she . . . well . . ." Mom pauses to look over both shoulders, making sure no one can hear her. "She got a *you know what*," she whispers.

"Wait." I shake myself out of my state of disbelief. "But what does that have to do with her mom not doing the spaghetti dinner?"

"You really think Mrs. O'Doyle could keep a leadership position after that? You know how the congregation can be, Stevie."

"Judgmental?" I ask.

"Straitlaced," she corrects, looking away from me. "Anyway, Mrs. O'Doyle technically stepped down of her *own* volition."

"I bet," I mumble under my breath. It's not that I don't want my mom to run the spaghetti dinner. I know she'd be great at it and she's wanted to do it for so long, but it seems kind of crappy to me that Mrs. O'Doyle was basically forced into stepping down from a position she's held for over ten years because of a choice her daughter made that doesn't involve anyone else. My mom might be able to talk herself into believing the Church is always right, but we Catholics claim to be the most welcoming of people, and lately it feels to me like we're the exact opposite.

I wonder where I stand now with it all . . .

"I recognize those faces!" Sue the waitress says, pointing her pen between the two of us as she approaches the table. "It's been so long since you've been in." She slips a notepad out of her apron pocket and holds it up to take our orders.

"It has?" I ask.

"It has," my mom says simultaneously. "It's good to be back, I've missed that pastrami on rye," she adds, and Sue scribbles it down. "With an iced tea? Thanks."

I order my favorite with an iced tea as well, and Sue heads back into the kitchen.

"Jeez, Mom, I know two weeks might seem like a long time away from your pastrami sandwich, but—"

"It's been a little longer than that," she replies.

"It has? Like how long?" I ask as she folds her maroon napkin wrapper into a tiny square.

She shrugs. "Maybe a little over a year."

"Over a *year*? I went a whole year without a chicken Caesar sandwich?"

"Well, I don't know about that. Maybe you came with your

friends or something." She sits back against the booth, looking like a deflated balloon.

I watch her for a minute, waiting for her to elaborate, but she doesn't.

"Mom?" I hate seeing her like this and I hate it even more that I don't know why. "What's going on?" I ask, but she doesn't even look up at me. "Did something happen between us or something?"

"No, honey, of course not." She shakes her head, unfolding the napkin across her lap.

"Mom—"

"Okay, I've got two sandwiches for two lovely ladies," Sue announces, setting two plates down in front of us.

"Thanks," I say, waiting for her to leave so I can talk to my mom, but the second she does, my mom changes the subject.

"Hey, I got you something. Yours didn't make it through your accident." She reaches into her purse and slides a brand-new iPhone across the glazed table. "I couldn't figure out how to get into iCloud to back anything up, but I added a few numbers in there that I had."

"Oh, cool. Thanks." Whatever it is we need to talk about, it's clear she doesn't want to do it now. So instead I take the phone and scroll through the short contact list. "Savannah and Rory! Oh my gosh. I have to see them. They must be so worried."

I remember in sixth grade when Savannah had to get her tonsils out, Rory was having panic attacks all day at school, thinking the doctor was going to slip and somehow leave Savannah unable to speak for the rest of her life. It wasn't until we got to her house after school and saw her pounding down a pint of Neapolitan ice cream that Rory was finally able to relax.

"Did they come to the hospital a lot?" I ask my mom as she sips on her iced tea.

"They came . . ." She sits up straighter in her seat. "Oh, that reminds me, why don't we get Nora something to go on our way out and take it over?"

"Who's Nora?" I ask, sinking my teeth into a sandwich that could end world wars. *Much* needed after all the hospital food.

"Nora Martin. The girl who pulled you out of the water?"

"Oh yeah." I shake my head, remembering the girl with the homemade jean shorts who hovered over my bed before disappearing out the door without a word. "I feel bad she saved my life and I forgot about her. That day was such a blur."

"I think it'd be a nice gesture to take her a little something," Mom says, flagging down our waitress to order an Italian sub to go. You can never go wrong with that.

I replay that night in my head as we wait, how odd the girl was acting and the way her eyes never strayed from mine. I have no idea why, but I guess seeing someone almost die would be pretty intense.

"Did you guys talk to her? Get to know her at all?" I ask my mom.

"Not really. We invited her into the room with us to eat a few times, but she always declined. She must be a pretty special person to come check on you just because she saw you hurt. Though I did overhear a couple of conversations on the phone with what sounded like her mom. I think she's pretty . . . tough on Nora. Maybe she also wanted to get away." Mom shrugs.

"But either way, she was there in that waiting room. Every single day."

"Huh." I can't imagine not being close with my mom, especially to the extent of visiting a stranger in the hospital just to get away from her. But still . . . if she spent all that time in the hospital waiting for me to wake up, why did she just bolt out of the room without even saying a word when I finally did? Why didn't she come back?

It doesn't make any sense, but my mom's right.

I'd say bringing her a sandwich is the absolute least I can do for her, and maybe while I'm there, I can find out more about what actually happened to me.

CHAPTER 10

MY FEET CRUNCH ACROSS THE EMPTY GRAVEL parking lot as I follow my mom through a faded wooden door marked MARTIN'S MEATS in red paint. We're the only ones here, which is a good thing because there's only enough room for a few customers. We walk around a homemade set of plywood shelves stuffed to the gills with hot sauces, steak rubs, and grill tools.

I hope she doesn't think it's weird us just showing up with a random sandwich, because now that I think about it . . . yeah, it's kinda weird.

Well, we're here now.

As we approach the counter, there's a woman about Nora's height but heavier-set behind it, her graying hair pulled back into a low ponytail. I set the bag down on the counter, watching her work with her back to us, grabbing handfuls of ground beef and dropping them onto an old-school metal scale.

"Excuse me, are you Mrs. Martin?" my mom asks, stepping up to the counter next to me. The lady glances over her shoulder just long enough to see the paper takeout bag.

"I'm not interested in whatever you're selling." She wraps the meat up in a sheet of butcher paper in one fluid motion. "If you're here for a fundraiser, we're already getting involved at the county fair."

"Oh no. That's not why we're here," my mom responds.

"What can I get for you, then?" The woman turns to face us, peeling off her clear plastic gloves. "We're running a special on stew beef, three ninety-nine a pound. Chuck eyes are—"

"I'm sorry," my mom interrupts her, looking more apologetic than she should. "We're actually here to drop this sandwich off for Nora. It's from Lola's." She picks the bag up off the counter and holds it out.

Mrs. Martin looks skeptically between the bag and my mom. "Why is it you've brought my daughter a sandwich?" she says with a suspicious drawl.

My mom looks more than a little uncomfortable, but her politeness instincts kick in and she plows ahead.

"I'm Julia Green. And this is Stevie, the girl she—"

"Stevie Green," Mrs. Martin announces, before my mom even finishes. "Now, *there's* a name I recognize." She crosses her arms over her chest, leaving my mom still holding the bag halfway over the counter between the two of them.

"Yes, well, we're *so* grateful for what your daughter did that day. I know it's not much, but we thought we'd stop by and say hi. Bring her a little something for dinner," my mom says, glancing over at me and then back again.

"Well, isn't *that* nice of you." Mrs. Martin's voice is dripping with sarcasm. Now I'm *really* feeling like we shouldn't have come here. I don't know what's going on, but I don't like it.

My mom shakes her head, confused. "I'm sorry, did I do something?"

"Nora has slacked off on *every single job* I've asked of her these last two weeks and chosen instead to wait around a hospital for some silly stranger who fell into the crick she had no business being near in the first place." She directs her attention to me, her dull hazel eyes making my knees shake.

"I'm sorry. I—I can't remember anything."

"Amnesia, huh? That's shocking. I was actually expecting you to be blind. Or did you just ignore the hundreds of No Trespassing signs posted all through the wood?"

"Hey. Don't speak to her like that," my mom interjects firmly. It's enough to make me jump, but Mrs. Martin doesn't even blink.

She just stares at my mom with a slightly amused smirk, like she's won something. "Leave it on the counter," she says finally, turning her back to us and grabbing another hunk of meat to drop onto the scale. "Although she won't eat it. She's too good for regular-people food these days."

I want to ask what that means but I don't want to prolong this conversation any further.

My mom hesitates for a second, burning a hole in the back of Mrs. Martin's head with her look. I tug on her sleeve, and she breaks her stare, locking eyes with me. She takes a breath and when I flick my head toward the door she nods and drops the sandwich onto the counter with a thud.

"You okay?" I ask when we're safely back in the car.

"*God, that woman!*" She curls her hand into a fist in her lap. "What *was* that? Not even a concern for the fact that you could have died. No wonder Nora spent every day at the hospital."

"Yeah, I don't know. She was pretty scary, but so are

hospitals." I laugh to try to lighten the mood, but it falls a little short. That's not a lady I'd want to have to spend any time at all around.

"How dare she talk to *you* like that!" my mom responds, still hyped up on her frustration. "She wants to talk to *me* like that? Fine! But you? I could've . . . I could've *socked* her." And at the idea of my mom "socking" anyone, I let out a real laugh. "What? I'm serious!" she exclaims.

"It's okay, Mom." I pat her leg, stifling another laugh. "I mean, she *was* a jerk, but . . . I don't know. She had a point," I admit.

"She had *no* point," Mom scoffs, and I look over at her.

"She did. Mom, what the heck was I doing out here?" I ask, shaking my head and motioning to the endless fields all around us. "I mean, how did I end up in the middle of the woods, falling into a ravine? I've never even been here before." I tighten my hands around my knees, looking out the front windshield. "At least I don't think I've been here. I just don't get it."

"It'll be okay," she says unconvincingly. Normally she'd know exactly what to say, a plausible solution to make me feel a bit better, but instead she's chosen the most generic statement on earth.

"Will it?" I ask. "What if I don't get my memories back? What if I never remember?"

"Then . . ." She sputters for a second. "Then I'll help you find your place again."

"What if you can't?" I look out the passenger window, nervous that I'm about to open a can of worms, but I can't get the thought out of my head. "Mom, things feel different between us."

"No. I don't think so," she replies, almost automatically.

"Really? You don't feel it? I mean, what's with Lola's? We've been going there all my life, and suddenly we just stopped?"

"Stevie." She shakes her head. "We just got busy. You had school and soccer and Savannah and Rory, and I've been doing my thing at the church. It's nothing more than that."

"Promise?"

"Promise," she replies. I study her face, looking for signs that she might be hiding something more, but I just find a soft familiar smile.

She starts up the car and pulls out onto the road. Our conversation feels finished, but I'm not sure it put me any more at ease. I don't *want* to find my place again. I want to remember the life I've already lived.

June 30

Stevie,

I can't believe you and your mom brought me dinner! And I wasn't even there to receive it . . . DAMN. I would have given anything to see you. Even if you still don't know me, even if I don't get to talk to you, even if it's through a window or across the street. I just want to see you again.

I still can't believe I just ran out of your room without saying anything. I just . . . don't know what I'm supposed to do. You're the only one that really knows me at all, babe. If you don't remember me, it almost feels like I don't even exist. I've been glued to my phone, waiting for any sign that you've remembered. A call, an Instagram message, anything, but so far it's been radio silence.

If you're up and about, you must be feeling pretty good. Maybe your memory won't be far behind. My mom barely lets me out of her sight now that I'm back working basically full-time on the farm, but somehow I'm going to find time to start going to your coffee shop, in case you start back there.

I have no idea what the heck I'm going to do if I do see you there, though. I mean, what could I possibly say? How is this even happening to us? I can't imagine ever forgetting you, Stevie, so I don't know how to fix it. I don't know what the right move is here. I don't know how to make you remember me.

Love,
Nora

CHAPTER 11

THE NEXT DAY, I WALK THROUGH THE SCREEN DOOR out onto our back deck to find my mom reading a paperback in the afternoon sun.

"You're still reading smut, I see," I say, trying to hide my smile.

"It's a romance!" she says defensively, holding the book closer to her chest.

"I'm *sure*. Let me see the cover," I insist, knowing it's going to be some scantily dressed lady in the arms of an oiled-up beefcake. I don't get the appeal, but she always says one day I will.

"No." She laughs as she closes the book and sets it facedown on the armrest of her Adirondack chair. I kick my Birkenstocks off and plop down in the one next to her. "What have you been up to? How's your head feeling today?" she asks.

"It's pretty good, actually. I took an Aleve this morning, but it's definitely feeling better every day. I was just looking through my laptop, trying to learn something about myself."

"Oh? Anything interesting?" she asks, shielding her eyes from the sun.

"Not really," I reply. I was disappointed to find that my search history had been erased. I can't imagine why I would do that, unless I was trying to hide something. "It's weird scrolling through my Instagram, though. Seeing myself doing things that I don't remember doing."

"Yeah, I imagine that *would* be a little unsettling."

"So since that didn't really help, I think the next step is starting back at the coffee shop," I tell her.

"Really? You don't think it's too soon?" she asks.

"The sooner I can get back to normal life, the more likely I am to get my memory back. That's what the pamphlets say, anyway. Sitting around here, looking at old photographs . . . it's not enough."

"I just don't want you rushing into—"

Ding dong. Ding. Ding. Ding dong. Ding . . .

Someone is going ham on the doorbell, and they're not stopping. We look at each other for a second and then behind us inside.

"I'll get it. You just get back to your steamy *romance*," I tell her, and she smacks me on the butt with it as I squeeze by.

When I open the front door, I'm greeted by two somewhat-familiar faces grinning back at me.

"Oh my God!" is all I can say as I look back and forth between my two best friends.

Savannah's hair is . . . so perfectly straight now. I always thought her curls were so beautiful, so *her*. They were an entity entirely on their own. She seems . . . smaller now. Her makeup has changed too. It's heavier, thick black eyeliner against her pale skin, her freckles painted over with foundation. If I hadn't known her my whole life, I honestly might be a little intimidated by her.

Rory lost her braces and well, she, uhh . . . filled out. The deep V of her thin T-shirt really accentuates her ultimate victory over puberty.

I'm still having trouble forming words so I just lift my arms up, and they both step into me for a hug, all of us holding on to each other tight.

"You guys look different." I laugh, giving them one more squeeze before letting go.

"Stevie, don't speak to Rory's cans like that," Savannah says, dodging a slap in the arm from Rory.

"Oh my God! Do *not* call my boobs *cans*, Van."

Van? That's new.

Savannah cocks her head at me. "So you like, really don't remember anything?" she asks, brushing her silky red hair backward.

"Not from the past two-ish years. It's really weird. Kinda scary," I reply.

"We're sorry we didn't visit more," Rory says, crossing her foot behind her other leg to rub her calf. "It's just, well, we came once and you were kinda . . . in a coma."

"I mean it's not like you knew we were there, anyways. Plus, hospitals skeeve me out. You know?" Savannah asks, twisting her face up to show me just how gross they are to her.

I nod, even though it does sting a little. I thought they would've been there all the time, but I guess she *is* right. It's not like I knew either way.

"Hi, girls! I didn't know you were coming over," my mom says as she steps in off the deck.

"We thought we'd come surprise her," Rory replies, throwing her arm around my shoulders.

"You want me to make you all a snack or something?"

"That's okay, Mom. We're just going to hang out in my room. Come on, guys." I head upstairs and the two of them follow me.

"Thanks anyways, Mrs. Green," Rory says over her shoulder.

They both flop down on my bed while I turn my desk chair around to face them. The two of them look like they feel more comfortable in my room than *I* do.

"I saw on Instagram about UNC," I say, pointing to Rory's baby-blue T-shirt. "I can't believe you're actually doing it. You've been talking about going there since like seventh grade."

Rory beams, glancing down at her shirt. "Thanks! Yeah, I can't freaking wait."

"I'll have to come visit you. It'll give me a good reason to get the heck out of Wyatt once in a while." I let out a sigh. "You guys . . . I can't believe I'm going to Bower. *Why* am I going to Bower?" I ask, looking between the two of them.

Rory shrugs. "Honestly, I don't know. It made no sense to us, either, but you made it seem like you *wanted* to stay close to home."

We never talked about it?

Savannah rolls over onto her back and hangs her head off the bed, looking at me upside down.

"So, you like . . . *really* don't remember the past two years . . ." She pauses, raising one eyebrow. When I shake my head, she continues, "Then you don't remember losing your v-card after prom?"

"*What?*" I drop my jaw, my eyes widening so much, it feels

like they're going to pop out of my head. *I had sex?! I've never even kissed anyone!*

"And if you don't remember that, then you *definitely* wouldn't remember your pregnancy scare. Right?" Rory asks. Savannah drops her face into my comforter.

"My *what?*" I yell, breaking out in a sweat all over my body. *Does my mom know? She would've blown a gasket. Is that . . . is that why things feel so off between us?*

"*Rory,*" Savannah says into my mattress, and that's when I notice her whole body shaking with laughter. I take a breath, letting all my muscles relax. Rory bursts out giggling, and Savannah lifts her head up and meets my eyes.

I'm not finding it funny right now, but I force out a laugh anyway while I blink the tears out of my eyes. I wouldn't have expected that kind of joke from them, considering the circumstances. It feels a little too far.

"I can't believe you bought that. Puh-lease, Little Miss Goody-Two-Shoes?" She squints at me. "You didn't even *go* to prom."

"I didn't?" I ask, the room still spinning a little from their joke.

"No, you had to work," Rory answers.

"Oh, at that coffee shop?" I ask. "My parents told me about that, but I can't believe I really missed senior prom. Damn." I was never the type of girl to spend her nights dreaming of prom, but still, I never thought I'd *not* go.

"Yeah, well, you've missed a lot of stuff this past year. Dances, parties, and basically every weekend when we ask you to hang out," Savannah says lightly, but there's a pointed edge to it I've never heard before.

"Oh." I pick at the wood of my chair. "What was I doing? I couldn't have been working *that* many hours."

She shrugs. "That was always the excuse you gave us. If I didn't know you, I'd have guessed you were sneaking around with some boy . . ." She narrows her eyes at me suspiciously.

"Look, I might not remember the last two years, but I'm *pretty sure* if I was, you guys would be the first to know," I reply with a laugh. What I'm really thinking is that I literally have never had a crush on a single guy in my life. I've never told *them* that, though. I mean, it's always felt so . . . not normal. Almost embarrassing, like there might be something wrong with me. But maybe that finally *did* change. I hope so, at least.

"Really? Because we never really bought into the whole *I have to work* thing. You would've been working like sixty hours per week, which isn't even legal," Rory says.

"Guys, I don't . . . remember. I don't know what to tell you." I shrug, at a loss for words, and almost a little frustrated. It's like they care more about getting answers than what happened to me. But I shake it off and try to move on. "Who'd you guys go with? To prom?"

"Van's dating Jake Mackey," Rory sings.

"You are not," I say, surprised, remembering the scruffy guy in our class with a comically lifted pickup truck. "Does he have to boost you up into his truck or do you bring your own stepladder?" I ask, but neither of them laughs.

"You're just jealous." Savannah rolls her eyes. "He's actually really great and really hot now."

"I was just kidding." I shrug, but nobody says anything for a little while and the silence is getting painful, so I spin around slowly in my chair to avoid their eyes for a second. But then it gets worse because the two of them start talking quietly behind me about something that happened this past weekend at Truck Night. Truck Night, the monthly gathering where country boys measure dicks by showing off their big trucks. So I obviously don't know anything about it. Nor would I want to. I can't believe Savannah and Rory go to that now. We used to make fun of the fact that something like that even exists.

My attention drifts to the top of my desk, where the stack of booklets sits from the hospital. I think of my mom and our talk outside the meat shop yesterday, how she didn't have many answers for me. She didn't know what I was doing in those woods, but Savannah and Rory . . . they have to know. Right?

"Hey, guys." I spin my chair back around to them and see they're now sitting up on my bed facing each other. "When I had my accident, I was in the woods on the Martin farm. Do you have any idea what I was doing there?"

They both shake their heads.

"All I know is that you told *us* you were going to work when you left the Dinor that morning," Rory says.

I slump, disappointed. But they have to know something more than I know already.

"Well, what about in general? Is there anything major or important that happened the past couple of years? Anything I should know? Other than me almost getting pregnant," I add, to let them know I can take a joke, that they don't need to walk on eggshells with me. Not that they seem to be.

"I don't think major," Rory says, looking across my bed at Savannah.

"Well, I don't know . . . though you probably wouldn't consider this important," Savannah says, shaking her head.

"What? Tell me. I want to know everything." I scoot to the edge of my chair, leaning toward her.

"There's this guy you kinda, sorta have a huge crush on, and he *definitely* likes you back," she says to me, and then looks at Rory. "Dinor boy?"

Rory smiles and nods. "Oh yeahhhh. Ryan."

"Are you serious? I . . . really had a crush on him?" I ask. It almost feels like a relief. At least something went right in the last two years. Maybe I'm not as messed up as I thought.

"Oh my God, *big-time*," Savannah answers.

"Well, is he cute?" I ask, interested to hear more about this missing part of my life.

They look at each other and then back at me, both raising one shoulder simultaneously and nodding. Cool. So obviously cute, but not rock-your-world cute.

"He works at the Dinor. We should go soon to see him. You can use your new lease on life to finally make a move. Unless you're too busy hunting down your other mystery guy, of course."

"I have a checkup at the hospital tomorrow. How about next week?" I reply, before I can chicken out. They exchange a look I don't quite understand, then nod excitedly.

Good. I said I was going to go back to my normal routine to get my old self back. Maybe this is a good place to start. Even if it means jumping in headfirst. Even if the idea of going to see this boy scares the crap out of me. Even if I don't know why.

CHAPTER 12

THE NEXT MORNING, MY MOM PLACES TWO MUGS OF fresh coffee on the kitchen table.

"Hey, Dad, your coffee's ready!" I call out, but he doesn't answer. "He must be outside? I'll get him." I start to stand up, but my mom catches my arm.

"Actually, honey, your dad had to go into work," she says, frowning.

"But he said he was going to the appointment with us." I plop back down in my chair.

"He really wanted to. Work has just been so busy."

"It feels like he *lives* there now. I've been home for days but I never see him," I reply.

"He's been taking as many appointments as he can at the garage."

"Does that have anything to do with those?" I flick my eyes to the hospital bills that my mom has tactfully hidden behind a fruit basket on the counter. I don't know much about health care, but I imagine a two-week stay paired with whatever they did to my head doesn't come cheap.

She pulls the chair out across from me and slides onto it.

"That's not for you to worry about. Okay? Here." She slides the orange mug toward me. "Drink your coffee."

"*My* coffee? Absolutely not. No thank you," I reply, scrunching my nose up.

"Oh, just try it. I added your favorite hazelnut creamer."

"Fine." I huff out a big sigh before I take a small sip and immediately drop the disgusted expression from my face. "Okay, that's actually not bad," I tell her, going in for a second slurp as her eyes crinkle over her green WORLD'S BEST MOM mug. I can't believe she *still* has that.

"Hey, speaking of your dad, I have to run over to the church before your appointment. Why don't I drop you off at the garage to have lunch with him? Then I'll pick you up when I'm done and we'll go to the doctor."

I remember all the times Mom and I would pack up dinner and bring it to him on nights when he was stuck there late. The three of us would huddle together in his tiny back office, before he would take me through the garage to show me all the cars he was working on at the time. I was never *particularly* interested in how to replace brake pads, but it was always nice to see him in his element, wanting to teach me a thing or two. Plus, it's somewhere new to try to jog a memory. "Yeah, that sounds really good," I reply.

I know I don't have to worry about what will be different about Green's Auto Repair, because that place hasn't been updated since my dad bought it ten, or I guess twelve, years ago. Sure enough, I spy the same blue plastic chairs in the waiting room. Same chunky television sitting in the corner of the office next to the same rust-stained refrigerator with the door you have to lift with your foot to shut.

"I'll be right there." A man's voice calls from underneath an old Ford pickup. Gruff and smoky.

"Hey, Uncle Chuck, it's just me," I reply. I have no idea why I call him that since he's not really my uncle, but immediately the sound of the ratchet stops and he rolls into view on a mechanic's creeper.

"Stevie?" he says as he sits up. His face is even more leathery than I remember, but his smile is still the same oddly endearing one I've always known.

"Is my dad around?" I ask, wondering why he's looking at me that way, until I remember everything that's happened.

"You're okay!" He hops up quicker than an old man should and wraps me up in a hug. "I was so worried about you. My God, you grew up, kiddo." He holds me out at arm's length to get a good look at me before tugging me into another hug. He's acting like he hasn't seen me in a decade, but *I'm* the one who's basically watched him age two years overnight.

"It's been longer for me than it has for you, trust me," I say, my face squished against his chest that's laced with the smell of motor oil and cigarettes.

He lets me go, knitting his eyebrows together, each scraggly white hair sprouting out in a different direction. "Last I seen you, you was just a kid."

"Okay, Uncle Chuck." I laugh him off, shaking my head. "I gotta go. Brought my dad lunch," I say, moving toward the back of the garage and into his office.

As I step in through the doorway, Dad looks up at me,

surprised. *What are you doing here?* he mouths, a corded telephone tucked under his jaw. I hold up the two sandwiches in Ziploc bags that I made this morning and a big bag of salt-and-vinegar chips to share.

"Okay, Mrs. L, we'll get you on the schedule. I'll see you Saturday," he says into the telephone before dropping it onto its base in the corner of his messy desk, almost every paper stained with black fingerprints.

I guess he really does work weekends now.

"Haven't seen much of you the past few days, thought we could have lunch," I say.

"I know." He runs his hand over the top of his bald head, the bags under his eyes even more apparent than they were at the hospital. "Sorry about that. Just playing catchup." His eyes flick to the food in my hands. "Is that ham and cheese?"

"With mustard and extra mayo."

He makes some space on his desk and I grab two cans of root beer out of the fridge before sitting down across from him.

We start eating in silence, the sound of our chewing the only noise in my dad's cramped office. It feels awkward, but I can't quite put my finger on why. It's not like we were ever big talkers, not like Mom and me anyway, but we've never had trouble finding things to chat about over a meal.

"How's business?" I ask, popping a salt-and-vinegar chip into my mouth, but I don't think he hears me. His attention is trained on something over my shoulder. I turn to find Fox News muted on the TV, closed captions scrolling across the bottom of the screen. "Dad," I repeat a little louder, rolling my chair to the right to cut off his line of sight until his attention is on me. "How's work been?"

"Oh, it's fine. It's good. Busy, you know," he replies, and subtly rolls his chair in the opposite direction to get a view of the TV again. This . . . is not what I had in mind for our lunch date.

"Pfft," he scoffs. "Yeah, because he's barely a man!" I spin my chair to see the pixelated screen, where a clean-cut guy in a tan suit and a pink tie is sitting at a round table with the regular hosts. "Just leave the queers to CNN, Joe. That's your problem."

"Dad!" I say, sitting back in surprise. I know he subscribes to the Church's views, but I've never heard him say something like *that* before.

"What? Come on. Why even bring *those people* on television?"

"They're just regular people, Dad. Not any different from you and me," I reply, but he's leaning around me again to get a clear view of the screen. "And since when do we eat meals with the TV on? That's like . . . your golden rule."

That finally gets his attention. He looks at me confused and then at the TV before turning it off with a guilty look on his face.

"You're right. I'm sorry. How are you doing? You've got your appointment today?" he asks.

"Yeah. Mom should be picking me up soon to take me," I reply, my skin still prickling after that comment he made, but I push through it. "I'm starting back at the coffee shop this coming week. I—"

"That's good to hear, Stevie." He laughs, shaking his head. "Glad you're not like these other yahoo kids who think they deserve everything fed to them on a silver spoon."

"Uh . . . yeah, I guess." I have more to say. I want to tell him that I'm trying to get back to my routine to try to recover my memories. I want to talk to him about how nervous I am for my first day, and tell him I'm meeting Savannah and Rory for breakfast next week at the Dinor. I want to know if I've ever mentioned the boy who works there. But even with the TV turned off now, things just . . . aren't feeling right between us, like we're operating on different wavelengths. And it's like he can't even hear the one I'm on.

This garage may not have changed. But my dad definitely seems different. So we end up eating our sandwiches in almost complete silence until my mom honks her horn from outside.

"Everything is looking good," Dr. Reicher says, sitting down across from my mom and me in her office after my checkup. "Your latest scans show things progressing just as we'd like them to. Incision is healing well too. How have you been feeling?"

"I'm okay, I guess. I haven't had to take the prescription pain meds at all and the headaches are getting better," I reply, squeezing my hands between my knees as I try to quiet the anxiety that's been building in my chest since we got here.

"That's great to hear! Well then, I'm happy to tell you that you have my full permission to get back behind the wheel. Your mother tells me that you've been chomping at the bit. Just take it slow and . . ."

"Look. I still haven't gotten *any* of my memories back," I interrupt her. "What does that mean? Is it bad? Does it mean I never will?"

I don't care about the scans. I don't care that my incision is healing or that I can drive. I care that my own dad and I can't even manage to hold a conversation now and I have no recollection of *why*. No memory of what has changed about me or him, or between the two of us.

She tilts her head in concern and folds her hands on top of her wooden desk. "Well, to be honest with you . . . most times, people do start to recover them within those first few days . . ."

Shit.

"Look, Stevie. You might want to consider the possibility that this is something you may need to make peace with. I know starting fresh sounds really scary, but it also might be a much healthier way for you to move through your life at this point. Okay?"

I nod, too frustrated to say anything back to her. My own doctor doesn't even believe I can do this, but I am not giving up. I'm not *starting fresh*. Not when everyone else can remember a version of me that I can't.

I'm going back to work at the coffee shop and that's all I need to focus on. I won't stop until I remember. Until I prove Dr. Reicher wrong.

CHAPTER 13

EVEN THOUGH DR. REICHER GAVE ME THE GO-AHEAD to start driving again, my mom still insisted I drive with her in the car first. So I drove to the coffee shop in her car for my first day of work and she drove it back home.

As expected, I passed her test with flying colors, and so far I seem to be doing the same at work.

I don't know why I was up half the night worrying about today. Well, I guess I do. This is my very first job ever, but now that I'm here . . . it isn't so scary.

Green buttons for food. Blue buttons for drinks. Total. Take payment. Write the order on the appropriate cup for the barista down the line. Easy peasy.

With each customer who trickles in, the process gets a little smoother. The locations of the buttons aren't there in my memory when I search for them, but they start to stick and my descriptions on each cup get shorter and more efficient.

"Decaf hazelnut latte," I announce, writing *de Haz Lat* on a paper cup before sliding it down the line to Cal, a guy around my age who's crafting each drink as if he was born to do this. His hands fly to different flavor pumps and milk cartons and levers, without ever taking his eyes off the espresso machine. I wonder if I was ever able to do that.

"Hey, Stevie. How are you doing?" Kendra, my manager, appears out of the back during a lull.

Her graying roots are giving way to long bleached-blond hair twisted into a bun using two pens. I straighten up even more.

"Pretty good, I think. Hey, quick question. When I emailed you about cutting my hours back to ten per week, you said that's what I was already working? My mom told me I was doing twenty."

She gives me a weird look, cocking her head to the side. "No. You've only ever worked ten per week," she replies.

"Oh, okay. Perfect, then." That's weird, though. I know the sixty was just Savannah and Rory being dramatic, but ten doesn't seem like too many hours at all. Definitely not enough to justify missing *prom*.

"Hey, I've been dying to ask you a few questions," Kendra says eagerly.

"Okay?" I reply, giving her the floor. I don't know what sort of relationship we have, but it must be good if she wants to chat.

"I've got to know. What was it like waking up from that coma?" she asks, leaning on the counter, her eyes wide with . . . excitement?

"Oh, umm . . ." I wasn't really expecting to talk about this here, with people I don't know anymore. I remind myself that to her, we've been coworkers for years—we might even be friends.

"I mean, two entire years of your life missing? What does that feel like?"

"I . . ." I think back to that horrible night when I woke up in the hospital, expecting to be at home in my bed but instead opening my eyes to fluorescent lights and voices I didn't recognize. Tubes and needles sticking out of my arm, my head searing.

"It was really weird. Confusing, I guess," I tell her, too nervous to simply say I don't want to talk about it.

"In a way, I actually think it'd be pretty cool to have a clean slate, though. I wouldn't mind being able to forget the majority of my high school years." She laughs.

I clench my jaw and force a closed-lipped smile. "I'm just hoping to get back to some form of normalcy, honestly."

"Well, I think that's really brave of you. How are things going here on the register?" Kendra asks.

"I think I've got the hang of it," I reply, feeling slightly proud of myself and also relieved not to be talking about the accident anymore.

"That's great. It's pretty slow now, so why don't you switch with Cal for a bit so you can dip your toes back in."

Cal lets out a dramatic sigh, clearly not thrilled to be giving up his designated post.

"Oh, some face-to-face with the public isn't going to kill you, Cal." She smiles.

"It just might," he replies, slamming the hazelnut latte down on the pickup counter a little too aggressively.

"Okay, Stevie, let me show you a few things," Kendra says, ignoring Cal's attitude as he drags his feet toward the register. She directs me to the monstrous espresso machine, which looks *a lot* scarier up close. "You got those cards?" she asks, and I reach into my back pocket and pull out the laminated cheat sheets she gave me earlier with the different measurements of each ingredient for every drink on the menu.

She gives me a tutorial on all the knobs and levers, making sure I understand the order of operations. I watch her make the next drink and then she watches me make two, patiently guiding me in the right direction when I get lost.

"I'm going to let you do it on your own for a bit while I take some inventory in the back," she tells me, and I look back at her with wide eyes. "Don't be nervous, okay? Just getting you back to that normal routine you're after." She winks and then lowers her voice to a whisper so Cal doesn't hear. "You've always been my hardest-working employee. Maybe now that you're done with school we *can* get you up to twenty hours finally. You got this down really quickly the first time around and we'll both be here to help if you need it."

"Okay," I reply with a smile as she heads into the back and sends Cal a glare on her way by. I'm flattered by what she said, but it also leaves me with a question . . . if I wasn't hanging out with Savannah and Rory and I wasn't here: what *was* I doing with all my free time? Was I working somewhere else?

Pretty soon two teen girls come in and order vanilla iced coffees, forcing me to stop thinking about it.

Here we go.

I check my cheat sheet and scoop some ice into two clear plastic cups. But while I'm pumping the three squirts of vanilla in, another customer enters. And then another one.

Cups slide down the counter to me, stamped with Cal's even more extreme shorthand. I squint, trying to read them as I set the first two on the pickup counter.

I grab the next cup and examine it closer. *L2BS.* What does that mean? *Two lattes . . . latte with two . . . two what?*

I squeeze my eyes shut and will myself to remember, but *nothing* comes from my memory bank.

"What does L2BS mean?" I ask Cal as quietly as I can, but everyone still hears me. The place isn't big by anyone's standards.

"Latte with two pumps of brown sugar," he says, without looking over at me. I didn't even know brown sugar could be in liquid form.

I go back to my cheat sheet to make sure I'm getting the ratios correct. By the time I get the drink finished, though, there are four more cups lined up for me. And by the way he just picks at his nails when no one's ordering, it's clear that despite how gung ho he was before, Cal has no intention of helping me even though we have expectant customers waiting.

The next one is a simple Americano. No problem. Espresso and hot water. *I can do this.*

But after that the next plastic cup reads *V ice blend.*

Crap.

"Kendra never showed me how to use the blender," I say, a sweat breaking out on my brow.

"You press blend and it blends," Cal replies as yet another person steps up to the counter. *What is up with this rush?*

I take a deep breath, turn toward the back counter to figure it out myself, and get to work adding ingredients into the pitcher. It takes me a second to understand that you have to lower the outer shield, but when I do that, it finally starts up. When the ice and milk and vanilla powder are blended perfectly into a white puree, I dump it into the cup. A bunch of it sloshes onto the counter, but I still manage to fill it to almost the top.

I go to turn on the sink to wash my hands off and *of course* the spray bounces right off a cup and directly into my face. *Fan-fucking-tastic.* I towel myself off as best I can, but the top of my shirt is still soaked.

My heart just about stops when I turn around to see six more cups on the counter and impatient-looking customers lined up along the barrier separating us. I look back at the mess I made on the counter, which is now dripping onto the floor, but decide to leave it. I need to catch up first.

CC w/ O.

Not even daring to interrupt Cal while he's taking a customer's order, I run through all the possibilities in my head until I come up with cinnamon cappuccino with oat milk.

That has to be it, it's one of the specials of the month. I step up to get started, but everything is so scattered now, milk cartons and dirty silver pitchers all over the place. My cheat sheets are God only knows where, but . . . it's fine. It's fine. I can do it without them.

You were good at this. You did it all the time. Just remember.

I start steaming the oat milk, trying to recall how much cinnamon goes into it. One, two, three teaspoons? I decide to go with three because who doesn't want more flavor, and scoop it in from a glass jar. The steam kicks some of it back in my face, though, and I cough.

Maybe I should've stirred it in at the end.

After I put it all together, I try to add a fancy little cinnamon sprinkle, but the whole glob falls off the spoon and lands in a big pile of powder on top of the foam. I do *not* have the time to redo it, though, so this will just have to do. On my way over to the pickup counter, I find one of my cheat sheets when I freaking *slip* on it. Thank God I manage to keep the drink upright while I end up a heap on the floor.

"*What* is going on here?" Kendra's voice booms from the back doorway, hands planted on her hips. She's not accusatory, I think she's more just genuinely shocked to see her shop in such disarray.

"I—I . . . ," I stutter, trying my best not to just start crying right there on the spot as I quickly shuffle up onto my feet.

"Stevie, I told you I was here to help if you needed me. Cal . . ." She looks like she's about to let him have it but she takes a breath, looking around at all the customers, who are all whispering to each other now. "It's okay, Stevie," she says to me finally. "Cal, make the drinks. I'll take orders." She steps up to the counter. "I am so sorry about this, folks. We'll have you out of here in no time and we appreciate your patience."

Cal walks down to the barista station, avoiding a few puddles of milk on the floor.

"Move." He steps into me, forcing me away from his beloved espresso machine.

"Here, this is—" I go to hand him the latte and he all but knocks it out of my hands.

"Just get out of my way, we need to catch up."

"I can help," I say to both of them, tears pressing against my eyes.

"Stevie, how about you just take your fifteen," Kendra says firmly, nodding toward the back room. But I can't be here right now, not even in the back. I can't be anywhere near here. Taking my crappy drink with me, I move quickly around the front counter, tears blurring my vision. My sticky shoes squeak shamefully against the floor as the customers part so I can get to the door.

I want to remember my life more than *anything*, but nothing about this feels familiar. I know they say routine helps, but I can't even remember why I wanted this stupid job, let alone how to do it. I wanted to prove Dr. Reicher wrong, but how can I if I can't even remember how to make coffee?

"Sorry!" I say, sucking in a quick breath as I almost run smack into someone trying to come inside. Their hands grab onto my shoulders so we don't collide.

"Hey, are you okay?" she asks, and something about her voice is familiar. I pick up my head, blinking the tears out of my eyes so I can see her more clearly. Short, dirty-blond hair and freckles under piercing hazel eyes that take me right back to the hospital.

Nora Martin. Perfect. The very last thing I want right now is for someone I know, even the tiniest bit, to see me like this. First unconscious, now crying at work? Talk about embarrassing.

"I'm sorry," I repeat, pushing past her until her hands fall off my arms. I fly out the door and then turn the corner before walking to the back of the building, where I plop down on the curb. I set the drink down next to me and drop my head into my hands, finally letting my tears fall now that I'm all alone. Maybe I came back too soon or maybe I shouldn't have come back at all. Even *without* a brain injury this must have been impossible. How did I ever like working here? It's so much pressure and Cal is *such* a jerk.

All of a sudden there are footsteps coming toward me down the alley, so I snort everything back inside and dry my face as best I can.

A pair of well-worn boots steps down off the curb beside me, the laces broken and knotted back together again in several places. I look above me, and Nora's head eclipses the sun.

"I'm fine," I tell her even though she hasn't asked, turning away to wipe my face one more time.

"Yeah, I was just thinking that. I was thinking, that girl? Crying and running away? She seems fine. She seems *great*, actually." She sits down on the curb a couple of feet away and holds out a few napkins. I look over at her and see a hint of a friendly smirk starting at the corners of her lips as I take them. She watches me for a second, but when I don't laugh, she keeps talking. "What's this?" she asks, picking up the drink by the lid.

"I have no idea." I shrug, defeated. "Oat milk something."

"Sounds delicious." She takes a gulp out of it without a second thought, and then just as quickly spits it out onto the pavement with a dramatic cough. "Oh my God." More coughing. "I think I just did the cinnamon challenge," she says, making me laugh even as a couple more tears roll down my cheeks. "My God . . ." She pauses and looks up to meet my eyes.

"You could've at least *pretended* to like it," I say.

"Yeah, you might want to try it before saying that," she jokes, her mouth cracking open into a wide smile, revealing a small gap between her two front teeth.

"Aren't you supposed to be nice to people when they're crying?" I ask, drying the last of my tears.

"Eh, I don't know." She shrugs. "Probably, but I already saved your life and it's also not super normal to give someone a sandwich in exchange for that. So . . ." She giggles, leaning out of the way of my attempted shove.

"It was my mom's idea," I admit. I *knew* it was a weird move. "Was it good, at least?"

"I actually didn't eat it," Nora replies, sounding a little guilty. "I went vegan a little bit ago."

"*Oh*. That's what your mom meant."

"Oof. Sorry you had to meet her." She cringes.

"Your mom? Yeah, she was . . . uh." I wrap my arms around my knees at the thought of her.

"Easygoing? Tenderhearted? Charismatic?" Nora fills in.

"All of the above," I answer, and both of us share a knowing smile. Nora seems to be about the opposite of whatever her mom is and not at all the awkward girl who walked into my room that night. "Hey, I didn't really get a chance to like . . . talk to you at the hospital. You kinda . . ."

"Yeah, sorry I disappeared." She pauses for a little while, kicking her boot into a few scattered stones. "I just realized it was probably a bad time. For you guys."

I think of that night, my dad getting emotional as he told me what Nora did for me, how she carried me *over a mile* through the woods.

"How did you do it?" I ask. She definitely looks stronger than most girls, but she's still at least a couple of inches shorter than me. "How did you get me out of there?"

She shrugs, staring at the brick wall across from us. "I never had another option. I was either going to get you out of there or . . ." She bites the inside of her mouth, the skin of her cheek hollowing. "I just . . . I couldn't leave you."

Being here at the coffee shop hasn't done anything to jog my memory, but maybe routine isn't enough. Maybe if I saw the place where it happened. Maybe I could at least remember why I was there in the first place.

"Can you show me sometime? Where it happened?" She doesn't answer me right away, like she's deciding. "Please," I add, and finally she nods.

I hand her my new phone from my pocket and she hesitates for a second before finally inputting her number. I half expect her to ask me about it, my lost memories, my recovery. Everyone else seems to have questions, but she doesn't.

I take a deep breath of fresh air, feeling surprisingly better after sitting here with her, and even though I don't like talking about it with strangers, even though she hasn't asked, there's this urge to tell her.

"Maybe it'll help because right now . . . I can't remember the last two years of my life," I admit. She doesn't look at me like I'm some kind of alien, or ask me a thousand questions. She looks almost like she understands. "You know, I think you're the first person I've talked to, like *really* talked to, who didn't know me before. Who doesn't know all these things about me that I don't even know myself. It's kinda nice."

She opens her mouth, closes it, then opens it again. "I . . . I'm glad," she says, checking her watch. I check my phone too and notice that my fifteen minutes are almost up.

"Oh my God. I can never go back in there." Kendra and Cal and all those customers flash in front of my eyes. "I need to leave. Move to a new country under a new name. You want to come with me?" I ask, turning to Nora.

She laughs, but her smile slowly disappears before she speaks. "I wish I could . . ." She pauses for a long time, her eyes scanning every part of my face again in a way that makes my cheeks heat up, then clears her throat. "But I've gotta get back to the farm," she finishes, standing up and turning her back to me.

"Wait, don't you want a drink?"

"I think your concoction just about did me in. I'm glad you're okay, Stevie," she says over her shoulder, then walks quickly around the front of the building.

I glance down at her phone number lit up on my screen and then up to the empty space where she just disappeared around the corner.

I know I'm supposed to be getting back to normal but being with Nora, this girl who I've never met before, feels more normal than anything I've tried so far. I feel like I can actually talk to her about stuff without any danger of stirring up the past, because, well, unlike everyone else I know, we have no past to stir up.

We're a completely clean slate.

Maybe a nice and simple friendship like that could be good for me, let me start living my life without giving up the way Dr. Reicher suggested. Maybe I need that just as much as I need to remember.

July 3

WHAT AM I DOING, STEVIE?

I just flat-out lied straight to your face.

But also like what was I supposed to say? "Well, actually, Stevie, funny story, you and I have been dating for two years and we're madly in love."

If you really have lost two years, then you would've freaked out at just the idea that you could be with a girl, let alone me.

I thought if I could just see you I would feel . . . I don't know . . . relieved? Like if I could only be near you, everything would be okay, but things feel more complicated than ever. I hope something comes back to you when you get to the farm. Maybe it's a bad idea having you come when I still haven't figured this out, but I couldn't say no . . . I mean, I didn't want to. I want to be with you. It's just that I don't know how to be around you like this . . . It hurts. I miss you. I miss YOU. The you that remembers me. The you that's in love with me. I wanted to reach over and wipe those tears away myself, not just pass you a stupid wad of napkins.

This is so fucking frustrating, but we'll figure it out. I know we will.

Just hang in there, babe.

Love,
Nora

CHAPTER 14

⟶

SO HOW WAS 'WORK'?" RORY ASKS, TAKING A LONG slurp of coffee from a classic chunky mug stamped with the Dinor's red-and-yellow logo. I can hear the air quotes, like she's still not sure she believes that's where I was, but I decide to ignore them.

"It was so bad that I literally am not ready to talk about it yet," I reply. I consider telling them about Nora, but they probably wouldn't appreciate me making plans to hang out with her when I've apparently been a crappy friend to them recently. "What have you guys been—"

"Shut up, shut up, shut up!" Savannah tries to whisper, while somehow managing to shout. I watch her blue eyes track something coming up behind me, and I turn around to find a boy our age, with a red apron tied around his waist.

"Hey." He looks right at me, recognition filling his brown eyes, but none fills me. In fact I don't think I've *ever* seen another Asian kid in this town, or even in the county. I can't help but be surprised. "I heard what happened. Holy shit, I'm so glad you're okay," he continues.

"Oh, uhh." I look away, confused. "How did you hear?"

"Small town." He shrugs, flicking his head to get the hair

out of his eyes. "And this place is like gossip central, so I'm basically Wyatt's Keeper of Secrets." He shakes his head, laughing, but something in my face must make him pause. "Anyway, sorry. It's probably not something you want to talk about. What can I get for you guys?" he asks, holding up his notepad and turning to my friends.

As Savannah and Rory order our usual short stacks of pancakes, my eyes float down to his name tag.

Ryan.

Oh my God. This is him. The guy I supposedly like. I look at him again with fresh eyes. He *is* actually cute, and that joke was pretty funny. I look up at his face again, waiting for some spark to hit or a flutter in my stomach, all the telltale signs I've read about and watched in movies. I try to really take in his angular jaw and sparkly smile and eyes that are . . . looking right at me, waiting. Oh, right. "Uh, same. Short stack," I say.

"Really? Not your usual?" He taps his pen against the pad. "You've been getting the same thing for as long as I've worked here. Two eggs over medium, bacon, hash browns, and wheat with no butter."

"Well, I'm glad *you* remember, because I definitely don't." I try to force out a flirty-sounding laugh, glancing at Savannah and Rory across the table.

"Just stuck in my head for some reason," he says with a nervous laugh, almost like he's embarrassed, tapping his pen against his temple.

"I'll take that instead," I say, smiling. "Maybe it'll help something stick in mine."

"This is Stevie, by the way," Savannah cuts in, pointing to

me. "I'm Savannah and this is Rory. We just graduated from Central Catholic."

"Hi." He gives a little wave. "Nice to officially meet you guys. I actually just graduated from Wyatt," he says, mostly to me. "I'll have these right out for you." By the time he disappears back into the kitchen, Rory is basically vibrating in the booth as Savannah's hands fly across the table to grab mine.

"See," she says. "You do like him, don't you!" Their eyes are on me and my cheeks are hot and I can't think of anything to do but smile to cover my nerves. And she immediately takes it as confirmation. "I knew it. You love him."

"I didn't say that!" I pull my hands out of hers and lean back against the booth.

"Well, you didn't have to. It was all over your face."

"It was?" I ask, and Rory nods her head dramatically. But I don't know how anything could be on my face when I don't really feel anything inside. Maybe . . . maybe I just need to give him a chance, get to know him all over again.

Still, I do wonder . . . "If I liked him as much as you two say I did, what stopped me before from like . . . doing something about it?"

"You? Talk to a boy of your own volition? Slim chance," Savannah says, "but we're not going to let that happen again. So when he comes back, you're going to ask him to hang out with the three of us. I'll invite Jake, too, so it's not weird."

"I am *not* interested in fifth-wheeling it. Hard pass," Rory cuts in.

"So we'll double. Okay?" Savannah's blue eyes flash at me expectantly, and I let out a sigh but don't respond.

"*God*, my life is depressing. Stevie somehow has an almost-boyfriend she doesn't even remember, and I'm still single," Rory mutters into her cup of coffee.

Savannah ignores her, eyes still trained on me.

"Savannah, I can't just *ask* him. I mean, isn't he supposed to ask me?"

"Well, clearly he's just as timid as you are about expressing his feelings, so you're going to have to step up if you want this to happen," she replies bluntly.

Maybe she's right and I should just do it. I've spent most of my teenage life not understanding how everyone except me was developing crushes or falling in love, thinking something was wrong with me because it just wasn't happening for me. But now apparently it has. If Rory and Savannah say I had a crush on him before, then I'm *sure* I can have a crush on him again.

I want to keep pushing forward, and if this was the path my life was headed on before the accident, I need to take it. Plus, Rory and Savannah would never steer me wrong.

Soon Ryan comes back with our three plates piled high with food. I watch him carefully set each one down on the table, the light smell of his laundry detergent swirling around as he leans across me.

"Ow!" I grunt, gritting my teeth as a foot collides with my shin under the table. Savannah's wide eyes look as intimidating as ever, but when I reach for the words, I have no idea what to say. This is all happening too fast. So I just thank him and pick up my fork as he starts to leave. I can try again another time.

"Hey, Ryan?" Savannah speaks up, and he reappears beside the table.

"What can I get for you?"

"Actually, *we*"—she gestures to me across the table—"want to know if you'd like to hang out with us. Well, me and my boyfriend, and you and Stevie," she clarifies, and I slink down in the booth a couple of inches, trying not to die from embarrassment.

"Yeah, totally," Ryan answers quickly, and I look up to find him beaming down at me.

"Really?" I ask.

"The county fair is in town this weekend. I don't know if that's your thing or not?" He raises his eyebrows at me. *Oh my God*. Is he . . . kind of asking *me* out now? I try to keep calm.

"I've always been a sucker for overpriced games," I joke. "Savannah?"

She brushes her perfect hair behind her ear and purses her lips as she digs into her pancakes. "Mmm. Rusty rides, mud, and fried food. *Love* that for me."

"Friday, six p.m. by the Ferris wheel?" Ryan asks me, ignoring Savannah's sarcasm.

"Yeah. Here. Let me get your number just in case," I say, handing him my phone. He inputs his number and hands it back to me.

"See you there," he says, then turns to check on his other tables.

"Girl." Savannah smiles crazily at me.

"I know!" I reply, trying to match her excitement.

"What are you going to wear? Ryan strikes me as the type of guy to like something a little more casual, you know?" Rory asks animatedly, even though she isn't coming.

"Uh, yeah. Whatever you think," I tell her.

The two of them start telling me what they think I should and shouldn't wear on Friday, how to do my makeup, and tips on how to be flirty . . . "but not slutty," Rory adds.

I know I should be paying attention. I should be interested in this conversation. I should be on cloud nine that this boy I like likes me back.

But I can't stop thinking about how much easier this would all be if I could only just *remember* how it felt. I look down at my phone, which is still lit up with Ryan's contact. A few lines above it I spy Nora's.

Maybe if Nora can show me the site of the accident, it'll all just come back to me. My two years of lost memories, my crush on Ryan, the reason I was in the woods that day, the reason things feel slightly off with just about everyone in my life.

I nod my head and laugh and say, "Sounds good" when it's necessary as we talk our way through the rest of breakfast. But the moment we part ways outside the Dinor, I pull out my phone and scroll right past Ryan's contact and up to Nora's name.

Hey, you free tomorrow? I text her.

It's time to find out what I was doing in the woods that day.

CHAPTER 15

BY THE TIME I ARRIVE AT THE MARTIN FARM THE following morning, the sun is already blazing hot, hanging from a cloudless blue sky. I pull out my phone and send my mom a text.

Hey, I made it. Only took out two kids.

The only way she would let me drive myself to Nora's today was if I updated her on my whereabouts, which . . . I would've done anyway. Well, except for why I'm here.

Not funny, she replies.

I juggle two iced vanilla lattes in one hand as I step out of my car and spot Nora on the other side of a few beat-up pickup trucks. She's sitting on a fence, facing the fields, her legs dangling over the other side. My shoulders relax a little—I'm thankful that I didn't have to park outside the meat shop and risk running into her mom again. Maybe Nora was thinking the same thing when she told me to pull all the way back here in between two gigantic grain silos.

As I approach from behind, I notice that the green cut-off Class of 2023 shirt she's wearing is from Wyatt High. She must've graduated this year too.

I lean against the fence beside her and she looks down at me.

"To make up for the other day. It's oat, so it's vegan." I hand her one of the drinks and she lifts the lid to give it a precautionary sniff. "I didn't make them," I say, rolling my eyes.

"Had to be sure." She grins, taking a sip. "Well, you ready?" She flicks her head to some far-off point across the field.

Am I ready to see the place where I almost died? I'm not exactly sure. I mean, is it even safe? I fell once, so I don't think it's out of the realm of possibility that it could happen again. But I take a deep breath and nod anyway, because I'm still holding out hope that when I see it, I'll remember why I was even there in the first place. Besides, this time I won't be alone. I'll be with Nora.

We walk side by side, away from the road and along the split-rail fence, which soon turns into welded wire laced around thick wooden posts. I try my best not to make eye contact with the hundreds of cows that lift their heads to look in our direction as we pass by. Our local grocery store stocks Martin's meat, so I'd say about 100 percent of the beef I've consumed in my life is probably from this farm, and unlike Nora, I don't have any plans to go vegan, so I'd prefer not to look my food in the eye.

"So what exactly is it that you do on the farm?" I ask as we walk past a couple of grain silos.

She shrugs. "Whatever my mom asks. Right now I'm putting up a new fence along the eastern field. So that'll probably take me another two months or so. Sometimes I work the shop when they need a fill-in, but I prefer to be out here if I can." She squints at me, holding her hand to her forehead to block the sun, and I notice a couple of bruises on the inside of her forearm.

"Hey, what happened there?" I ask.

"What?" She turns her arm to inspect it. "Oh. Just one of the perks of the job." She shrugs and tucks her hand into her pocket. "How'd the rest of your shift go?"

"A bit better. They let me stay on register the rest of the time. Thanks for . . . uhh . . ." I'm actually not sure what she did to make me feel so much better, so I don't know what to thank her for.

"Sure thing," she replies anyway. I swipe my arm across my brow to mop away the sweat. It feels like the temperature has gone up about twenty degrees since we left the parking lot, and it's got me wishing I had brought water instead of lattes.

I watch my feet as we wade through the tall grass; then I come to a stop, recognizing something sticking out of the dirt.

"What is this?" I ask, bending down to pick up a small orange-striped rock, just like the one I found on my desk. I drop it into Nora's outstretched hand.

"Granite. There's a whole bunch of it under the dirt all over the farm. Sometimes the rototillers pull it up." She underhands it back to me. "Why do you ask?"

"No reason," I reply, but really I'm wondering how it made its way onto *my* desk and if it means I've been here more than just that one time.

"Come on, we're almost there," she says, and I let the rock fall back into the grass.

I let out a big sigh of relief as we make it to the tree line, beyond thankful for the beautiful, *beautiful* shade. Nora laughs, shaking her head as she takes a few more steps, using her boot to stomp down a jagger bush for me. I hop over it and then drop back behind her, letting her lead me through the trees. Soon the leaves are so thick overhead that barely a single ray of sun breaks through.

How could I have found myself all the way out here alone?

Under the sounds of birds whistling and crickets chirping, I begin to hear the rush of water. It grows louder as we head deeper into the woods, sounding more like a river than a crick, until finally, we break through an opening. Nora looks back at me hesitantly and then steps to the side to reveal a massive tree lying across a ravine that I can't even see the bottom of from this angle. I carefully step closer to the bank, my heart jumping up into my throat as I look over the edge.

"Oh my God, Nora. How did I end up down there? What the . . . It's gotta be fifteen, twenty feet to the bottom. How the hell did you get me out of there?" I ask as she steps up beside me.

"I, uh . . . I don't know how it happened. But given the placement, it seems like maybe you tried to walk across the tree trunk and fell. Like I told your parents and the paramedics, though, I just heard you scream and when I got here, you were at the bottom, unconscious. So I used those to climb down." She points at some scattered tree roots poking out of the wall of dirt and creeping down toward the water. "By the time I got down there, you were completely underwater. I—I thought you were . . ." She looks away, clearing her throat as she digs the toe of her right boot into the mud. Her eyes are slightly glassy when she looks back at me.

Dead. She thought I was *dead.*

"You *really* don't recognize any of this?" she asks.

I look all around us, then close my eyes and breathe in as I listen to the sounds of the birds chirping overhead, the wind rustling through the trees.

"I thought once I got here, maybe I would, maybe I'd know why I was here, but . . ."

Goddammit. I really thought this would work.

"I've been doing everything I can to get back to my routine, but *nothing* is working. It felt like if anything was going to work, it was going to be coming here, seeing where it all started, but I'm here and . . . nothing." Tears press against my eyes as I look back at Nora, and something inside me crumples.

"What are the other things you've been doing to try to remember?" she asks.

"Starting back at the coffee shop, hanging out with my best friends. Although *apparently* I wasn't even doing that much anymore so maybe it's not a surprise that didn't work. They told me I'm always working and barely have time for them anymore, so I don't even know." I shrug. "I even went to see my dad at his garage, but we barely had anything to talk about. So I guess I've mostly just been hanging out with my mom and going to our favorite spots."

"Oh. Are you two close?" she asks.

"My mom and I? Yeah, we're like . . ." I cross my middle and pointer fingers. Nora furrows her brow at me and does one slow nod. Instantly I feel bad saying that, when she can't even stand to be around hers.

She looks away at an animal rustling in some brush, and then she gets real quiet. *Mental note: Don't bring up moms.*

"You want to get out of here?" I ask. But as I turn to take

my first step away, my foot catches on a branch and it pulls me down until my knee collides with a rock. *"Son of a—!"* I yell as blood begins to seep through my scraped skin.

"Stevie. Oh my God." Nora crouches down in front of me as I plop my butt down on the ground, a laugh already escaping my lips. "I will straight-up bubble-wrap your ass. Jesus Christ." She wipes a hand down her face, trying and failing to hide a smile as she sits back on the rock.

"Sorry," I say. "Ow." I pluck a few pieces of dirt out of my knee.

"Come on. We have a first aid kit up at the house," she says, pulling me up off the ground.

Before we go I look back down at the water and the near-vertical wall of mud on the other side, keeping my feet safely planted where they are.

What she did seems almost impossible.

I can't even imagine being able to pull *myself* out of there, let alone someone else.

It must have almost killed her.

I don't think many people would do that for a complete stranger.

I can't believe she did it for me.

I always pictured farmhouses as big and cozy. Lots of family photos lining the walls of every room and heaps of antiques cluttering old wooden hutches.

Nora's house isn't anything like that. It's big but . . . empty, lacking any sort of warmth.

"Okay, hop up and swing your leg over the sink," she says, smacking the countertop as she rifles through a metal first aid kit. I do as she says, watching her pull out what seems like way too many things for just a scraped-up knee, but I don't say anything.

She unscrews the white cap off a brown bottle and moves to pour it over my knee. All of a sudden I'm transported back to my mom holding the same bottle over a cut when I was real little.

"Wait, is that the one that bur—*Oh my—Nora!*" I clutch my knee as the clear liquid sizzles over my scrape.

"Sorry, sorry, sorry, sorry." She winces up at me. "I thought it would be better if you didn't know it was coming." She dabs a paper towel over it and then finishes up by carefully spreading Neosporin over a rectangular Band-Aid and sticking it onto my knee. "There."

"Ow," I moan as I inspect my knee.

"Oh, you survived a fifteen-foot drop onto your head. You'll be all right," she says bluntly. I hop down off the counter, testing the bend in my knee.

"Has anyone ever told you that you're incredibly sensitive?" I ask.

"You'd be the first, and *thank you so much.*" She turns around, grinning innocently, and I shake my head at her. I'd never admit it to her, but I kinda love the way she talks to me, like I'm just a regular person. Like she's not afraid I'll break.

"How about lunch?" she asks, opening the fridge and slapping down a package of . . . uh . . . I don't know what.

"That looks . . ." I swallow hard as I inspect the package more closely. Tofurky. "Actually, I'm not that hu—"

"Relax," she replies, tossing a pack of honey ham right on top.

"Oh, thank God." I breathe a sigh of relief.

I watch as Nora slaps a few pieces of very wet-looking Tofurky onto her bread. She stops assembling to throw me an irritated look, but I can still see half of an amused smile underneath it.

"Can you stop looking at my food like it's a pile of cow shit on a plate? I will actually be eating it soon."

"Sorry," I reply with a laugh, trying to smooth out the wrinkles from my look of disgust.

"You really can't even tell the difference once I get done," she says.

"Oh, I'm sure," I reply as she adds lettuce, tomato, and then mayonnaise and Dijon mustard onto mine.

"That's my favorite combo, the ultimate condiments," I say in approval. "My dad loves it that way too."

She stills and looks at me and then back at the sandwich.

"Just one of my many talents," she says, but then her eyes shift just left of my head as a door creaks. I peek behind me through the doorway to see Mrs. Martin kicking her shoes off inside the heavy front door.

"Come on," Nora whispers, sliding me the plate with my sandwich on it. She leads me out of the kitchen, up an old wooden staircase, then down a narrow hallway whose gray walls are completely bare.

I follow her through a door and up a steeper set of uneven stairs, each one creaking underneath us with a different sound. It opens up to a large room with wood-slatted, sloped ceilings that peak in the center along the roofline. A finished attic. Cool.

"This is my room," Nora says, watching as I pick up my sandwich and take a small bite.

"Mmm. It's good. Thanks," I tell her, then dig in for a bigger mouthful.

I walk farther into the room, the faded floorboards almost bending under my shoes. The walls are just about as empty as the rest of the house except for three small Polaroids taped above her bed.

"Oh, I always love these instant photographs," I say. Leaving Nora standing in the doorway holding her untouched sandwich, I walk over to get a closer look at the photos.

The first is a shot of an open field, brown cows dotting the background. The second is Pittsburgh, the closest city to us, about an hour and a half away, with its big yellow bridge stretching across a wide river. And the third looks like it was maybe taken back in the woods where we just were. There's a girl sitting on a stump, facing away from the camera. It takes me a second to realize it's Nora. Hmm, that's a little odd.

Taking another bite of my sandwich, I step past her bed, and my eyes land on her side table. I swap my plate for the book that's lying on top, a California travel guide packed full of sticky notes. I open it up, fanning through the pages until another Polaroid falls out and floats toward my feet, landing facedown on the floor.

"Ooh, California. Are you taking a trip?" I ask, bending down to pick it back up, but before I can, Nora practically dives on the floor to grab it out from under me. She nabs it, holding it close to her chest.

"Sorry," I say, realizing I maybe shouldn't just be rifling through this girl's things when I just met her. I hand the book back to her.

"No, I'm . . ." She plops down on her bed, dropping her head as she runs her thumb over the worn cover. "I'm staying right here," she says disappointedly.

If there's one thing I can relate to, it's that. I sit down beside her on the bed.

"It's funny, I actually always thought I might like to live somewhere like California, but apparently I'm going to Bower. I guess we'll both be stuck in Wyatt," I say, looking over at her.

"You're going to Bower?" she asks, looking almost as surprised as I was when I first found out.

"Yeah. Are you?"

"No. I'm not going to college," she replies. "I'm going to work here full-time."

"Oh. Well . . . I'll be around if you want to hang out." I shrug, letting out a big sigh.

"Maybe you'll still make it out there someday. To California," she tells me.

"Maybe you will too," I reply, nudging my leg into hers.

We sit on her bed, eating the rest of our sandwiches in a comfortable silence, until Nora finishes her last bite and breaks it.

"Hey, uh, what are you doing this weekend?" she asks.

"Nothing, really," I reply before thinking.

"Maybe we—"

"Oh!" I cut her off, remembering the plans I made just yesterday. "Actually, I have a date with this guy, Ryan. He works at the Dinor. I wasn't really sure at first, since I can't remember meeting him, but he actually seems pretty cool, and—"

"You what?" Nora interjects.

"I have a—"

"No." She shakes her head, hopping up off the bed and standing right in front of me. "You can't . . . You . . ."

I don't know what reaction I was expecting, but it wasn't this. I remember Ryan saying he went to Wyatt. Does she know something about him?

"He was in your class, right? Is he like . . . a jerk or something? Because he seemed like a really good guy," I reply, giving her a confused look.

"No, he's not a jerk, I just . . ." She lets out a frustrated grunt and paces across the room, then stops to look at me again. "You don't even *like* him."

"How do *you* know if I like him? *I* don't even know if I like him yet." She turns away from me and I stand up to make my way over to her. "Why are you being like this? What, do *you* like have a crush on him or something?"

She turns her back to me. "Forget it. Actually just . . . Can you just go?"

"What?"

"Stevie, please just go." Her voice is low, shaky, but final.

So I do. I just . . . leave. Even though I have no idea what just happened. She must have a crush on him, that's the only thing that makes sense. But why not just say it, then?

Maybe this was a mistake, thinking Nora would be the right person to help me through this. Clearly, she's got some shit of her own to straighten out.

And whatever it is, she doesn't want me involved in it. At least not anymore.

July 5

A DATE? Are you kidding me, Stevie? Why are you pretending to like this guy? Why are you even thinking about dating, anyway? I feel like you have plenty on your plate right now trying to remember the last two years. It literally makes no sense.

Unless you're giving up.

God.

Please don't give up.

Because with how I just reacted I don't think you're going to want to be hanging out with me unless you do remember. It just took me by surprise . . . and well, what was I supposed to say when I hear my girlfriend is going out with some dude? Plus you told me coming right off the heels of our conversation about the future we almost had together. I just couldn't take it. And I can't explain how I know you won't like him, because I can't tell you any of this. This whole situation is impossible, Stevie.

I look at that photograph I have of you every single night, the one you almost found today, and I tell myself that we've already faced so much together, we can overcome this, too. But with each passing day . . . it feels like you're slipping further and further away from me.

I won't give up, though. I will never give up on you.

Being back in the woods did nothing to jog your memory like we both hoped, but I have to believe that something will. This Ryan thing is just temporary. Maybe it'll even be a good thing. Maybe when it falls flat, you'll realize why. You'll remember that this isn't you. You'll remember me.

Nora

CHAPTER 16

D ICE, STEVIE. *DICE!*" MY MOM YELLS FROM BEHIND me.

"I am dicing!" I turn around to face her, but she's just a big blur of colors through the stinging tears streaming down my cheeks. I swipe my sleeve across my face to clear my vision and see her vigorously stirring two pots of spaghetti sauce simultaneously.

"No. You're chopping," she says, eyes wide.

"Oh my gosh, Mom. *What* is the difference?" I ask, looking back at my pile of apparently *chopped* onions on the cutting board, my eyes practically burning out of their sockets.

"They need to be smaller. Like one-third that size."

"My God. She's becoming the Spaghetti Dinner Menace," I mumble under my breath as I get back to it.

"I heard that!" she replies with a laugh, trying and failing to knock her bare foot into me from her post at the stove. "I just want everything to be perfect."

"It will be. We're trying three different meatball recipes. One of them has to be a winner."

When she finally deems my pile of vegetables *diced*, we get to work assembling each of the three types, spreading them out evenly over a few sheet pans.

The first batch is 100 percent beef, the second is all pork, and the third is the two mixed together. Honestly, all of them smell *delicious* already, even raw. Probably thanks to all the garlic and parsley.

"So what did you and Nora do yesterday?" she asks, rolling a meatball between her palms.

"We—" Probably wouldn't be the best thing to tell my mom that I went right back to the place where I almost died. That sounds like a good way to *actually* die, since she'd kill me herself. "We just hung out at her house. She made us sandwiches and we talked."

"Well, she seems like a nice girl. You're welcome to have her over anytime."

"Okay," I reply, but I'm not so sure Nora and I will be hanging out again. Not after how the last time ended. Which reminds me, I've been wanting to ask my mom about Ryan, but I haven't been sure how to start. I guess I'm surprised that *she* hasn't brought him up to me. The only way she wouldn't is if I never told her.

"So, you know how I went to the Dinor with Savannah and Rory the other day? Well, they told me something . . . about, you know, before."

My mom sets her meatball down and looks over at me. "Oh?"

"Yeah, they told me about this . . . boy, Ryan. I guess I kinda really liked him."

She doesn't say anything at first, but I can feel her eyes on me. *"Really?"* she says finally, a surprised lightness in her voice, then excitement. Like this is the first she's hearing that he exists.

"Yeah." I look over to find a genuine look of shock covering her face that answers that, but I press on first. "I wanted to ask . . . can I go to the fair with him tomorrow? Savannah would be there too, and—"

"Yes," she replies before I can even finish. "Yes!" She throws her arms around me and squeals as she squeezes the breath out of me.

She finally releases me and picks her meatball back up, shaking her head with a huge smile still plastered onto her face. "See. I knew you'd find someone."

"What does that mean?" I ask, furrowing my eyebrows.

"Oh, n-nothing," she stutters. "I just . . . I'm happy for you, baby. Tell—"

"Mom, but how do you not already know about him? I have always told you literally *everything.*" I'm looking right at her, but her eyes are on the countertop now. "But that clearly hasn't been the case, and I just keep brushing it off, because you tell me everything is fine, but . . . *something* doesn't feel right."

"I don't know what you mean." She shrugs.

"Really? You didn't know the answer when I asked why Savannah and Rory quit soccer. You reacted so weird when I told you to come sleep in the hospital bed with me. We haven't gone to Lola's in over a year and you could barely give me an explanation why. And then *this.* What aren't you telling me?" I raise my voice, pleading with her to finally come clean.

"Stevie, just drop it."

"*Why?* I deserve to know! Maybe it would even help me remember."

"You shut me out!" she replies, her shaky voice echoing through the kitchen. When she looks up at me, her eyes are shining with tears just like that night in bed at the hospital.

"What?" I ask, my voice softer now.

She sniffles, turning away from me to look out the window. "You just stopped talking to me." Her words stab me right through the heart.

"What do you mean? I wouldn't. We're so close." I shake my head, blinking hard.

"We don't spend time together, Stevie. We don't talk. We barely ever even sit in the same room."

I try to process this. Try to imagine me just drifting away from her. But I can't. Does it have something to do with me lying about work and ditching Savannah and Rory? Is it all connected?

"Mom, *something* must have happened. I wouldn't just . . ."

"You grew up, Stevie. That's what happened. I mean, I knew it had to happen eventually, but . . ." She shrugs. "You just . . . you wouldn't talk to me. I tried so many times. You have no idea how many times." She pulls her sleeve over the end of her thumb to wipe a tear off her cheek. "I'm sorry. I know more questions isn't what you need right now. I know you're trying to get back on track so I didn't want to say anything."

"No, I want you to be honest. I *need* you to be." I reach across to squeeze her forearm, hoping she'll look at me, but she doesn't. And even if I can't remember why, I can feel it in my chest, how deeply I've hurt her. Guilt washes over me.

"But whatever it was, it's in the past," she replies quietly. "We can start over."

I genuinely can't imagine a scenario that would cause me to completely stop talking to my mom, but even just thinking about it scares me. I've been trying so hard to get the past back, because I thought it would solve all of my problems, but maybe I'm wrong.

Maybe some things are better left forgotten.

CHAPTER 17

WHAT IN THE SAM HILL IS THAT KID DRIVING? Looks like a monster truck," my dad says, looking out the front window at Jake Mackey's pickup truck pulling into the driveway. Good Lord, and he's still got his gigantic and offensive Confederate flag hanging off the back. Not that Confederate flags are particularly hard to find around here, but most people don't have flagpole-sized ones billowing from their mode of transportation. It looks even bigger than I remember. I absolutely should've insisted on just driving myself, but it's too late now.

"See, I could be going on a date with that guy instead of Ryan," I say, standing up next to Dad.

"At least he would then have the balls to pick you up himself and shake my hand."

"Dad, he doesn't even know you want to meet him. We'd already agreed to just meet there," I tell him, rolling my eyes.

"Well, I'm sorry that I don't trust some guy I've never met to not break my daughter's heart."

"Your dad's just having trouble letting his little girl go on her first date," my mom says from behind me. Then she turns me around and wraps me in a hug. "But if you want to leave early, just text and I can come get you, and *no* crazy rides, okay? Just take it easy." She gently touches my head before letting me go. It's been almost two weeks since I woke up in the hospital. My stitches haven't quite dissolved yet, but I can tell they're *really* close.

"Got it. See you guys tonight," I say before heading out the door.

"Text me when you get there!" my mom shouts while I barely manage to yank myself up into the backseat of Jake's truck.

"Hey, bitch," Savannah greets me as Jake turns around to look at me.

"Hi, my name's Jake," he says over a lower lip full of dip.

"Yeah, I know, we've been in school together since pre-school, Jake," I reply, squinting at him.

"I *told* you. She just can't remember the last two years, dummy," Savannah says, slapping her hand into his chest.

"Oh, word. Okay. 'Sup, Stevie."

Something tells me this is going to be a long ride.

"You ready?" Savannah asks, smiling back at me and shimmying her shoulders. I laugh and throw my hands up in the air. *I guess so.*

"Kind of cute that the only two Chinese kids in Wyatt are dating each other," Jake says, his blue eyes finding me in the rearview.

"I'm Korean," I tell him, fighting the urge to roll my eyes.

"Same thing." He shrugs and then turns his country music up.

Definitely going to be a long ride.

• • •

Venturing out to the county fair on opening night is a little bit like being caught in the middle of the Black Friday stampede at Walmart. Except people aren't after flat-screen TVs or the newest PlayStation. They're just after a shred of excitement, since the fair is pretty much the only novelty that goes on within a thirty-mile radius of Wyatt. It's the event of the year, and tonight, everyone and their cousin are here and on the move.

I've barely stepped past the chain link fence and already I've seen about thirty kids from my high school. Some who are currently attending, and others who just couldn't escape Wyatt's gravitational pull.

I guess I fall into that category now too.

"He said he'd meet us by the . . . ," I start to say, but I turn around to find Savannah and Jake standing in line at the ticket counter with their backs to me, his hand planted firmly around her ass and his lips on hers. I guess I'll have to meet Ryan alone. I roll my eyes and leave them behind me, weaving through the rivers of people until I find the Ferris wheel exactly where it always is, right between the Roundup and the Gee Wizz, which actually looks a lot smaller than it used to.

"Hey," a voice says from behind me as a hand lightly grazes my shoulder. I turn around to find Ryan looking down at me like I've just made his day by showing up here, even though he knew I was coming.

"Hi," I reply, suddenly a little nervous as I tuck my hands into my back pockets. As I was getting ready tonight, I didn't feel very nervous, or much of anything. But now, standing here in front of Ryan, his red apron swapped for faded blue jeans and a plain white pocket T that shows off his tan arms . . . my palms are at least feeling a little sweaty, which has to mean I'm feeling something. Right?

"Thanks for coming. Do you want to walk around?" he asks, his smile matching the white of his shirt.

"Uhh . . ." I consider telling him we should go meet back up with Savannah, but I just don't know if I want to hang out with Jake all night. Savannah might be offended that I didn't text her, but that's what she gets for dating Jake Mackey. "Yeah. I still have to buy tickets, though," I reply, craning my neck to look around for the peeling pink paint of the ticket shacks scattered around the grounds.

"Got it covered." He holds up a neat stack of what has to be over a hundred tickets, enough for about thirty rides or in my case fifty games, since I'm only a games girl tonight. I hope he doesn't mind that I won't be able to ride anything other than maybe a slow spin around the Ferris wheel.

"Holy shit, Ryan," I say with a laugh.

"I like games," he says guiltily, and it feels like everything is coming together.

An idea for the perfect place to start pops into my head. It's a game I've always wanted to play but have never been able to. Not until now, because *I'm an adult.*

"Are you eighteen?" I ask.

"Yeah, why?"

"Have you ever played the ring toss here?"

"We just moved here at the end of last summer." *So that's why I haven't seen him before.* "I've never been here. Why?"

A knowing smirk spreads across my face as I hand the stack of tickets back to him but don't say anything.

"You're scaring me. Should I be scared?" he asks, eyeballing me suspiciously.

"Possibly," I reply, my smile widening as I picture the most ridiculous, most unbelievable game in the history of county fairs.

We walk across the grass, which is destined to become a giant mud pit by the end of the night, and toward the stalls at the far end of the grounds.

"Stevie? Where are we going?" Ryan asks, just as I finally catch a glimpse of the ring toss booth through an opening in the crowd.

"Give me four tickets and your ID," I tell him, digging my own out of my back pocket. He hands everything to me, following on my heels until I spin around to face him right in front of the booth.

"Ta-da!" I say, as we both take in the glorious weirdness in front of us.

One hundred pocketknives are stuck blade down into a spinning contraption shaped like a giant tiered wedding cake. People are crowded around it, shoulder to shoulder, tossing red plastic rings out in the hope of landing one around a knife and being lucky enough to take it home. Screams of celebration ring out all around us as a woman on the other side wins a neon-orange one with a deer head stamped into the plastic.

"Oh my God." Ryan looks on, eyes wide in utter shock as he steps closer to me, lowering his voice. "How is this legal?" he asks.

I laugh as I turn to the game attendant who's approaching us. "We'll take a full bucket." I raise my voice so he can hear me, handing him our IDs and the tickets. He hands them right back to me without even looking. I glance over and see a guy with a big beard and a beer belly pick his toddler up so that he can throw one. Maybe I could've been playing this game all along. Savannah and Rory never understood why I was so stuck on playing this one day. It's not that I'm particularly obsessed with knives, but *come on*. Who wouldn't want to play this weird-ass game?

The attendant tucks the tickets into his pouch and hands me a bucket filled to the brim with rings. It takes us three full buckets to actually win, but *finally* one of Ryan's rings captures a small pocketknife with a wooden handle, stuck into the second tier.

"Oh my God, Ryan! You did it! You got one!" I yell, thrilled.

"WOOOO!" he hollers, the sound coming from somewhere deep in his throat.

"Hell yeah, dude!" I give him a double high five and then we quickly get the attendant's attention, trying to point out our knife as the poor guy dodges rings being thrown all around him and, I suspect, *at* him as well.

After he drops the knife into Ryan's hand, we duck out of the crowd and into an open spot beside the basketball hoops.

"For you," he says, handing me the knife, the blade tucked safely away in the handle.

"Wow. Every girl's dream. There's nothing more romantic than a boy winning you a knife," I joke, taking it from him. But my cheeks turn red when I realize I've just mentioned *romance*. "Thanks," I add with a smile, and tuck it into my pocket.

Luckily my mention of romance doesn't make things weird.

After our first win there's no stopping us, and we make our way to each of the booths. Darts, we win a wonky Minion from *Despicable Me* that looks a little different than I remember from the movie, and Ryan gives it to a little girl playing beside us, which is adorable. Basketball, neither of us has any luck at. Then we find our way to the Rope Ladder, four rotating, wobbly ladders hanging over a sloped, inflatable base. The goal: to hold on for dear life as you climb up to the buzzer at the very top.

"Aww man. I *gotta* try this," Ryan says, already pulling ahead of me with excitement. I watch as he hands the attendant ticket after ticket, falling time and time again.

He bounces down with a grunt for the tenth time and slides back down to the ground. "Okay. This is the last time," he says to me, completely out of breath but still excited. As he hands over another ticket and takes a second to formulate a game plan, the attendant eggs him on by bunny-hopping up onto a middle rung right in front of him and then somehow manages to walk right up to the top, pressing the buzzer without his hands ever touching the ladder.

"Yeah, real nice, buddy," Ryan says as he steps up again. His legs are already shaking like a leaf before he even makes it to the second rung, but to my surprise, he steadies himself and manages to go farther than he ever has before. I take a step forward, holding my breath as he lowers himself to the ladder, as close as he can get. *What is he . . .*

All at once he makes a full-body lunge toward the button at the top but misses by about seven feet and slams down onto the base with a thud. I bust out laughing as he rolls his way back down and onto his feet.

"Did you see how close I was that time?!" He holds his thumb and pointer finger about an inch apart. "*This close*. I was *this close* to that buzzer," he says.

"Sure, 'this close.'" I laugh.

Now I can't remember what I was so nervous about. This is just like hanging out with a friend. Maybe I've been making too big a deal out of it.

"You want to get something to eat?" he asks.

"Yeah, I've been dying for a caramel apple all year. So for like three years, I guess. Which is *way* too long to be wanting a caramel apple," I reply.

"You know, you can get those at the grocery store."

"It's not the same. I need the full experience," I tell him as we head out of the games section.

"The exorbitant prices, the hundreds of sweaty people around you, the smell of mud and porta-potties," he jokes.

"*Exactly,*" I say as we pass a gun raffle right next to a couple of people handing out free Bibles.

We take our time walking through the food stands, neither of us attempting to overtake the group of older ladies ahead of us. We slow our pace, listening to them bicker about whether or not the malt vinegar on their fresh-cut fries was watered down this year, as the smell of greasy funnel cakes swirls all around us.

"So why did you and your family move here?" I ask, looking up at him, about half a head taller than me.

"My dad got a job a couple of towns over and my mom really liked the house they found here." He shrugs. "Although they're gone more than they're home."

"I'm sorry, that sucks. How do you like Wyatt so far?" I ask.

"It's . . . nice." I meet eyes with him. I can see his face starting to break, and soon we're both laughing. *Wyatt. Nice. HA.* "I don't know. The people here all seem kinda . . . the same, I guess. It sorta felt like I would never really belong. I mean, until I met you, of course."

"No, I know what you mean. I feel like that sometimes and I was born and raised here, so you're not alone," I reply.

"It's been okay, but I'll be more than ready to get out of here in the fall," he says.

"Oh, where are you going?" I ask.

"I'm doing my first semester in Rome."

"No *way!*" I say, excited for him, but also a little bummed that he'll be leaving at the end of summer too and I'll be staying right here.

"How about you? What are you doing?" he asks.

"Staying here. Going to Bower, the community college," I reply, feeling a little crushed again just saying it.

"You don't seem too thrilled."

"It's fine, I guess. My dad thinks it'll be good for me to stay close to home after . . . you know." I point vaguely to my head, and suddenly, I realize for the first time that I haven't thought about any of that all night, partially thanks to Ryan not bringing it up. "Bower just isn't exactly what I had in mind for myself," I add.

"What *did* you have in mind?" he asks.

"Basically anything that doesn't involve Wyatt. It's not that I ever had any concrete dreams or plans, but this town is like . . . dead. It has been for as long as I've been alive. There will never be any new ideas or beliefs. Never any room for change. It's just . . . stuck. And the people are stuck, and now I'm going to be stuck." I shake my head in frustration. "College would've been the perfect opportunity to experience somewhere new. So I don't understand why I would choose to stay."

"You're not stuck, Stevie. It's not too late." He shrugs. "I'm positive there are some colleges still taking applications for the fall. Maybe especially with your circumstances."

"Yeah, that's—" I stop when I hear a familiar voice yelling something ahead of us and find Savannah standing in front of the Ring of Fire with Jake. Somehow while Ryan and I have been talking, we've managed to walk the whole way through the food and back into the rides section.

"Stevie, where the *hell* have you been? I've been texting you *all* night," Savannah says as we approach her, sounding much more annoyed than worried.

"Sorry. I must have my phone on silent," I lie.

"Well, we're about to ride this. You guys coming?" she asks, pointing straight up in the air.

"Yeah! Totally. Stevie? You seem like the adventurous type. I've seen you slather your entire breakfast in hot sauce on more than one occasion," Ryan says, reminding me that the two of us have a past. However big or small, we interacted, got to know each other, enough for me to develop feelings for him. He's not a clean slate like Nora. He remembers things that I don't, and for the first time all night that scares me a little.

"I think I'm going to pass, but you guys go ahead," I reply, looking up at the gigantic circular roller coaster looming over us against the night sky. I'm going to go ahead and guess that this is exactly the type of ride my mom would consider off-limits.

"You sure? I'll stay back. We could go eat or play some more games or—"

"No, go ahead. I'll . . ." I look around until I spot the attraction my mom and I always loved. "I'll take a walk through the animal barn. Come find me after you ride a few of these." I can tell by how quickly he gives in that he really does want to ride, but I can't help feeling a little bummed about it.

I walk to the darkest corner of the fairgrounds, away from the music and the lights and the screams of laughter, where there's a big wooden barn. String lights line the wide-open sliding doors, revealing rows of rabbit cages and stalls of horses, donkeys, cows, and goats. There are a lot fewer people over here, mostly parents with their small kids, pointing out the blue ribbons hanging on various gates.

I make my way around slowly, looking in each cage at every rabbit, giving a couple of pats to a big white scraggly one that didn't even score an honorable mention. Behind me, a horse sticks his muzzle out and nips at my hair. I step around to the side of him and run my hand down the white diamond between his eyes, before turning the corner to find a perfectly groomed brown cow lying down on a pile of hay outside of his stall.

"Hey, buddy," I say, squatting down in front of him, his ears flicking as a fly hops back and forth between them. I hear the rip of tickets off the roll and pick my head up, looking over him to the source.

"Nora?" I ask, before I can even process what I'm doing, before I remember our last encounter.

As she hands a man an arm's length of red raffle tickets, she looks back at me, startled.

"Stevie. What are you doing here?" she asks as she drops the other halves of the tickets into a plastic container.

"Just . . ." I shrug, shaking my head. "Riding some rides, playing some games. What about you?" I ask as she adjusts her faded-red Martin's Meats baseball cap.

"We're raffling off some beef to raise money for the fire station," she replies, motioning to the brown cow that I just made friends with . . . *Oh. Oh no.*

She points behind her out the door. "I think maybe the gun raffle out there is having a little more success with ticket sales, though."

"Welcome to Wyatt," I add, and we sigh in unison.

"Hey." She stands up, setting the roll of tickets on her folding chair. "Uh, listen. I'm sorry I was so weird the other day. I was just dealing with something. It didn't have anything to do with you. Okay?" she says, but I can still see it in her eyes. Like . . . a lingering sadness.

"Are you sure? Because it kinda seemed like it," I reply. "I'm sorry if I was being too nosy looking around your room. I wasn't trying—"

"No, no, no." She shakes her head. "Really. It wasn't you. I was just trying to find something to do tonight so I had an excuse not to be here selling tickets. And I really liked talking to you. We should do it again sometime, maybe without you getting injured, though. If you think you could manage that."

"Yeah." I grin. "I can at least try."

"So did you win anything?" she asks.

"Yeah, we actually managed to win this in the ring toss," I tell her, pulling the small knife out of my pocket.

She cocks her head at me. "We?"

With perfect timing, Ryan comes around the corner, stepping up beside Nora with a giant caramel apple in hand. A big smile breaks out across my face. *He found my apple.*

"Nora, I think you and Ryan went to school together. Ryan, Nora," I say, motioning between the two of them.

"Yeah. Hey, Nora," Ryan says, throwing her a head nod.

"Oh. H-Hey, Ryan. Good to see you," she replies, readjusting her hat.

"Stevie, you want to walk around some more? I've got my eye on some deep-fried Oreos," Ryan says, already starting to backpedal toward the exit.

"Uh, sure," I reply. "Just a sec." I hang back with Nora for a moment, noticing her shoulders sagging slightly.

"Are . . . you okay?" I ask her.

"Yeah," she says quickly, her cheeks pulling up into a smile, but it drops just as fast.

"You sure?" I ask again, and this time, she meets my eyes. There's a look in them that for some reason makes me not want to leave her here all alone.

"I'm sure." She scratches the cow's neck as she plops down into her chair.

"Stevie, you coming?" Ryan calls from halfway down the barn.

"Okay, well, maybe we can hang out soon? You'll call me?" I ask as I take a step past Nora.

"Yeah, totally," she replies, crossing her legs and turning away from me.

A few minutes later, as Ryan snacks on his paper boat of deep-fried Oreos and I eat all of the crushed peanuts and caramel off the outside of my Granny Smith apple, he tells me about the rides he went on. I try to listen, to stay present, but my mind keeps wandering back to Nora and why she seemed so . . . down.

"Hey, there's nothing going on between you two, right?" I ask Ryan.

"Who? Me and *Nora*?" He snorts out a laugh. "What gave us away? Our lustful greeting? Our palpable chemistry?" he asks sarcastically. "I barely know her."

I don't get it, then. . . . Why did she seem so upset just now? What could—

Oh. It hits me as we're walking past a burger stand.

"It's the cow!" I stop, slapping Ryan in the chest, and he looks at me like I just told him I want to buy tickets for the gun raffle. "Nora. She seemed really down and I couldn't figure out why, but it's because she's vegan."

"I mean, I know living a vegan lifestyle probably isn't the *most* enjoyable, but . . ."

"No. I mean, she's selling tickets to raffle off the cow that's just been lying at her feet all day. She's probably bummed about having to kill the cow for meat," I tell him, proud of myself for solving this very inconsequential case. "She did save my life. I wish I could help her save the cow."

Ryan pops another Oreo into his mouth.

"You could try to win it. And then it can just live on her family's farm?" he suggests casually, trying to talk over his mouthful of food.

"Would that work? Like you think they could keep it and not kill it?" I ask.

He shrugs. "They have like a million acres, I'm sure there's space for it."

"Wait, that might actually be a good idea," I reply, my eyes lighting up as I put the plastic back over my apple and pull my cash out of my pocket. "I've got thirty-three dollars."

"I've got . . ." He empties his wallet. "Twenty-seven."

"You don't have to spend your own money on this, Ryan."

He shrugs. "It supports the fire hall, right?"

"Are we really about to spend sixty bucks on a *chance* to win a cow for a girl neither of us really knows?" I ask, but the answer is already clear based on the mischievous look on his face, the one I'm sure is plastered on my own, too.

When we make it back to the animal barn, Nora is gone. In her place is a young Amish guy with a short beard and a straw hat, the short sleeves of his button-down cuffed at the ends. I hand him the money and he hands us a string of tickets so long that it drags against the dusty barn floor. I give Ryan half and we get to work writing my name and phone number on each one.

After we drop them into the bucket, we head outside through the open doors, both of us shaking out our right hands.

"This was really fun. Well, not just trying to buy a cow. I mean the whole night. Thanks for . . . everything," I tell him honestly.

"Thanks for coming with me," he says, looking down at me, the back of his hand brushing against mine as I suddenly remember that this is a *date*, not just two friends hanging out, even though that's what it has felt like all night long. And dates come with certain expectations that even with as much fun as we had . . . I'm not at all ready for. But the way he's looking at me tells me that *he* is.

I reach down deep to try to pull out that feeling that I always thought was supposed to come when you want to kiss someone. That feeling from the movies where time slows down and lights seem to dim and maybe your chest feels a little floaty.

But even with the bright lights flashing all around us and the warm summer air, it just isn't quite there yet. I'm sure I just need a little more time. I mean, not everyone kisses on the first date, right? I feel like I'm just finally starting to get to know him.

"Uhh, I should probably find Savannah, I think they're about to start closing down for the night," I tell him, even though I know the fair stays open until midnight opening night.

"Oh, sure. Okay. Yeah, I should be getting home too, probably."

I give him a quick hug, patting him twice on the back before I disappear into the crowd. My heart is beating a mile a minute as I weave my way through an opening and lean up against the cool concrete behind the bathrooms, filled with disappointment.

I thought it would be easier than this. I thought it would be instant just like my newfound love of coffee with hazelnut creamer. I *had* a crush on him before, so I should have a crush on him now. I'm still the same person.

But where are those feelings?

And why aren't they coming back?

July 7

Stevie,

I realized something tonight at the fair. I can't sit here and wait anymore. I can't do nothing or keep lying, waiting for you to call me on it. I can't keep watching other people lie to you.

I need to find a way to tell you the truth.

About us. About you.

I should have from the start. But I didn't. So now . . . I need to figure out how to do it without making you hate me.

Please don't hate me.

Nora

CHAPTER 18

M Y FIRST SUNDAY BACK AT ST. JOE'S THIS MORNING felt more like some sort of funeral service than it did Mass. In the hundred-yard walk from our pew to my mom's car, about thirty people stopped to touch my shoulder and tell me how sorry they were for what happened. Like I'd died or something.

Samantha McDonald from the year below me asked if I was okay and then immediately tried to touch my scar.

My kindergarten teacher asked suspiciously if I really drove my car into the reservoir.

Mr. Yardley told me about his cousin who went into a coma and never woke up.

Old Monsignor Becker, who I can't even believe has made it two more years, told me it's all part of His plan.

Not a single one of them said something that might actually make me feel even slightly better. They wanted to make themselves feel better, or even worse, get the gossip on Wyatt's latest news.

I've been going to Mass my whole life, so I'm used to sitting through the fifty minutes of monotony and the gossip that spreads after, but today . . . I just wanted to get the hell out of there.

"Stevie." My mom presses her hand down on my knee until my heel settles onto the cracked pavement underneath our picnic table at the farmers' market.

"Sorry," I say. I didn't even realize I was bouncing it up and down.

"You haven't touched your food," she says, her eyes flicking down to my hot dog smothered in yellow mustard and mayo. It turns my stomach. I don't even know if I like hot dogs anymore, but the longer I look at it, the sicker I feel. So I push it away from me to the other side of the wooden table. "I'm not hungry," I tell her as a big German shepherd strolls by on a leash, sticking his nose out for a hopeful sniff.

"Stevie." She swings one leg to the outside of the bench to face me. "What's going on in your head right now? You haven't said a thing since we got here."

That's the problem. I don't know what's going on in my head. I don't know what I want. Part of me wants desperately to move on with my life, just accept this clean slate, but everywhere I go everyone keeps reminding me of this unknowable past and the questions that I don't have answers to. That I might not like the answers to if I did find them.

I changed. Sometime over these last two years, I became someone who ditches her best friends and skips out on senior prom. Someone who is totally fine with staying in Wyatt for college. Someone who has a crush on a boy but doesn't tell her mom about it. Someone who has grown apart from her dad, and who sneaks off into the woods in the middle of nowhere without telling any of her friends or family.

I can't just forget that all of these things happened in my

life even though I don't know why they did, because they still affect all my relationships now. And most of all, I can't forget the way my mom looked at me in the kitchen that day. I will never get that look out of my head, no matter how much I want to forget it.

"Talk to me. What's wrong?" she asks as I pick at a peeling wood chip on the table.

"What if what happened between us happens again? I don't ever want to hurt you like that again, Mom, but if I can't remember what happened, how do I know I won't just do it again?" I ask, pulling back.

My mom stutters around her words for a moment before saying, "Stevie, nothing is going to magically happen that makes you and me grow apart. *You* get to choose how you want to live your life now. *You* get to choose who you want to spend time with. You and me? We're going to be fine. Just . . . *look* at us. Hanging out like old times. Making meatballs and talking about *boys*. Stevie, I know you've been really focused on remembering, but . . . would it be so bad if you just . . . didn't? I mean, of course if it happens it'll be amazing, but if it doesn't, well, sometimes we all need a fresh start," she says sheepishly.

I sit back, a little shocked to hear her say that not having my memories could be a good thing, but . . . the longer I sit with it, the more I see where she's coming from. I don't know what it was like when things were bad between us, and I can't change that it happened, but I know that sitting here with her in the sunshine in the middle of the summer farmers' market . . . feels right. It makes me think maybe some good could come out of all this after all. Maybe she's right. Maybe I've been chasing after the wrong thing. Maybe I can use this as a second chance . . . to do things right this time. And maybe I don't need the answers to do that.

I reach across and wrap my hand around the back of hers on top of the table.

"Maybe a fresh start would be nice," I tell her.

Perhaps starting off with a clean slate could mean also applying to some other colleges, maybe even some out of state, instead of just trying to figure out why I chose Bower.

"One day at a time, right?" she says, touching her hand gently to my cheek. "You want to walk around with me?"

"Sure," I reply as she gathers up my untouched hot dog and stands. "Hey, Mom, actually . . . I'll eat that."

"I thought you weren't hungry," she says, furrowing her brow.

"Changed my mind." I pick it up, taking a big bite as I climb out of the table to follow her.

Yep. I still like hot dogs.

Maybe the last two years were just a detour, not a path I have to figure out why I was following in the first place. Maybe I can still be the person I wanted to be.

An hour later we've almost made it to the end of the twenty or so tents set up around the parking lot.

"Well, I guess you're not going to tell me how your date went," Mom says, inspecting a basket of fresh-picked apples.

"You know, it was actually a lot of fun. I really like hanging out with Ryan."

"Yeah? You like him?" she asks, smiling over at me.

"Well . . . I'm not really sure. I'm kinda just getting to know him. You know?"

"Just take it slow. Sometimes it just takes a bit. That's sort of how it was with me and your dad."

"Really? What do you mean?"

She laughs, getting lost in the memories. "He would come into Billie's, where I used to bartend. Him and all his rowdy friends. I bet your dad asked me out *ten times* over the course of that couple of weeks, always right in front of his buddies. I thought he was just some jerk who was looking for a hookup, but . . . then he started coming in alone and he'd sit up at the bar and try all my new drinks I was concocting. Give me feedback. We did that for a few months and then I don't know. It wasn't some big spark between us or anything. He just . . . grew on me. My big Johnny."

"Ew." I audibly gag. "Mom, please, I just ate."

She laughs. "Just hang in there. Give Ryan a chance."

"I will," I reply, feeling encouraged.

"So what all did you guys do at the fair?"

"Lots of games. And I got a caramel apple."

"And you only ate the peanuts and caramel off, right?" she asks.

"How else would I eat it?" I joke as we try a few chips-and-salsa samples. "Then we actually ran into Nora Martin in the animal barn."

"Oh, how is she?" she asks, before her eyes go wide and she starts fanning her mouth. "Oh my lanta. That's hotter than Hades." I roll my eyes and hand her my water bottle.

"She's okay, I think, but she seemed sort of sad. We might hang out again. I don't really know."

"I think you should. She seems like a nice girl who could probably use a friend like you," Mom replies, panting like a dog between words.

Huh. I feel guilty. I hadn't really put a lot of thought into what Nora might need. I could use a fresh start, but from what I saw with her mom, maybe Nora needs that too.

Maybe she could use a friend like me just as much as I could use a friend like her.

CHAPTER 19

MOCHA ICE BLEND WITH TWO SHOTS AND EXTRA whip," I call out into the coffee shop, sliding a perfectly made drink onto the pickup counter. A five-hour shift and zero mistakes. Progress. Mostly thanks to Kendra not scheduling me with Cal anymore.

"You're really getting it down again, Stevie," Kendra says with a satisfied look.

"Thanks for being so patient with me," I reply, feeling like I'm finally starting to settle in now that I'm not spending all my time trying to remember the past.

"Oh please, you're killing it." She looks at the analog clock on the decorative brick wall behind us. Noon. "Go on. Get out of here. I'll see you tomorrow," she says.

"Sweet. I convinced my dad to rent a boat today to take my mom and me out on the reservoir," I reply, with a stupid smile plastered onto my face. We haven't actually done anything together all three of us since the accident, which feels so weird. So I think it's the perfect time for our annual summer boat outing. I think it's exactly what we need.

"Well, have a good time! You've got a great day for it," she replies.

I pull my phone out of my pocket to let them know I'm going to head to the marina, but before I can, I find a voice mail from an unknown number and a different kind of text from my dad.

Hey kiddo, not going to be able to get out on the water today. Swamped at the garage and Uncle Chuck called out sick. Maybe see you tonight if I'm not home too late.

Damn.

I peel off my apron and then head out the back door toward my Volvo.

I press play on that voice mail and hold it up to my ear. I'm assuming it's a telemarketer since who really leaves voicemails anymore, so I'm not expecting it to improve my mood. But my mouth drops open slightly as the guy on the other end talks and my disappointment is temporarily forgotten.

I can't actually believe it.

The second he's finished, I quickly dial Ryan's number, strapping my seat belt around me at the same time. With each ring, my smile grows a little wider.

Pick up. Pick up.

"Hello?" he says finally.

"Ryan . . . we won! We freaking won a cow!" I scream into the phone, and he laughs.

"You're kidding me. That's amazing! Where are you?" he asks, incredulous.

"I'm on my way to the farm to like . . . I don't know, tell Nora it's hers, I guess?"

I can figure out the logistics of picking up and re-delivering a cow later.

"You *have* to call me after and tell me what she says."

"I will," I reply as I turn the key over, switching my phone to the other ear.

"Maybe we could do it again sometime," he says.

"Win another cow? I'm not sure we should press our luck," I joke.

"I was thinking more like lunch. I work the next two days, but maybe Thursday?" he asks.

"I don't think I can," I reply.

"Oh . . . okay. Yeah, that's cool. I—"

I cut him off before he spirals. "I have to work the lunch shift on Thursday. How about Friday?"

"Friday." I can almost hear his smile widening through the phone and it brings nerves to my stomach. "Okay. I'll text you."

"Bye, Ryan," I say before hanging up and trying not to think too much about what a second date might entail. Instead, I focus on what my mom said about giving him a chance, about how it might take time like it did with my parents.

I shake it off and shoot Nora a text.

Meet me at the meat shop. I've got something for you.

When I arrive twenty minutes later, I'm so caught up in the excitement of telling Nora that I totally forget that there might be someone else working here today. Luckily, when I walk through the worn door, it's not her mom. Instead, the guy I bought the tickets from is standing behind the counter. Nora is nowhere to be seen, but he is staring expectantly at me, waiting for me to order or something.

"Uh, hi. I'm Stevie. I won the cow." *Never thought I'd say those particular words in my entire life.*

"'Ey, congrats! I'll be right back . . ." His voice trails off as he points behind him. I nod and he disappears through the doorframe. God, I hope he doesn't walk it out here and expect me to put it in my backseat.

"Is Nora here?" I call out. If he brings it, I guess I'll walk it out to her.

"I think she's out working on the fence right now," he says. I can hear him rummaging around back there.

"Okay. Do you know when she'll be done?" I ask, checking my phone, but there's no reply from her.

"I'm not sure. But it's taking her forever. If you ask me, I bet she's been sneaking around with some boy instead, but she keeps denying it," he replies, emerging from the back, dragging a cart behind him.

Nora never mentioned a boy, but I guess it's possible.

"Okay, well, I actually won the cow for—" Before I can finish, a giant vacuum-sealed slab of red meat smacks down onto the counter in front of me with a thud . . . followed by another and then another. I watch with horror as he empties the whole cart, until the counter is covered with enough meat to fill the entire display case at our local grocery store.

"Oh my God," I gasp as I picture the cute brown cow that was lying on the barn floor at the fair and then fully take in the pile that's stacking up in front of me. Ribs, ground beef, steaks, tenderloin, roast . . .

What have I done?!

"Stevie?" a voice asks from behind me, making sweat break out across my brow and goose bumps rise to the surface of my skin. *Oh no.*

Sure enough, I turn around to find Nora stepping in through the front door.

"Nora!" I quickly slide in front of the counter, as if my 120-pound frame and stick arms could even come *close* to covering the enormous pile of raw beef behind me. "I-I," I stutter, unable to string an explanation together. What started as an idea to do something nice for her by saving this cow's life has ended with her seeing me take home five hundred pounds of meat. She's going to think I'm a *murderer*.

"I got your text. What are you doing here? What's that?" she asks, her eyes shifting to look behind me. This was a *bad* idea. I should never even have bought tickets for it. Why did I ever think they would give me the opportunity to take a *live* cow from a meat farm? But she's standing there looking at me, waiting for an answer, so I *have* to get myself together.

"I won the cow at the raffle . . . for you," I tell her, and she twists her face up in confusion.

"Why the hell would you do that?" she asks, walking across the small space to stand next to me.

"Well, it was supposed to be *alive*," I explain, trying to clear everything up, but she looks even more lost, if that's possible.

"Again . . . why would you do that?" she repeats, and now *I'm* the one looking at *her* like she's not making any sense. The answer is so clear.

"You seemed super bummed at the fair that night and I know you're vegan, so I thought maybe it was your favorite cow or something and it was about to get . . . you know." I run my thumb across my neck, clicking my tongue.

Nice, Stevie. Way to be delicate.

But then to my surprise, Nora laughs. "You know I live on a beef farm, right? We slaughter hundreds of cattle every single year. You think I'd have a problem with *one* cow?"

My eyes shift from her to the pile of meat and then back to her. "Well, *why* are you vegan, then?!"

"Yeah, I don't get it either," the guy working the counter cuts in.

"Albert, how many times am I going to have to explain it to you?" Nora asks, throwing her hands up in the air before turning to face me. Then she checks her watch and glances at the front door again. "I'm really sorry, Stevie, but I gotta get back to work or my mom is going to kill me. Can we talk later?" she asks.

Later. I don't really want to wait until later. After talking to my mom, I'm done waiting to uncover things. I want to start living my second chance, to be an actual friend to Nora, after everything she did for me. She's different than everyone else here. Definitely way different than Savannah and Rory. Somehow, hanging out with Nora feels more effortless than spending time with the two people I've known my entire life. I can't quite put my finger on why yet, but I want to figure it out. Not that *I* should be giving anyone relationship advice, but maybe I can lend an ear for her boy drama.

"Wait, what are you working on out there?" I ask as she wipes the sweat off her brow.

"Just putting up that new fence that I was telling you about the other day."

"Well, could you use an extra set of hands?"

She looks over her shoulder at the wall, thinking, and then back to me. Finally she takes in a deep breath and lets it out. "Come on."

CHAPTER 20

A FTER NORA ASKS ALBERT TO PUT MY "WINNINGS" back in the walk-in, I follow her out the squeaky front door and around the side of the shop, where a four-wheeler is parked in the shade. It's obviously been *through* it. The green paint is faded and scuffed, and the tires are heavily caked with mud.

I expect to walk right by, but then Nora plants her boot on the foothold and swings her leg over the seat to the other side. She turns and flicks her head at me as if to say *Hop on*, but I've never ridden one before and to be honest, I'm a little nervous.

"Don't worry. I have my license." She smirks, dimples forming in her cheeks that I've never noticed before.

Her expression doesn't reassure me one bit, but I guess it beats walking, considering I almost died of heat exhaustion when we hiked out to the woods the other day.

I step up beside it, unsure of exactly where to get on. It must be obvious by the look on my face, because she reaches back and pats the small space behind her. I climb up about 10 percent as gracefully but finally settle in where I think I'm supposed to be.

She stands up and kicks her foot down onto a metal pedal,

throwing her whole weight behind it. The thing doesn't start so she does it again and again, until finally, the motor growls to life under us. As she plops down on the vinyl seat in front of me, I scoot back to give her as much room as possible, but I'm not sure this thing was meant for two people.

I fumble around behind me, trying to find a spot to grab onto, but nothing feels sturdy enough.

"Hold on to me," Nora says, raising her voice over the sound of the idling motor as she readjusts the bottom of her cutoff shirt.

I start to reach for her waist, but just the thought of holding on to her like that makes me feel a little . . . weird. So instead, I clamp my hands over her shoulders, leaving about half a foot of space between the two of us. She turns her face to the side, and the sun lights up her hazel eyes as she peeks back at me.

"Ready?"

"Ready," I reply.

I was NOT ready.

Nora twists the throttle and my weight gets thrown backward all of a sudden, sending a screech from my throat that I don't even recognize as my own voice. Just as I start to lose my grip on her shoulders, she releases the throttle and I fly forward into her back, completely eliminating the six inches I had left between us.

"I told you to *hold on* to me," she says, bringing us to a stop.

"Well, I didn't know you meant for dear life!" I yell back at her.

I slide backward on the seat, but then this time, I plant my hands on either side of her waist, wondering if it feels as odd for her as it does for me.

"Ready?" she asks sarcastically, and I roll my eyes from behind her.

"Ready," I reply, sinking my fingers into her skin, my chest tingling as I prepare for takeoff again.

Nora hits the throttle a little softer this time, and soon we're flying across the field, racing the big puffy clouds as the wind blows them east. When we run over small uneven patches of dirt and rocks, I tuck my head in behind her, blocking the wind from my face.

As we find our way onto more of a path, Nora pulls back on the throttle a little harder and my stomach jumps up into my throat, my hair whipping all around my face.

I let out a gasp as we take a sharp curve, thinking of my stitches that have just healed. "Nora! Slow down!" I yell, and immediately, she lets off the gas a little.

Weird or not, I pull myself forward on the seat until I'm right up against Nora's back. I slide my hands all the way around her, locking them in front of her body almost like a hug. And for the first time since I got on this thing, I actually feel safe.

A few wisps of blond hair fall out of her ponytail, lightly tickling my face. I close my eyes and rest my chin on her shoulder blade, letting every turn and bump in the path be a surprise. She smells like her room up on the third floor and like peaches and maybe a little like dirt, too.

She smells nice.

There's this rush in my stomach, now that I don't feel like I'm about to catapult off this thing. It's actually pretty fun.

Soon we slow to a stop and everything goes quiet enough

to hear the crows and the wind blowing through the tall grass, and the sunshine just feels so perfect and warm on my face.

"Uh . . . Stevie?" Nora's voice startles me as my eyes fly open and I realize we're parked by a roll of wire fence, at our destination.

"Shit. Sorry." I unclasp my hands and slide them back across her stomach, into the dip of her waist, and then into my own lap as I sit up straight. She twists around halfway, a smile turning into a soft laugh.

"You've got, umm . . . Your hair looks kinda crazy." She reaches out, takes a strand from in front of my eyes, and tucks it behind my ear. The feel of her fingertips against my skin makes my whole body go rigid. As she switches focus from my hair to my eyes, she quickly pulls away and turns back around to face the front.

My face feels hot and I'm glad she's not looking at me still, because I have no idea why I'm being so weird. "What can I do to help?" I ask as she scratches at her eye.

"Right." She hops off the four-wheeler and into the grass, which has grown up well past her knees. "I've been working on pulling some new fence," she says, pointing down the field at a line of freshly placed wooden posts stretching as far as the eye can see. I follow her over to the roll of new wire fence and a pile of tools beside it. Soon she's explaining to me how all the tools function and what she needs me to do.

Basically, I stand by the "puller," ratcheting it tighter when she tells me to, and Nora does . . . well, everything else. She hooks up the chains between the puller and the stretcher bar, which grabs onto the wire fence so we can pull it evenly around each post. She staples it in when it's in just the right spot. And then she moves the heavy-looking roll of the new fencing from post to post.

"Are you doing this whole thing by yourself?" I ask incredulously as she finishes stapling the wire to the next post.

"Albert, that guy in the shop, works on it too, but yeah, mostly. This is basically my entire job for the summer."

"Speaking of Albert, he said he thought you've been sneaking around with some boy this summer. That true?"

Nora snorts out a laugh. "Albert needs to mind his own damn business."

"Is that a yes, then?"

She drops the staple gun to the ground and gives me a deadpan look. "Stevie, I can't think of a single thing that I would rather do *less* than run around with some dumb boy this summer."

"I believe you," I tell her, and I do. It's odd, though. Most girls our age are at least *thinking* about boys, even me . . . now.

Nora doesn't seem like most girls, though.

I watch as she wipes her forehead off on her forearm and then drags it across the front of her homemade cutoff shirt.

"You don't really care what people think about you, do you?" I ask.

"No. Why would I?" she asks, dragging the heavy wire down to the next post.

"I don't know," I reply. She's so *sure* of herself. So confident in who she is . . . unlike me. "Most people do."

"Sorry to disappoint you," she says.

"No, that's not what I meant. I actually kinda love it." I

smile, squinting at her through the sun. Sweat is starting to roll down my back, even though I'm barely doing anything. I don't know how she does this all day.

"Do you really like this job?" I ask, having a hard time imagining how anyone could.

"Be more specific," she replies.

I don't know what other job I could be talking about, but okay.

"Do you like being out here in the blazing sun, pulling a wire fence around an endless line of posts?" I ask.

"Yeah. I do." She lets out a grunt as she unrolls the fence, her toned biceps flexing underneath her tan skin. "I like being outside and I like working with my hands, building something. It makes me feel accomplished at the end of the day in a way that nothing else ever has . . . like school, for example. That was never really for me."

I haven't ever really done anything like this, but as I look down the fence line at the hundreds of yards she's already finished . . . I find I can understand that.

"Do you think you'll work here forever? Take the farm over from your mom?" I ask.

"God, I hope not. I was serious the other day about wanting to get out of here someday. I can't live in Wyatt forever, and if you haven't picked up on it, my mom and I don't exactly . . . mesh," she says as she squeezes the trigger on the staple gun with a loud click.

"Yeah . . . I kinda did. You can tell me about it if you want, but you don't have to."

"Pull that tighter," she says, and I pull on my tool until the fence straightens out. "There's not a whole lot to tell. I just don't think she was ever really meant to be a mom." She stops to look at me. "I don't think it's in her blood, to be able to care about someone the way a mom probably should."

"So why stay? Now that you're done with school? I mean, if you really want out of here."

Huh. There's a question I can't even answer about myself . . .

She stops and looks at me, squinting like she's trying to figure me out or something. "You ask a lot of questions."

I shrug. "Just trying to get to know you. Have you never had a friend before?"

She shakes her head, a smile playing on her lips. "Well, if I leave Wyatt, who are you going to have around to come bother?"

"Hey, I'm helping!" I yell back, dropping my tool slightly to try to shove her in the shoulder, but she dodges me.

"And you're doing *such* a good job." She points back at my post. "*Get over there* and keep that tight!"

I like this. Talking to her feels so . . . freeing. No history to bog us down. No underhanded comments or pressure to do something I might not be ready for. No overthinking what I'm saying in case it might not be right.

"So why *did* you go vegan? If not to hashtag 'freethecows'?"

She looks over at me and her eyes *completely* light up.

"Oh my God. Okay. You *have* to watch this documentary I found. It's all about the meat industry and its effect on the environment, and how . . ."

She goes on and on, her voice practically buzzing as she tells me all about it for the next twenty or so minutes while we make our way down the fence line.

"Did you know that giving up meat is the number one thing you can do to help protect the environment?" she says before finally pausing dramatically.

"I did not know that," I reply with a smile.

"Well, it is. *One* burger uses up over six hundred gallons of water. *Six hundred gallons!*"

"That's a lot of water," I reply.

"That is *a lot* of water, Stevie. Anyway, I could literally go on forever about this, but I just . . . I just wanted to do something good," she says as she kneels down on the other side of the fence from me.

I don't think I've ever seen someone speak so passionately about anything before. It's honestly kinda . . . cute? I don't know. My heart feels happy listening to her, like I could do it forever.

"Why not just go vegetarian, though?" I ask, reaching out to help her connect the chain, my left hand slightly overlapping her right.

"I'm sort of an all-or-nothing type of person." She picks her head up, inches from mine, and looks right into my eyes in a way that makes me feel guilty, like I should look away. But I don't. "When I'm in . . . I'm all in," she finishes.

I'm not sure if it's just the weight of the chain or if she's actually pressing her hand down into mine, but I can't seem to look away from her face to check.

Her eyes flick down to my mouth as a lump forms in my throat. I try to slow my breathing so the rising and falling of my chest isn't as apparent, but it's just not possible.

This feeling is . . . well, I don't know what it is, but it feels familiar. It takes a few seconds to place it but finally I do.

It's what I expected to feel when Ryan wanted to kiss me. That *thing* that I've never felt. The feeling that I was starting to think didn't actually exist.

And I'm feeling it right now.

With Nora.

I sit back on my heels and force myself to look away from her as I stand up and drop the chain. The full weight of it sags and pulls Nora's hands to the ground. I turn my back to her as the heat of the sun starts to make me feel a little light-headed.

What was that?

She's just being nice. I just think she's cool and I like being around her. That's it.

"Stevie, why are you here? I mean, what are you really doing out here with me?" Nora asks from behind me. "You chose to be out here, working in the middle of a field in the heat of summer, when you could be doing literally *anything else.*"

"I don't know. I just—"

. . . like the person I get to be with you.

. . . want to get to know you.

. . . want to ride on the back of your four-wheeler again.

All of it sounds weird. "I—wanted to give you a cow. And then suddenly it wasn't a cow anymore and . . . I guess I don't know why I'm here." I turn around to face her, pulling my hair off my sticky neck. "I'm actually not feeling super well."

Nora's face fills with concern as she takes a step toward me.

"Is it your head? Are you—"

I shake my head, cutting her off.

"Can you just take me back to my car?" I ask, already heading back toward the four-wheeler. "Please?"

"Uh, yeah. Sure," she replies, but her voice is more distant now. She hops on in front of me without ever meeting my eyes.

She starts it up in one solid kick down, but this time she doesn't tell me to hold on to her, and I don't. Instead, I wrap my fingers around the metal rack behind us and hold on tight as she flies across the field, toward the buildings in the distance.

Why did *I come out here? Why did I win a freaking cow for this girl? Why do I only feel normal when I'm around her?*

I remind myself that it all comes back to the fact that we didn't know each other before. That's why I like being around her. I just need a friend for this version of me. She *is* my friend. And just my friend.

My brain must still be slightly broken. Maybe it's just sending the wrong signals at the wrong time or something, because I know I can like Ryan. I mean . . . I *do* like Ryan. I think.

I just . . . need to spend more time with him, too.

July 10

Stevie,

I felt it today, by the fence.

The way you looked at me . . . people don't just go around looking at each other like that.

There was something electric between us. And I think it scared you enough to want to leave.

You fell in love with me once. Maybe you can do it again.

I'm not saying that I'm not going to tell you the truth, because I am. If you do get your memories back, you'll probably be pretty pissed at me for not telling you. But maybe the best thing for me to do is let you fall for me again and then it might be easier to believe. I feel so guilty having all the answers you want, but . . . I can't risk you not being ready to hear them. Especially in this town. You'll understand why I had to wait. Right?

The moment when we first held hands in the gym was when every-thing clicked into place for you. I just need to wait for that moment to happen again. Our moment. It's coming, I know it is.

I love you,

Nora

PS: The cow, Stevie? Really? It was cute that you did it for me, it felt like something <u>my</u> Stevie would do, but I don't even want to know how much of our California money you spent on tickets to win that thing.

CHAPTER 21

WHY DID YOU MAKE ME CHANGE MY PLANS WITH Ryan today?" I ask Rory, one of my many questions as she and Savannah follow me into my room a few days later.

"Lunch, Stevie? Really? Lunch is what you get with your great-aunt so she keeps giving you fifty bucks on your birthday, not something you get with the guy you're trying to bone."

"Rory, *shut up*," I whisper. "That's not what I'm trying to . . . I'm not . . ." I shake my head, at a loss for words.

"My point is, you need to take him somewhere fun. Somewhere you can look hot."

As if on cue, both of them unzip their jackets to reveal matching American flag bras and booty shorts.

Oh. No, no, please no. They are really going full tilt into this.

"I'm not sure Ryan would exactly consider Truck Night *fun.*" *I* wouldn't even consider it fun, and I grew up here.

"Well, he agreed to go, didn't he?" she presses.

"I guess," I reply, but it doesn't do anything to reassure me.

Truck Night takes place after dark the second Friday of every month through the summer at Creed Lake, which actually isn't a lake at all. It's a town with a population of under a hundred people, and their claim to fame is literally just a giant pit of mud, and if you're *real* lucky, it's slightly filled with water from a recent rain. Even more shocking, people travel from all over the tricounty area to drive their pickup trucks around in it. People like Savannah's boyfriend, Jake, and all his friends. And inexplicably, they apparently all dress like the flag even though there's nothing particularly patriotic about it.

"Let's get you dressed," Savannah says as she dumps out a duffel bag of red, white, and blue clothes onto my bed.

"I love you guys. I do. But *please* tell me you are not expecting me to match you," I say.

"Excuse you, we look hot as fuck," Rory says, giving me an overly dramatic offended look. "It's Truck Night, girl. You gotta dress the part . . . but no. I do know you better than that, Stevie."

It puts a smile on my face to hear that. Despite how off things have felt among the three of us, they do still know me. Maybe our friendship can really get back on the right track tonight. After all, I didn't switch my date with Ryan because I thought he'd find me hotter there or something. I did it for them.

"How about these jean shorts and this red-white-and-blue tank top?" Rory asks, holding them both up.

I let out a big sigh. I feel like my butt cheeks are still going to be hanging out the bottom of the shorts, but at least the tank top has a high neckline.

Suck it up, Stevie. For your friends. This is how you fix this.

Savannah pulls up right next to Ryan in the gravel parking lot, and I'm already embarrassed before I even step out of the car.

What am I getting myself into?

We all get out and Savannah and Rory greet Ryan before the two of them run ahead to find Jake and his friends, including a guy Jake is setting Rory up with who graduated a few years ahead of us, which honestly doesn't feel that promising.

Ryan steps up to walk alongside me as we head toward the stadium lights and the sounds of country music *blasting* through oversized speakers. He hasn't said anything, but I saw him look me up and down and not in the way Savannah and Rory were intending. He's had a smirk on his face ever since.

"Just say it." I roll my eyes, tugging on the bottom of my shorts.

"I'm just not sure if I should be turned on or reciting the Pledge of Allegiance," he says with a laugh, and even though that's my thought exactly, my cheeks flush out of embarrassment.

"Well, if you think *my* outfit is something, you're in for a big surprise, buddy," I tell him as we reach the end of the parking lot, where the mosh of pickup trucks comes into view. "I know I tried to warn you over text earlier, but you really have no idea what we're about to walk into. Honestly, *I* don't even have any idea what we're walking into. I've never actually been here. I've only seen pictures posted online."

"Truck Night." He shrugs. "How bad can it be?"

He quickly gets his answer as we crest the hill and everything opens up to a mud pit the size of a football field, filled with trucks so caked in it that you can't even tell what color they are. I don't know what's louder, the trucks' exhausts or the music.

"What on earth . . . ," Ryan says out of the side of his mouth as we walk through the slew of trucks parked on the side, waiting for their turn. Shirtless guys sit on top of each one, with girls on the tailgate, beer coolers wide open beside them. One Ford Raptor's bed is filled to the brim with thirty-something-year-old women dancing in cowboy boots and hats. One of them *only* has those on; her nipples are just covered with tassels, little Liberty Bells hanging off the ends.

God Bless America, I guess.

"Yeah, so I feel like you did not properly prepare me for this *at all*," Ryan says as I spot Jake's truck looming over the others around it.

"I don't think I properly prepared myself," I reply. I don't know if I feel fifteen or eighteen right now, but neither age feels particularly appropriate to be here. Thank *God* I didn't tell my mom the truth about where I was going when we were baking cookies together this morning, or she never would've let me come. I wasn't thrilled about lying to her, but I did it for the sake of rebuilding my friendship with Savannah and Rory. And it was just a small lie, one that any normal eighteen-year-old would tell.

"Stevie!" Before I know it, something is whizzing through the air right at my head from the bed of Jake's truck. Thankfully Ryan sticks his hand out just in time to snatch it. I turn and see him holding a can of Bud Light.

"Nice catch! Sorry!" Rory yells, but she doesn't really sound all that sorry. *Great.* Very thoughtful of my best friend. The last thing my head needs is to be nailed by a full can of beer. "Here, Stevie." She winds up to toss another one, but I stop her.

"No, no, I'm good," I reply, looking between Savannah and Rory both up there, double-fisting.

I have no problem with them drinking, I can drive us home, it just throws me off-balance a little. It feels like just a couple of months ago that the three of us drank a six-pack of beer together for the first time and then hated how we felt after. I think I remember Rory swearing off the stuff for the rest of her life, even in the afterlife. But I guess that wasn't recently . . . it was years ago, and obviously things have changed since then.

I wonder if there's some version of me that could have grown up to be more like them, to be up there dancing and drinking and not worrying if my ass is hanging out of these shorts right now.

"Laaaame," Savannah sings into one of her beer cans along with the melody of the song, pointing at me and making me feel even more uncomfortable than I already do, standing here with Jake's Confederate flag waving in my face.

I look up at Rory dancing in front of that guy she came to meet, who . . . actually seems more than a few years older than us. I visibly cringe as I read his shirt.

I LIKE MY WOMEN THE WAY I LIKE MY DEER. HORNY.

Savannah being with Jake I guess I could understand at least a little. But Rory with *this* guy? She's like the smartest person I've ever met. I mean, she got into UNC's biomedical research program. The Rory I knew wouldn't have come within a hundred yards of a shirt like that. But here she is, grinding on him like her life depends on it.

Ryan cracks his beer and takes a small sip, and the two of us awkwardly stand there as everyone else dances and sings around us. This was supposed to be an opportunity to get to know him more, to catch feelings again, but I can barely hear myself think here. I should've just let him take me to lunch like we originally planned. Savannah and Rory used to give me the best advice, but despite what Rory said earlier . . . it feels like they don't even know me now, not just that I don't remember them.

And then it gets worse.

"Yo, Bruce Lee!" A deep voice shouts from behind me, pulling my attention away.

I turn around to find a man old enough to grow a full beard sliding down over the side of his truck toward us.

"Come on, let's see what you got." The guy laughs, holding his fists up in front of him like a boxer . . . a very drunk boxer.

Ryan turns his back to him and so do I, but he doesn't give up.

"Who wants to see me fight Bruce Lee?!" he yells, and the people around his truck erupt with cheers behind us.

"He can't understand you!" a woman yells.

My blood is freaking boiling and there are a thousand things running through my head that I could say, but everything feels caught in my throat. I look up at Savannah and Rory and Jake and all the other people here with us, hoping maybe someone else will speak up or jump down to help, but they all just keep dancing.

The guy comes right up behind us then. I see him out of my peripheral vision, hopping back and forth between both feet before he throws a few light jabs into Ryan's back. Ryan closes his eyes as his face goes beet red. But the guy doesn't let up at all until finally Ryan turns around. He gives him one shove. It isn't very hard, more like he's trying to create distance than fight, but it's enough to knock him off-balance in his inebriated state. He stumbles backward until he ends up on his ass, still laughing the whole way.

Jake clangs two empty beer bottles together and yells, "Round one! Bruce!"

My face drops as I watch both Savannah and Rory not only paying attention now but *laughing* along with everyone else surrounding us.

I don't even recognize them at all anymore. I watch the relationship I was trying so hard to save crumble right in front of my eyes.

What the fuck am I doing here?

"Let's go," I say to Ryan above all the noise, placing my hand on his shoulder. He sets his can of beer down on Jake's tailgate and then we head off toward the parking lot, a chorus of boos directed at us as we go.

"Thanks, Pat," Ryan says as the waitress sets down chocolate milkshakes and two burgers in front of us at the Dinor. It's after ten, and the place is almost empty. Ryan hasn't said much of anything since we got here.

"Are you okay?" I ask as he stirs his straw around in the shake. He nods. "I'm sorry I took you there. I didn't . . . I mean—"

"I'm okay, Stevie," he says, finally looking up at me. "But why did we go there instead of just grabbing something to eat in the first place?"

"My friends thought lunch wasn't *fun* enough or something . . . ," I reply.

"And *that* is?" He scoffs.

I give a pathetic grimace and shake my head. "No."

"Has that stuff happened to you a lot growing up here?" he asks.

"You mean do drunk men often try to fight me?" I joke, trying to lighten the mood.

"You don't have to talk about it if you don't—"

"No, no. I just . . . I guess I've never had anyone to really discuss it with." I pause to take a sip of my milkshake. "It's not that I've encountered a ton of very direct abuse or anything like that, I think mostly because people here have known me my whole life, but . . . you know, there are still stupid things that I hear. People making racist jokes about me doing their nails, or pulling their eyes back asking how I can even see. Moments that remind me I'm different from everyone else here and that people around me see me differently. Even Savannah and Rory. My whole life, they've never really seen me as Asian, because to them . . . being Asian is a bad thing. You know? But it's not. It's just . . . a thing. I don't really think it has to be good or bad. It just *is*."

Ryan nods. "I get that. I felt that a little bit growing up in Pittsburgh, but then when I came here, it was like . . . *much* more apparent. Also, since I didn't know anyone, I felt like there were really no moments when I *didn't* feel like that . . . until I met you."

"Really?" I ask, taking a bite of my burger.

"Yeah, I mean, even before we started hanging out, like when you would just come into the Dinor with your friends, there was this awareness that someone else in that space was like me. It made me feel less . . . other, I guess." He offers me a sad sort of smile and a shrug.

"I kinda had the same feeling. I mean, I don't remember, you know . . . most of it, but when we made plans to go to the fair that day . . . it was almost comforting? Is that the right word?" I ask.

He nods hard in agreement. "That's it."

"Like I knew I could take you to that knife game at the fair and you'd find it just as ridiculous as I did. There was something really nice about that," I say.

"I think any sane person would agree with us." He laughs.

We slurp down our drinks and eat our burgers, and the whole time I can't stop thinking about how even after the horrible start tonight, things might *actually* be finally falling into place between the two of us. We're really talking about some real stuff, and . . . things seem to be clicking so easily. Maybe I did just need to try a little harder with him.

When we finish our meals, he offers to drive me home, and I don't hesitate to accept.

On the way to his car, a text buzzes into my phone from Rory.

Hey, did you really leave?

Yeah . . . , I reply. It's been over an hour, is she just noticing now?

Seriously? Stevie, come on. That guy was drunk. I mean, it was a joke.

It seemed like you and Savannah found it real funny.

I silence my phone and slip it back into my pocket as I climb into the car. I'm not going to let them mess this night up again.

We pull out and I sit in the passenger seat tracing random shapes into the top of my white Styrofoam container with my nail as we shuffle through one of Ryan's Spotify playlists. On the other side of the glass, the endless fields roll by, thick with eight-foot-tall cornstalks and dark-green soybeans waiting to turn brown before harvest. As we make our way back to my house, each farm blurs into the next, somehow all looking like the Martins' to me now.

I dig my nails deeper into the Styrofoam as I think about the other day there. The tingling lightness in my stomach when I finally wrapped myself around Nora. The way she made me feel safe even though we were riding on an absolute death trap. The way my face felt when she moved the strand of hair, the feeling lingering long after she pulled her hand away.

I try to redirect the crossed signals where they're supposed to go. I imagine what it would feel like for Ryan to be standing on the other side of the fence line from me, his face inches from mine, or to have my arms wrapped around his waist as we rode through a field, his honey-brown eyes peeking over his shoulder at me. After tonight it should be easy. But no matter what I try, it just doesn't feel the same, not like I think it should.

"When do you have to work again?" Ryan asks from beside me, pulling me out of my thoughts, and my eyes refocus on the container in my lap.

On *N-O-R-A* etched into the top.

"Umm . . ." My eyes go wide as I casually cover the whole thing with my hand. "Wednesday, er, no, Thursday, actually."

"Me too," he says, bringing his left hand to the top of the steering wheel and resting his right arm on the center console between us. I watch his fingers tap against the gearshift with the rhythm of the electric guitar playing through the speakers. I like him. I do. I mean, we've never had trouble finding things to talk about. Maybe we have to be touching like I was with Nora. If I could just reach out and take his hand, I'd probably feel it then. My eyes trace the veins in the back of his hand, under his simple black watch, over his forearm, and up to his face.

I slowly pick my hand up and slide it under his. He looks over at me and smiles, closing his hand around mine.

I wait to feel something, anything, but the only thing that comes is a building tension in my shoulders that I can't seem to relax. My chest tightens but my stomach sinks. I want to let go, take my hand back into my lap and pretend I never did this, but the problem is I have no freaking clue how. I *really* don't want to hurt his feelings, but the longer we sit like this, the more I think about what might happen next and the harder it is for me to breathe.

I can't do it.

"I love this song," I say, slipping my hand out of his and turning the volume dial up a couple of notches.

"Me too." He nods, still smiling. Success.

I take a deep breath and tighten my hand into a fist before letting it rest back over my takeout container. Both of us are quiet for the last couple of minutes of the ride except for the directions I give him, until he pulls into my driveway, the house all dark except for the light on the front porch.

"Thanks, Ryan," I say, already unbuckling my seat belt. As I reach for the door handle, I feel him lean across to give me a hug. Quickly, I spin back around to face him, but by the time I get my arms up, he's holding one hand out for a handshake and then it becomes a small awkward wave.

"Uh . . ." I drop my arms back to my side, trying to figure out what the hell to do. "Bye," I say, deciding to just follow through with the hug after all, and it's about a million times more awkward than I ever thought possible.

When he lets go, he avoids my eyes, looking at the center console, at the radio, at my door handle, anywhere but at me.

"Next time, maybe we skip Truck Night." I laugh, hoping it doesn't sound too forced.

"Ha, yeah, maybe," he says, looking at me just long enough to offer a quick smile. "Good night, Stevie."

I hop out and close the door behind me, cringing all the way inside. I'm ruining it. This great thing my former self wanted, a relationship with Ryan. He's supposed to be a part of my fresh start, my second chance to get everything right this time. Why can't I make it work?

I kick my shoes off and lean against the front door, pulling out my phone. Maybe I just need to talk about it with someone who has more experience. But there's no way Savannah or Rory would understand, and even if they did, I don't really want to talk to them right now. I pull out my phone and hesitate for a second, until I remember Albert mentioning Nora's secret boy drama. This is totally normal. She'll get it.

You working tomorrow? I text Nora.

In the meat shop bright and early! she replies.

Alone?

Yeah.

Need some help? I ask, and I try not to smile as three dots blink across her text bubble right away.

You help out much more and my mom is going to have to start paying you, and she doesn't even like paying me, she replies first, but then,

I'll see you at open.

CHAPTER 22

NORA LOOKS OVER THE TOP OF THE DISPLAY CASE at me, the tiny gap in her teeth showing through her sleepy smile. I *am* here to talk to her about Ryan, but . . . maybe I should let us both wake up a little first.

"You feeling better?" she asks, leaning casually on the counter.

"What?" I ask, before remembering how we last left things. "Oh, yeah. Much better. Actually my stitches came out this morning in the shower," I tell her, holding my hair back to show her the now-visible scar.

"Oh, cool. That must feel good."

"It kinda does. I definitely feel a little more normal . . . or as normal as I can with amnesia."

"Well then, come on around, maybe you can set up the display case for me. I've got to do some stuff in the back real quick." She motions me around the counter and shows me all the trays of various meats that need to be put out. As soon as she goes to the back, I get to work.

She didn't really give me any specific direction, so I decide to have some fun with it and arrange each tray of steaks into the shape of flowers, a burger patty at the center of each.

Pretty. I step back to inspect my handiwork as Nora comes out of the back holding a tray of prewrapped orders labeled with each person's name.

"Stevie, what the hell am I looking at?" she asks, motioning to my masterpiece.

"What? It looks good!"

"Yeah, but this isn't a bakery." She laughs, sliding the case open to make it all boring again, but before she can, a lady walks in through the door.

"Morning," Nora says cheerily, popping up from behind the display.

"Hi, girls." She smiles at us both before inspecting the case. "Oh, what a cute display."

Nora gives me that deadpan look, making me snicker.

"It was all Nora. She's very creative," I tell the lady as I wink over my shoulder at Nora, who rolls her eyes at me.

As soon as the lady walks out the door, Nora reaches over and pinches my side, making me giggle and fold in half.

"See? She loved it," I tell her, stepping out of her reach.

"How about you just let me handle this part and you get on the register."

"Fine," I say with a sigh, but she doesn't touch the way I have the meat displayed.

After a quick tutorial on the cash register, which is a little different from the one at work, we fall into a comfortable rhythm as customers slowly trickle into the shop. Nora takes orders and weighs and packages up the meat while I check people out.

About an hour after open, I pull my phone out of my back pocket, surprised to see eight unread texts from my mom.

Hey did you get there okay?

Stevie?

Are you there?

Text me so I know.

Hello?

Helloooo?

Stevie, answer me.

Stevie???

I roll my eyes as I text back. Relax, Mom. Jeez. Yes, I'm fine.

It's not like much could've happened to me on the ten-minute drive here. I know she's worried, but I've been feeling *fine*. A little more space might be nice.

I tuck my phone back into my pocket as a customer comes in, asking for some kind of sauce that was on order for them, but when I turn around Nora is nowhere to be found. I start reversing toward the back room.

"I just have to ask about it." I round the corner. "Hey, Nor—"

Oof.

I run *smack* into her, and both of us lose our footing. I fall forward while she falls backward, until I have her pinned up against one of the stainless-steel carts. I start to push myself back.

"Shit. S—" I freeze when I see her face so close to mine, her freckled cheeks, her pupils wide in her greenish-brown eyes. My breath catches in my throat and I swallow hard as that tingly feeling I was searching for so hard all last night shows up without any effort at all. It runs all the way from my toes to my fingertips, which are gripped onto the cart on either side of her head.

I feel a warmth radiating from my right side, just above my hips, and it takes me a second to realize that it's her hand.

"Uh, hot sauce . . ." I blink hard and step backward, putting a couple of feet between us.

"Wh-what?" Nora asks, still glued up against the cart.

"The guy out there, he says he ordered some hot sauce," I tell her, pointing over my shoulder.

"Right. I'll just . . ." She points to the front, walking by me without another word.

When she's out of sight, I take in a deep breath and let it out, trying to get my head to stop swimming.

What the hell is going on with me? Why does this keep happening?

I lean my elbows on the cold steel table and rub the scar on my head, getting myself together before I have to go back out there. I just need to chill. And remember why I came here.

One more deep breath and then I head back out to run the register.

Neither of us says anything to the other for the next half hour or so, even when no one else is in the shop with us. The silence is deafening. I keep wanting to bring up Ryan, but after that weird moment . . . I don't know how to start.

Just as I'm about to lose my mind, a middle-aged couple comes in and asks for *thirty pounds* of lean ground beef.

"It'll just be a moment," Nora tells them. "Stevie, you want to help me?" she asks me, and I follow her into the back room, avoiding making eye contact with that particular metal cart.

"Here." She tosses a black pair of gloves at me and then disappears into the cooler. She emerges a minute later pushing a stack of hotel pans on a rolling cart.

"Okay, let's split it into two bags," she says, seeming completely normal. Okay. All right. Maybe it was just me.

She lifts up the lid to reveal more raw ground beef in one place than I've ever seen before, and I resist the urge to dry-heave as she opens up a large plastic bag over a metal scale.

I feel like I got the short end of the stick here.

"Ewww," I groan, sinking my gloved hands into the vat of meat and dropping a hunk into the bag.

"*Shhhh*, they can hear you!" Nora says, nudging me. "It's just meat."

"Yeah, but there's so much of it and it's all *squishy*," I complain, twisting my face up as I go in for seconds.

"Just . . . talk to me about something, then. Don't think about it."

Well, I guess that's my cue.

"So I hung out with Ryan again last night."

"Oh. What did you guys do?" she asks, keeping her eyes on the scale as I add the last chunk to make about fifteen pounds. She ties it up and holds the other bag out.

"We went to Truck Night," I say, embarrassed to admit it.

Nora snorts out a laugh. "*You* went to Truck Night?"

"Yeah, I know . . . it was a mistake. It was horrible."

"Uh, *yeah*. It's Truck Night. What did you expect?" she asks as I plop another hunk into her bag.

"It's a long story. Anyway, we ended up leaving early and just went to the Dinor, where he works, and . . . well, that was definitely better. We at least got to talk, and—"

"That's good. Come on," Nora interrupts, tying up the second bag and swinging it into my chest with a light thud.

I check the couple out at the register and Nora kneels down to restock the T-bones in the display case, balancing the tray on her knee.

I watch the couple leave, the door squeaking shut behind them.

"So, do you like him?" she asks without looking up at me. I let out a sigh, because even now after date number two, the truth is . . .

"I don't know."

I lean on the front counter as I replay my car ride with Ryan last night. The lack of any sort of *feelings at all* when I slid my hand into his, our uncomfortable hug goodbye.

"I feel like I *should* like him that way. He's great, but we just aren't clicking like . . ." I turn my head to look at her. "Well, like I think we should be. And I don't understand why."

"Are you going to keep going out with him?" she asks, moving on to rearrange some burger patties on the second shelf, still not looking at me. I open up the cash drawer, fixing each stack of bills so they all face the same direction.

"I guess so. I was wondering what you think actually. Sometimes it just takes time, right? I mean, my two friends told me I really liked him before the accident, so—"

"*What?*" She hops up onto her feet, completely forgoing the display and finally looking at me.

"What?" I repeat back, squinting at her in confusion.

"Which friends?" She takes a step toward me, tossing the empty metal tray onto the counter with a clatter.

"My best friends, Savannah and Rory. They've known me for like . . . ever," I reply, even though my stomach still turns at the thought of them just standing there last night while every-thing happened.

"I thought . . . you told me you weren't hanging out with them as much, during that gap in your memory . . ."

"Yeah, but . . . I guess it was still obvious enough for them to pick up on. So I think it's got to be on me and my stupid brain, that things aren't clicking with Ryan. I've just never dated anyone before so I don't really know how to. My mom says it wasn't instant for her and my dad either. Have you ever dealt with anything like this? How'd it feel for you?

"Stevie." Nora shakes her head. "You can't blame yourself for not feeling something. That's not really something you can force. You know? It kinda has to come naturally." She picks up the tray and walks it to the back counter next to the old metal scale. "I mean, when you find the right person, you just . . . you *know*." She grabs onto the butcher-block countertop, her knuck-les turning white as they clench around it. "When you find the right person, it feels so right that it's impossible to even ques-tion if it could be wrong."

"You sound like you might be speaking from experience," I say, leaning my back up against the front counter. This feeling of jealousy tugs at me because *that*, what she just described, is exactly what I want.

"Yeah," she says, her voice so quiet and small that it makes me feel sad. I stand there, watching her from behind for a long moment. It feels like she wants to say more, but I don't want to press her if she doesn't want to tell me about him.

Finally, after letting out a heavy breath, she continues, "I felt like that with my um . . . ex. We met in line for the porta-potties at a Friday-night football game when our high schools were facing off."

I try to imagine what type of guy she would date, tall or short, muscular or lanky, what color hair, but I can't see it.

"We both had to pee really bad and the line was like twenty people long, so . . ." Nora hesitates, then turns around to face me, but doesn't quite meet my eyes. "She snuck me into her school through this window that she said never really locked."

She.

My insides turn cold as I hold my breath in.

I can feel her eyes shift to mine, but now it's *me* that can't look at *her.* Instead, I focus on her hands, still wrenched around the counter behind her.

Nora's . . . gay? I can't believe she just told *me* that. I mean . . . I never thought . . . Not in Wyatt. I never even considered . . . Not that I could *ever* be . . .

I force myself to look back at her face again as my thoughts keep colliding, but she looks down at her shoes, her eyes shining with tears.

"After we left the bathroom, we didn't go back to the game. We just started walking around the empty hallways talking about . . . *everything.* It was so weird, I'd never clicked so easily with someone before and we had *just* met. When we ended up in the gym, standing at half-court, it was pitch-black and . . . I held her hand. I know that sounds so innocent, but . . . it didn't feel like it." Another pang of jealousy strikes me as I think of the hand meltdown last night. "It happened *so* organically. We didn't talk about it. I didn't ask her. It just happened and it was . . . I mean, I just . . ." She smiles as she stutters around her words, a tear rolling down her cheek as her voice grows shakier. "We spent so much time after that talking about getting out of this town, but honestly . . . I could've spent the rest of my life stuck in that school with her." She shakes her head, her eyes locked on the floor, and it doesn't even feel like she's talking to me anymore. "Now I wish we had."

And with that she stops fighting it and finally cries. She buries her face in her hands and slides down the back counter all at once. I reach out, trying to catch her by the arms, but instead, I end up on the floor right in front of her. On pure instinct, I pull her into me and she wraps both of her arms around me, burying her face in my neck.

"I just want to go back," she says, digging her nails practically through my T-shirt as she pulls me even closer. Listening to her cry makes my whole body ache. How could anyone do this to her? How did they even end up breaking up if Nora still feels so strongly about her?

"Nora," I whisper. "Maybe you shouldn't give up if she means so much to you." I'm trying to be helpful, but that only seems to make her cry harder.

"I *haven't* given up," she says over a shuddering breath. She pulls back slightly and I release my grip, but her hands slide up my back, over my shoulders, and down my arms until we're both looking at her hands enclosing mine. "That would be impossible," she says as we finally lock eyes.

"Stevie?" she says, her mouth trying to form words. I've never been looked at the way she's looking at me, and I'm so confused again.

"Yeah?" I whisper, my heartbeat pulsing in my ears.

"I have to tell—" She jumps, her attention jerking to the door as the bells jingle at the top, pulling both of us out of our trance. "Shit."

"I got it," I say quickly, pulling my hands out of Nora's grip before she shuffles across the small space to clean herself up.

"Can I help you?" I ask, standing up to greet a man and woman who are waiting expectantly.

"Jensen. Here to pick up an order. You must be new," the man says, approaching the counter.

"Yes, sir, uh . . . just helping out for the day." I open the display cooler and reach into the bottom shelf, trying to get him out the door as quickly as possible so Nora can finish telling me whatever she was going to say. I don't know what it is, but it feels really important.

I quickly bag up his order as he dips his card into the reader, then the two of them are out the door.

"Thanks," Nora says, popping out of the back, her face dry. She comes in to grab the tray off the back counter like the last ten minutes never happened.

"Nora, was there something you were going to tell me?" I ask, but she shakes her head.

"Sorry about"—she motions to the spot on the floor where we both were—"that." And then she disappears into the back. It feels . . . familiar.

Like for the first time she's treating me the same way everyone else in my life is.

Like she's hiding something.

July 15

Stevie,

Oh my God. I almost did it. I almost told you the truth. Why couldn't I? What am I so scared of?

Telling you our love story and having you not remember was . . . awful . . . Stevie, but it was even worse hearing that Savannah and Rory have been lying to you, taking advantage of your injury to mess with you. But am I really any better? Hanging out like we're just friends is lying to you too . . . it's fucking killing me. All this time I've been waiting for you to find your way back to me, but the truth is . . . that might not ever happen. Especially if you're still so determined to make it work with Ryan. Yeah, you'll realize eventually that it won't, but . . . when? A month from now? A year? No.

It's time for me to come clean, to take a risk for you, for us.

The next time I see you . . . I'm going to tell you the truth about everything. About our relationship and California. About how you gave up on your friendship with Savannah and Rory a long time ago. I don't know why they made up this lie that you like Ryan, but I'm going to put an end to it.

And hopefully . . . hopefully . . . you'll believe me.

Please believe me.

Please forgive me for hiding this for so long.

Please. Please. Please.

All my love,

N.

CHAPTER 23

"MOM, *AGAIN?* ARE YOU SERIOUS?" I ASK THE moment I step through my front door later that afternoon. I'm going to become *that* girl whose house and clothes just always smell like spaghetti and meatballs. We've literally eaten it *three* days this week.

"I know, I know, I know, but it has to be perfect because Monsignor just called and *guess* how many tickets have been sold for the dinner?" she asks as I round the corner into the kitchen.

"I don't know. How many?" I ask.

"Guess!" She clasps her hands in front of her chest.

"Two hundred?"

"More!" Now she's bouncing up and down on her toes.

"Three hundred?"

"Mo—"

"Oh my gosh, Mom, just tell me!"

"Six hundred tickets!" she screams. "Can you believe it? I went and invited a few other local churches and it really paid off! It's going to be the biggest one yet! We can't even fit that many at once in the hall, so we're going to have to do it in two shifts. Which means I have a favor to ask. I know you were supposed to help in the kitchen, but we really need more servers than anything. What do you think about asking some of your friends to do it with you, maybe Ryan, too?" she asks expectantly.

I don't know if Ryan will ever text me again after how I left things when he dropped me off. I don't even know if I *want* him to text me . . . but I have other friends I could ask.

"Uh, sure. Okay. I'll probably ask Nora next time I see her." I smile to myself, imagining her in the mandatory black pants and white button-down, serving the public, carrying a tray full of plates and pouring glasses of red wine. It could actually be really fun.

"Great, and I already recruited Savannah and Rory. I called their moms this morning," Mom says, and I deflate a little.

"Oh, uhh . . ." I try to imagine them hanging out with Nora, but I can't.

"What? Did something happen between you three?" she asks.

"I don't know. Not really, I guess. It just . . . feels like I'm growing apart from them," I tell her, leaning against the counter. She turns the burner off under her sauce and comes to stand beside me.

"How so?" she asks.

I can't very well tell her about Truck Night, because she thinks I went out to see a movie with them, but it really isn't just that night.

"Things just don't feel like they used to. They're just . . . different. We're different. We used to just be able to hang out at each other's houses and eat snacks and watch movies and stay up late, and that was enough. But now . . . well, they just like to spend their time in ways that I don't, really. And they don't seem to care what I want or how I feel," I tell her.

"Maybe it's just part of this adjustment period, you know?"

"Maybe. But it feels like it was already happening before. I just wonder when it started, and how. I wonder about a lot of things, still," I admit. I've tried so hard not to want to know any more, but it's impossible. I wonder what it was I used to feel with Ryan. I wonder what happened between my mom and me. And I wonder why all of a sudden, it feels very much like Nora, the person I thought was a clean slate, might be hiding something from me too. What *was* that at the meat shop today? She had something important to tell me and then she just completely shut down.

"Sweetheart, remember, whatever you're wondering is in the past. Just be thankful for a second chance with them. Move forward," she says, as if that's all there is to it. I feel a flash of annoyance at her. I don't want to, but I can't help it. Whatever happened between the two of us might have been my fault, but why is she assuming this thing with Savannah and Rory is too? Like I'm the only one who needs to do things differently.

"Do you want me to make you up a plate before I take some over to your dad?" she asks.

"I think I'll eat a little later."

"Okay. Well, maybe I'll make up two containers so I can eat with your dad, then."

"That's a good idea," I say, standing up. "I'm going to run up and take a shower, so I'll see you tonight."

I go upstairs to my room as my mom's voice calls out behind me, "There's something for you on the bed!"

I turn into my room, curious, and find . . . a Bower campus magazine, the cover featuring a group of students in navy-blue sweatshirts and matching beanies. Either those are natural smiles or they hired some grade-A models. I guess it doesn't look like the *worst* place for me to spend a year or so.

I toss it aside for now, though, my mind set on something else as I look around my room, *my* space. There has to be *something* in here that could help me make sense of some of the questions I can't get out of my head.

I can't just move on. There is no moving on from this. I need to figure out the missing pieces of this puzzle and how they're all connected.

I watch through the window as my mom pulls out of the driveway, then I get to work. I start again with my computer, hoping there's something I missed that might make sense now. I comb through every one of my social media profiles, then move on to my email, then I open each file I have saved on my laptop.

Still nothing. There's absolutely nothing here.

I rifle through my closet, digging to the bottom of each drawer and opening every box along my top shelf, but all I find are clothes and shoes and all the framed family photos that used to line the top of my desk. I clean out all the dirty clothes that got shoved under my bed. I open every drawer and fan through every book on my desk, but again, there's nothing of any new value to me. It's almost . . . too empty. Where are my mementos? Where are the things I've wanted to keep from my high school years? Where did I put *anything* that's personal to me? I'm an eighteen-year-old girl; surely I have *something* hidden around here that was just for me and no one else.

But the only thing that even sort of stands out is the little orange-and-black rock that matches the one I picked out of the grass at the farm that day. I let out a sigh, pick it up, and toss it up in the air over and over, catching it in my hand as I look around my room for more potential hiding places.

Why do I have this? Does it connect to why I was at the farm?

On the next toss the rock slips through my fingers and lands on the floor by the wall. As I bend over to pick it up, I notice that all four screws on the AC vent are stripped down to nothing. *Odd.*

I grab the pocketknife from the ring toss off my desk and use it to loosen each one until the vent falls onto the floor and . . .

What the fuck is that?

An orange Nike shoe box inside the duct sends my heart hammering in my chest.

I reach in and slide it out. The corners and hinges are so worn that it's been taped back together in several places, the brown cardboard showing through the orange outer coating on the sides.

I double-check that my mom's car is still gone as I place it on my bed. Whatever is in here, I certainly didn't want anyone to find it.

I reach for the lid but draw my hand back, too nervous to find out what's inside.

This box.

This tiny little shoe box could be holding *all* the answers to every question I've been asking. But what if I don't like them?

I close my eyes and take a deep breath, reaching for the lid again.

Please, God. Please. Please. Please.

Slowly I flip the lid back on its hinges, revealing . . .

Well . . . I'm not really sure.

It's a whole pile of all kinds of stuff. Papers and photos and other random things that I've never seen before.

Is all this stuff mine?

I pull out a yellow hair tie from the top, slipping it over my wrist before lifting up a pink Instax camera to reveal a popcorn bag underneath it, a Central Catholic football ticket, and a paperback book with a pressed violet between the pages. None of it means anything to me.

"What is all this shit?" I whisper to myself. *And why did I keep it hidden away?*

Underneath the book, though, I find a whole pile of small rectangular photographs.

The first one I flip up is a photo of me, surrounded by trees, a handful of wildflowers clutched in my hand. I'm about to flip to the next one, when I look more closely—the tall grass and those trees . . . I guess it *could* be a lot of places in Wyatt.

But . . . it could also be the woods on the Martin farm.

I slide it up to reveal the next one. A side-profile silhouette of a girl looking over her shoulder at the camera. I hold it closer, the smooth line of her nose feeling familiar, but the lighting is too dark to make out any features.

I flip again to the next one, and at first I'm not exactly sure what I'm looking at, but there's a lump in my throat that I can't seem to swallow.

I hold it closer, inspecting the blurry face in the corner of the photo.

Dirty-blond hair.

Freckled cheeks.

My palms break out in a nervous sweat.

I shuffle through the next few photos, holding my breath the whole time, my vision shaking.

Nora standing in the middle of two yellow lines running down a street, Pittsburgh's skyscrapers illuminating the background.

Nora swimming, greenery filling the space behind her, her bare shoulders peeking just above the waterline.

Nora sitting on the hood of *my* Volvo next to a plastic Sheetz bag filled with Doritos and pop.

Nora. Nora. Nora.

I put the stack down for a second, letting my breath out, my head aching for oxygen.

We were *friends.*

She's been lying to me this whole time.

Why would she lie to me?

When my head settles down, I move on to the next photograph, trying to make sense of this, and reveal Nora . . .

Nora and . . .

My jaw drops open.

The stack slips through my fingers, each photo floating down onto my bed, but my eyes are still glued onto the back of the photo I just saw. I reach down, but my fingers are shaking so bad that I have to use both hands to pick it back up.

I shake my head.

I don't . . . I can't . . .

It's . . . It's Nora . . .

And me.

She's . . .

We're . . .

Kissing.

What the fuck.

I can finally see where all the pieces of the puzzle belong, but I don't want to snap them into place. A chill crawls up my spine as I stand there frozen.

Move, Stevie!

All at once, my eyes are darting around my bed and my hands must've developed a mind of their own, because I am not in control of my own body right now. I watch as they manically gather up every last remnant and shove it back into the box as quickly as humanly possible.

I step backward away from it all until I knock into my desk. I jump, thinking it's my mom, and scare the absolute shit out of myself.

I need to get it out of here. Get rid of it before anyone sees.

I shouldn't have gone looking in the first place.

I should have just let it go.

Because now my clean slate is gone. For good.

CHAPTER 24

I DON'T KNOW WHAT THE HELL I'M DOING. I CAN'T THINK of a single safe place for this box of secrets and I don't have much of a plan, but I deserve to know the truth and there's only one person who can give that to me.

There has to be another explanation, because if there's one thing I am sure about, it's that I'm not .... gay. *I can't be.*

As I speed toward the countryside, I try to ignore the way that photo made me feel in the deepest parts of me. I try to ignore how it all makes so much sense.

It could be the reason I stopped hanging out with Savannah and Rory.

It could be the reason I was in the woods that day, and why Nora acts so strange sometimes.

Is this why I shut Mom out? Did Nora make me hide this from her? How could I ever choose *her* over my own mom?

I could never. I *would* never.

A stop sign comes out of nowhere and I slam my foot down on the brake. My backpack flies off the passenger seat and into the dash. I can hear the contents of the shoe box inside shuffle around as it hits the floor. I force my eyes back onto the road, my hand wrenching around the steering wheel so tight that my knuckles turn white, and instantly I'm reminded of Nora in the meat shop, her hands clamped down on the counter.

That fucking story . . .

She was talking about me right to my face knowing I'd never know.

When I arrive at the farm, I sling my backpack up onto my shoulder and step out of my car. The thick white clouds provide some cover from the late-July sun as I start across the field to the spot where we worked on the fence together last week, but I still feel hot all over.

I spend the entire walk trying to stop crying, but the tears just won't stop leaking out of my eyes, because every time the shoe box thumps against my back, I'm reminded of all the lies Nora has told me these past couple of weeks. All the secrets she's been keeping from me.

The one person I thought was a clean slate . . . and she knew everything the whole time. It's everything I was afraid of. The reason I decided to stop looking and turn over a new leaf for a second chance. I should never have changed my mind. I just never imagined that what I might uncover would be something this big.

By the time I spot her four-wheeler, I'm crying even harder, my breath a little ragged.

"Stevie?" she asks, surprised, as she tugs on the cord of her earbuds and they dangle from around her neck. "What are—" She stops. I can see that she registers that something is wrong. Every time it felt like she was somehow reading me, every time she would say exactly the thing I needed to hear. It makes sense now.

"What was I doing in the woods that day?" My voice shakes as I speak, but I enunciate every word, giving her one more opportunity to tell me the truth this time.

"Stevie, what are you talking about? I—I don't—"

"What, are you just gonna tell me the same bullshit story again?" I cut her off, trying to swallow my tears long enough to get this out. "You don't know? Huh? You don't know anything?" I swing my backpack around in front of me, unzipping it to reveal the orange shoe box.

With a shaking hand, I slip it out and let my backpack fall to the ground at my feet. I lock eyes with her and then throw the box onto the grass between us, and the contents go spilling out at her feet. The camera and photographs and a random lottery ticket and a ton of other things that don't mean *anything* to me.

But I can see it in her eyes as they shift frantically from item to item.

I can see that she knows exactly what all this stuff is.

And that it means something to her

I watch her chest rise and fall, sweat beading on her tan skin and pooling at her collarbone. She looks up at me, slowly, her mouth hanging open like she's going to say something, but she never does.

"This whole time . . ." I keep my voice low, because it's the only thing I can muster right now. "This whole *fucking* time . . ."

Nora lets her head fall backward, looking up at the sky. When she finally looks back at me again, tears are falling from her eyes just like that day in the butcher shop, and that's how I know for sure it's all true.

"You . . . forgot me," she says, her voice so small that I can barely hear her over the soft sound of the wind blowing through the grass.

"But you didn't forget! You knew and you didn't tell me." I shake my head and she presses her hand over her heart like she's in physical pain. "All those times I was going on and on like an *idiot* about how nice it was to talk to someone new. Someone who didn't know me before."

"I wanted to tell you. But *how* could I?" She throws her hands up. "I know you don't remember, but you told me that you never gave one thought to your sexuality before we met junior year. So how would you have reacted to me telling you something like that? I didn't know what to do. Then you kept coming by and we started hanging out and I thought maybe that meant something, that if I waited, it would all come back to you. Or that maybe we could just fall back into . . . and then our plan could still work." She takes a step toward me but I take a step back.

"What plan? What are you talking about?" I ask.

She bends down, her hands shuffling desperately through the mess I've made in the grass until she pulls out a thick piece of linen paper folded in thirds and tucked inside the popcorn bag. She holds it out to me, but I don't move to take it.

So she starts reading.

"Dear Ms. Green, Congratulations! It is our great pleasure to offer you admission to UCLA . . ."

"What the hell?" I grab the paper and run my hand over it, my thumb dipping into the imprint of the school crest at the top.

California.

I was *never* going to go to Bower.

I was never going to stay here.

But why would I hide getting into UCLA? Why didn't anyone know?

"We were going to get out of Wyatt, Stevie. You and me, we were going to a place we could actually be together. We were *so close*," Nora says. I remember the California travel guide on her side table that she didn't want me to see. It wasn't hers, it was ours. Just like the mess lying in the grass in front of me, proof of a secret life that I don't remember.

"Why would I go *anywhere* with you? Why would I leave my whole family, my friends behind without even telling them? I don't even know what you're talking about . . . I'm not . . . I'm not *gay*." Just saying the word feels wrong, it makes me feel scared, makes me check over my shoulder to be sure we're alone.

"You *chose* me, Stevie. You chose me over everyone else in your life who would never understand. Doesn't that tell you something?" she asks.

I crumple the acceptance letter in the fist at my side and look her dead in the eyes as she stands back up, just a couple of feet away from me now. "Well, whoever that was, it wasn't me. You don't know me. I would never. And I . . . I *like* Ryan," I tell her. The truth. It's the truth, no matter how much it doesn't feel like it in this moment.

"You don't like Ryan," Nora scoffs, confident, almost amused. "That's bullshit and you know it." She takes a step forward until she's one foot away, and my skin starts tingling.

"No. What's *bullshit* is being lied to by someone who you thought was your friend," I cut back.

"I'm not your friend, Stevie! I was never *just* your friend." She takes a deep breath. "I'm sorry that I lied to you. Okay? I'm so sorry." She gives it room to breathe between us. "But this has been *impossible* for me. You don't understand . . . we had *everything*. I mean, our relationship is something that shouldn't have survived this town. We could never share a milkshake at the Dinor. We could never hold hands at the mall or go to prom or even risk being seen together as friends because we were terrified of letting something slip and someone taking it all away. We spent all of our time tucked back in those woods together, and somehow, we didn't just survive there, we *thrived*. Our relationship blossomed all alone in the dark. And finally, *finally*, we were about to step into the light when in an instant, it was all taken away anyway." She pauses, her glassy eyes tracing every inch of my face. "Do you know what it's like? To have the only person you love standing right in front of you, but she has no idea who you are? No idea that she's your entire fucking heart."

My ribs ache as I watch fresh tears roll down her cheeks.

"I know you, Stevie Green. I know you hate grocery stores, because they're always too cold. I know you love when people scratch your back, but no one does it quite like your grandma used to. I know you don't like the feeling of your bare feet in the wet shower after the water is turned off. I know you won't talk to someone who raises their voice at you until they've calmed down." She moves still closer to me, her face inches from mine as my legs quiver underneath me. "I know you don't remember, but *I* do. And I know you feel it. Even now."

Her hand brushes against mine, but this time I don't pull

away, because as much as I know I should . . . I physically can't. I stand there, frozen in place by the truth in all her words as her fingers slip into mine, lacing between each one until our palms are flush against each other. A warmth ignites up my arm and burns all through my body. Suddenly, I understand how it could have happened, how holding hands in the middle of the gym during a football game could lead to all of this.

But I can't do this. I can't *be* this.

"Please just let me go," I whisper across the shrinking gap of space between us, which I find myself wishing wasn't there.

"I can't," Nora replies, leaning toward me until finally I give in to the magnetic pull between us, wrapping my arm around the back of her waist and pulling her up against me, her lips crashing into mine. Our heads twist and tilt and readjust clumsily. I breathe in hard against her salty skin as she drags her fingers down my jaw and off the end of my chin over and over again, trying to pull me impossibly closer.

What does it feel like to kiss her?

It feels like we've both been swallowed by flames.

It feels like my insides are so light that I wonder if we're actually floating.

It feels so right that it couldn't possibly be wrong.

I mean, it *shouldn't* be.

But whatever this is, it made a mess of all the other areas of my life.

So even if it's all I want, I know that this time I'm the one who can't. I can't do this with her.

I push her shoulders away from me and then force my

legs to stumble backward a few steps, putting some distance between us.

"This was a mistake," I say, wiping my mouth with the back of my hand, even though everything in my body is begging her to ignore me, begging her to kiss me again. "Please just leave me alone."

"Stevie . . ."

I can't bring myself to look at her, because I'm afraid that I won't be able to leave if I do. Instead, I close my eyes and see both of my parents' faces if they ever found out what I just did with a girl. I might've chosen Nora over them before, but that was another life. I couldn't possibly do it now.

"I can't do this. My parents would . . . I never should've come here." I bend down to scoop my backpack off the ground, but instead I toss it onto the pile of stuff. "Just . . . keep it. All of it."

"Wait, there's more. Just . . . just give me a second. I have to tell you—"

"I don't want to know, Nora," I reply, even though I want to know more than just about anything right now. The problem is, if I do, I'm scared I won't be able to walk away. And if I don't walk away, everyone is going to find out about me and I'll lose them all over again, just like these last two years. And I've already lost too much.

"Just wait," Nora says, reaching out to grab my arm as I stalk past her. "Stevie, wait! Just talk to me." I shake her off and keep moving. "Stevie, I'm sorry! Please don't leave!" she calls from behind me, her voice breaking.

It takes everything in me but I don't stop until I'm back to the safety of my car.

I don't need her. I don't need her. I don't need her.

I say it over and over again in my head until I convince myself that it's true.

Until I realize how I can prove it.

CHAPTER 25

I SWING INTO A PARKING SPACE ON MAIN STREET RIGHT outside the Dinor and make a beeline for the double swinging doors of the kitchen. As soon as I step through, it feels like a different place altogether. The wood floors turn into tan tile with dark grout. The quiet of the dining room instantly turns to pans clanging in the wash sink, fans venting smoke off the flattop, the cook's laugh booming across the kitchen. But I shut all of that out until I find him.

Ryan.

He's standing there looking at me, a plate ready to be served in each of his hands. I feel like I'm going to pass out, but I move toward him anyway, ignoring how suddenly silent it's gotten.

This is it. The moment I've been so scared of for the past few weeks. The moment that's going to fill my chest with air and prove that I'm not . . . like her.

I plant my right hand on his side and slide my left hand along my jaw until my fingers reach his silky black hair.

"Stevie, what are you—"

I start leaning into him, and I don't stop until my lips are pressed up against his. I stand up on my tippy-toes while his hands stay outstretched to the sides as he tries to keep the plates balanced.

I step in closer to him, press harder, hoping, *waiting* for that feeling.

It has to come.

But it won't.

"Stevie," he tries to say as he leans his head away, his brown eyes looking at me horrified. The exact opposite of what you want to see from the person you just kissed. I step back, finally looking around at his coworkers, who have all stopped what they're doing to stare at me.

"Uh, Ryan, why don't you take a break, man," the cook says, flicking his spatula toward a red exit sign glowing above a dented metal door.

Ryan sets the plates down and takes my hand. Then he leads me outside, next to the dumpsters, where the fan is blowing hot, smoky air up into the sky.

Okay, it must've just been weird because everyone was watching. I throw myself at him again, but he holds me back, away from him.

"Stevie, wait, what are you doing? What's wrong?" he asks, confused.

I wrap my hands around his bony arms and look up at him, trying to sound as genuine as possible. "I just . . . like you. Okay? I like *you*," I tell him.

"I—I like you, too," he replies. "Maybe, like, we can kiss a little slower and . . . not in front of my coworkers." He huffs out a laugh, but then his eyes soften and he's tilting his head toward me.

I let him kiss me this time.

As our lips meet and his arms wrap around me, I try to

ignore that he smells like onions and burger grease. I try to ignore the way his spiky upper lip makes me curl mine. I try to ignore how . . . wrong all of this feels.

Because now I know what a kiss is supposed to feel like and that scares the shit out of me.

My breathing hitches and I pull my lips off his as I stumble across the alley to lean on the opposite building.

"Stevie, please just talk to me," he says from behind me. "What is going on?"

"Do you like me?" I ask, unable to look at him.

He stutters for a while. "Wh-what? Yeah."

"What's it feel like?" I ask, my throat aching with every word.

"It feels . . . good. I mean, I don't know." I can hear him step off the curb, coming toward me.

"No, Ryan." I meet his eyes as his face searches mine for answers. "I mean, what does it *feel* like when you're with me?" I ask.

I remember the way it felt just sitting on the curb outside the coffee shop with Nora. Like just being near her calmed me down somehow.

"When you're close to me?"

The excitement and safety of being pressed up against her on the back of the four-wheeler.

"When you look at me?"

The way my breath caught when her eyes locked onto mine at the fence line.

"When you hold my hand?"

The way my hand felt in hers, like nothing could ever feel more *right*.

"What does it feel like to kiss me?"

My skin burns like oxygen on hot embers at just the memory of her lips against mine.

He stands there with a lingering shrug in his shoulders. "Stevie, why are you asking me all of this? I don't understand. I don't know how to answer *any* of that." He takes in a deep breath and lets it out in frustration. "I mean, we *just* started hanging out and I'm leaving in a month."

And that's exactly the problem. He doesn't understand.

Because he's not the one for me.

"I have to go. I'm . . . I'm sorry," I reply, shuffling backward down the alley, toward the street.

"Wait!" he yells, but it's too late. I'm already around the corner, in my car, and gone as quickly as I came.

That night, I pull my covers up over my head and try not to think about the shoe box or the lies, our kiss in the field, or my life before the accident.

After all this time of trying to remember, all I want to do is forget. But I can't. As many times as I force it out, everything just comes flooding back in again.

It was one thing to know that I had a hole in my life.

But it's a completely different thing to know exactly what was missing.

Especially when what was missing is something I can never let myself have again.

July 15

Stevie,

I'm sorry.

I'm sorry I just pretended like we didn't know each other.

I'm sorry I was too much of a coward to tell you the truth.

I'm sorry I didn't tell you everything in the field today.

Most of all . . . I'm sorry I made you walk out over the crick.

Hurting you was the last thing in the world that I wanted . . .

But now it seems like that's all I've done.

I can't believe I'm saying this, but . . . I can see now that things can't work out for us. That we can't go back and forget the accident ever happened and pick up where we left off.

You asked me to let you go, and maybe that's the punishment I deserve.

So . . . I won't contact you again.

But in my heart, I'll never let go. I never could. I will truly love you for the rest of my life.

Nora

CHAPTER 26

O
VER THE NEXT WEEK, I DO EVERYTHING I CAN TO
keep myself busy. I pick up a few extra shifts at work,
I drop off lunch to my dad a couple of times, I help my
mom stuff bulletins and we go see a movie and make plans to do
it every Wednesday from now on, even after I start at Bower. I
play music in the shower and fall asleep to Netflix on my laptop
every night, because whenever I find myself completely alone in
the quiet, all I do is think about her. And the more time I spend
thinking about her, the harder it gets to keep myself convinced
that being with her is a bad idea.

Because the truth is, while I was doing all that other shit
this week, the only thing I really wanted to do was go see her.

To ride a four-wheeler.

To fix a fence.

To stick my hand in a disgusting vat of ground meat.

Anything to just be near her.

She lit something in me that day in the field and despite my
best efforts to snuff it out, it's been burning ever since.

It burns even as I look between my parents in the front
seat of my mom's car while we drive back home from St. Joe's
on Sunday. It was weird being back at Mass after knowing the

truth. My freshman-year theology teacher was just a few pews ahead of us, and I kept replaying the entire stupid class period that he spent explaining why marriage should only take place between a man and a woman.

What would it even feel like to tell my parents?

Mom. Dad. I like Nora Martin.

My dad's head would probably just explode right here in the car, brain matter and blood all over my mom's fabric seats.

Kidding. *I'm kidding.* But it's an easier image for me to swallow than the truth. In reality, he'd probably just disown me. He didn't even want "the queers" on his television station, so I highly doubt he'd want one living in his house.

But my mom? She wouldn't, right? I'm the one who shut her out, she would never do that to me. I mean, I've seen her roll her eyes at my dad's political rants . . . but I guess she never stops him either. And more than that, there's the Church, and the truth is her status at St. Joe's means the world to her. If having a daughter who got an abortion was grounds for Mrs. O'Doyle to step down from her post, certainly having a gay daughter would be catastrophic to my mom's image and the progress she's finally making. Not that abortion and sexuality have *anything* to do with each other, but in the eyes of the Church, they're both basically a one-way ticket to the fiery pits of hell.

But would my mom *really* choose the Church over me? It's hard for me to believe, but I did choose to leave her behind for California . . . for Nora. So I must've really believed that she would.

It's so hard for me to understand how something that feels

so right could be seen as so wrong. If they could just get into my head for a second to feel how I feel about her, they would understand immediately. And maybe . . .

"Stevie?" my mom asks, adjusting the rearview mirror so she can see me in the backseat. "I asked if you want to get breakfast at the Dinor."

"No!" I reply too quickly and too loudly. "I mean, uh . . . I was actually going to look at my class schedule this morning and see what books I need." *Nice save.*

"I've gotta get into the garage by eleven, anyway." My dad wipes a hand down his face. I'm starting to wonder if he looks tired or if he actually just looks older than I remember.

"Do you really have to go into work *again*, John? It's Sunday," my mom says with an edge to her voice.

"Babe, we talked about this . . . I have to take every job I can right now," he replies, then the two of them start talking in hushed tones in the front seat while my attention wanders back out the window, grasping for something else to focus on. Like Ryan.

I haven't spoken to him since . . . the incident. He must think I'm actually nuts or something, to jump him like that and then disappear. I know I need to call him. Apologize. I just . . . don't know how to explain it.

He's not just going to settle for an *I'm sorry*, and really, I could never even ask that of him. He deserves a real explanation, which is the one thing I can't give him.

I think about that night at the Dinor, though, talking about growing up here, living here. If there's another human being in this town that I could possibly talk to about Nora . . . it's Ryan.

Maybe . . . maybe he might even be able to help me figure out what to do, too.

I just hope he can forgive me first.

I've been nervously looking out the front window of my house for the past twenty minutes. I texted Ryan to ask if he could come over today to talk, so now he's coming, but I still have no idea what the heck to say to him.

Hey, sorry I jumped you at work and made out with you beside a dumpster, but it was only because I actually really wanted to be doing it with a girl and was trying not to want that.

"Oh my God. I can't tell him that," I whisper under my breath, shaking my head at myself.

"Who you talkin' to?" My dad's voice scares the shit out of me as I whip around to find him directly behind me. He ducks his head to look out the window with me as he takes a big bite of a brownie from the batch my mom made yesterday.

"Dad. Jesus." I hold my hand over my pounding heart. "How long have you been standing there?"

He shrugs and then moves on. "What are you doing?"

"Ryan's coming over. I'm just waiting," I reply.

My dad grunts as he tosses the rest of the brownie into his mouth and wipes his hand on his coveralls.

"He could actually ring the doorbell and come in. Don't you think? Nobody does the right thing anymore."

"When did you get so pessimistic? You know people can't do the right thing if you don't actually give them a chance to," I say. He furrows his eyebrows at me. "We're just friends, Dad. So you can stop with the grumbling," I add with a sigh as Ryan's white Honda Civic swings into the driveway. I head out the door before he can say anything else.

As I approach the car, Ryan rolls his window down, but there isn't even a glimpse of his normal sparkly smile, which I've gotten used to seeing.

"You want to go for a walk around the neighborhood?" I ask, flicking my head down the road.

Ryan nods before climbing out of his car.

I know my dad is probably still standing at the window watching, so I don't say anything for the first minute as we make our way a few houses down. My street is so quiet that we walk right down the middle of the road, taking turns kicking a stone out ahead of us again and again until it tumbles into a storm drain.

"Thanks for coming," I say finally, looking over at him.

"Kinda left me hanging." He shrugs, his shoulders drooping more than usual.

"Yeah . . ." When I don't elaborate, he gives me a look like *Well, are you going to explain or what?* So I tell him the only thing I know for sure now.

"I'm sorry about what I did. I was just . . . having a really bad day. That's not an excuse, either. It was a really weird thing to do and I know I probably hurt you and embarrassed you in front of your coworkers. I really am sorry, Ryan."

"It's okay." He says it so easily. The words I couldn't say to Nora no matter how many times she apologized to me. "Pete, the cook, calls me Casanova now. So thanks for that," he adds, making us both laugh, and the air feels a little lighter between us as a result. But there's one more thing I have to say.

"So, uh . . . I was thinking maybe we could just be friends," I say.

"I think maybe that's a good idea," he replies without much hesitation. I expect it to sting, but it doesn't.

I lead us down a quieter street that's mostly empty lots that were never sold, overgrown weeds shooting up all around us.

"So that's it, huh? That's all you're going to give me? You know, now that we're friends, maybe you could talk to me about what was going on," he says.

I take a deep breath and open my mouth. I guess this is where I have to take a bit of a leap of faith that he's the guy I'm hoping he is.

"Can I, umm . . . ask you something that's kinda . . . well . . . Can I just ask you something?" My throat is suddenly almost too dry to speak.

"Sure," he replies, looking over at me as we move to the side of the street to avoid an oncoming pickup truck, black smoke rolling out of a rusty muffler. I swallow hard.

"Can you like . . . not look at me?" I ask, letting out a nervous laugh.

"Uh, okay." He looks down at his feet hitting the tar-and-chip road. I check over both of my shoulders and all around us to make sure no one is within hearing distance.

Every front yard is empty, but even so I keep my voice barely above a whisper. "Do you think it would be really weird if I liked . . . a . . . not a boy?" The second the words leave my lips, I instantly regret them and I clench my teeth so hard that I think my jaw might bust in two.

Why would I ask him that? Why would I ask *anyone* that? He's going to think I'm—

"I don't think it would be weird at all if you liked not a boy."
I see him swing his head over to me out of my peripheral vision.

"It's okay if you do," I reply, too embarrassed to make eye
contact.

"Well, first of all, it wouldn't be okay. And second, Stevie,
it's *not* weird." He puts his hand out, lightly catching the front
of my arm to stop me from walking. I sneak a glance to find him
squinting at me suspiciously. "Nora Martin?"

My cheeks instantly feel warm and I look away quickly,
panicked. "What? Why would you think that?"

"Uhh, let's see. You spent all of your money at the fair on
the chance to *possibly* cheer her up. Your entire face lit up the
couple of times you talked about her. And also, Nora doesn't
exactly strike me as the straightest pencil in the box . . . if you
know what I'm saying. I won't tell anyone, Stevie." I look up at
him and he looks back at me. "I promise," he adds, and I believe
him.

I take a deep breath and plop down on the side of the road,
wrapping my arms around my knees and pulling them in tight
to my chest.

"I guess we were like . . . together. Before the accident, in
the time that I can't remember."

"*Whoa.* Are you serious?" he asks, his eyes wide as he comes
to sit next to me.

"Right before I came to the Dinor, I found this box . . ." I tell
him everything that happened, about the photos, my confron-
tation with Nora, and finding out about UCLA and California,
the truth and all the lies Nora told me since I woke up. The only

thing I don't tell him about is the kiss, because somehow I know saying it out loud would just make it sound small.

"Holy shit. So what are you going to do?" he asks after I finish.

"I don't know. Nothing, I guess." I shrug, feeling frustrated.

"Well, didn't you say you like her?" he asks.

I let out a laugh at that. Of *course* I like her. I didn't even know it was possible for me to feel this way about another person, but . . . "It doesn't matter. It's not like I could ever actually . . ."

"Why not? You already did once," he replies.

"Well, for one thing, my parents would disown me, Ryan." I state the obvious. "I don't want to leave my whole life behind. I don't understand why I ever said I would."

"Did Nora tell you how you came to that decision?" he asks. "I imagine there's a reason."

I think back to how quickly I left that day, and her trying to tell me more. "I didn't really stick around long enough to get many answers."

"Well, maybe you should."

I think about that as my phone buzzes in my pocket and I pull it out to find a text from my mom.

Ribs will be done in 20. Ask Ryan to join us! I won't be weird I promise lol

"My dad's making BBQ ribs with our . . . winnings. You want to stay for dinner?" I ask.

He looks at me deadpan. "Oh my God. You want me to *eat* that adorable cow that I watched you *pet* at the fair?" I just stare back at him until his face breaks into a smirk. "Eh, why not. Sign me up," he finishes, making me laugh. I hop up onto my feet and pull him up off the ground.

"Just so you know, my dad kinda thinks we're dating. So he might be cleaning his shotgun or something when we walk in."

"And here I thought that only happened in the movies," he replies as we stand up to make our way back to my house.

CHAPTER 27

RYAN, WHAT DID YOU THINK OF MY MEATBALLS?" my mom asks, leaning eagerly across the table as he forks the last one on his plate and pops it into his mouth.

He chews eagerly so he can swallow before answering.

"Oh, they were really good, Mrs. Green. Meat with a side of meat. I love it," he says with a wink.

"I know, a little unconventional. I've been going a little crazy prepping for the spaghetti dinner."

"Spaghetti dinner?" Ryan asks.

"Stevie, you didn't tell him?" she asks, her eyes lighting up as she looks back at him. "Ryan! You have to come serve tables with us! We could use a pro like you out there. It's a fundraiser for our church's mission trip to Haiti. It's in a couple of weeks, August twelfth. Can you make it?"

I butt in. "Mom, don't drag him into . . . Ryan, you don't have to come *work* the fundraiser."

"No, it's okay. Really. I'd love to help," he replies, and my mom explodes with excited squeals.

"Ryan, you look like you could use a few more," my dad says

as he stands up from his chair and picks up the tongs lying on a spoon rest. Even after his shower, I can still smell the motor oil underneath the Ivory soap and aftershave.

"Oh, no thanks, Mr. Green. I'm pretty f—" Ryan stops when my dad leans across the table and plunks down three more ribs onto his empty plate anyway.

"John, don't force him," my mom says to my dad before directing her attention back to Ryan. "So Ryan, you graduated this year too, right?"

"Yes, ma'am," he replies, faking a bite before wiping his mouth with a napkin from my mom's rooster-shaped napkin holder.

"What are your plans for next year?" she asks.

"I'm actually heading to Italy at the end of the month for a year abroad," he replies.

"Oh, wow! That's so neat," she tells him, an excited smile spreading across her face.

"I'll tell you, kid. The grass isn't always greener on the other side," my dad says, his expression changing.

Ryan cocks his head. "How so?"

"Well, all you kids today think you have to go halfway across the world. I don't know. Maybe you think you've got something to prove. But you're not going to find anything better than you could find right here in Wyatt, with your family," Dad says, almost smug. "Like Stevie. She knows what's good for her. She understands family values and she knows that the best place for her is right here."

I've always known my dad had no interest in leaving Wyatt, even for vacation. But I didn't know he had such strong opinions about *me* leaving. In the hospital, he told me he wanted me close by so he could support me after my accident, but come to think of it . . . he hasn't actually done any supporting at all. Kind of hard to support someone when you're literally never around.

I'm the one who's *tried* to connect with him again. I've tried to hang out. I've tried to mend whatever broke down in our relationship . . . but it's like he doesn't even *want* to try to get back to how things were. He just wants to be . . . angry.

He goes back to his ribs, like the conversation is over.

I pick my fork back up to push some food around on my plate. I steal a quick glance at my mom, but she's doing the same.

"Well"—Ryan looks at me and then back to my dad—"respectfully, sir, not everyone is suited to live in a town like this."

Our eyes meet and I think he's talking about me as much as he's talking about himself.

"Well, I got a lot of years on you. You're young and young folks think they know everything, but I guess everyone has to figure out the truth on their own," Dad says dismissively.

"I guess so," Ryan replies, and my dad gets up to take his plate to the sink. Then he just keeps walking through the mudroom and out into the garage, pulling the door shut behind him.

After a few awkward moments of quiet, my mom speaks.

"Sorry about him. He thinks this place is the be-all and end-all." She fakes a laugh, shaking her head. "I think it's really admirable that you're going. Takes a lot of guts to move that far from home. I always thought I might like to do something like that, but I never had it in me."

"Really? You wanted to get out of Wyatt?" I ask, shocked. She's *never* told me anything like that before.

"When I was young I did, yeah, but then I met your dad, and then you came along and I don't know . . . Time just kind of got away from me," she says, with an almost faraway look in her eyes.

Huh.

My mom wanted to get out just like I do now. I wonder what she would've thought if I'd told her I wanted to go out to California or something. I wonder if she would've been supportive of that.

"Not that I regret any of it," she follows up quickly. "I love my life here, with you. And your grumpy old dad." She laughs. That statement may be true, but it doesn't mean she wouldn't have loved a different sort of life too. Maybe even a little more than this one. Now she'll never know. And something about that makes me really sad.

Maybe it wasn't fair of me before to just *decide* that she would react badly to me being with Nora. Maybe she deserves a chance. Maybe I deserve one too.

After dinner I follow Ryan out to his car.

"Hey, thanks for saying that stuff to my dad," I tell him.

"It's true." He nods and climbs into the car. I lean into his rolled-down front window and he looks right and left, and then back at me.

"So do you think you're going to try with Nora?" he whispers.

Nora.

It scares the absolute shit out of me, but . . . I've never felt these sorts of feelings for *anyone* before. And I don't want to live my life not knowing, like my mom. I really did get a second chance here. If the accident hadn't happened, I would have left everyone I cared about behind. If I hadn't found the box, I might have left Nora in my forgotten past. What if there could really be a way I don't have to give either one up? I won't know if I don't try.

"I think I have to," I reply, an uncontrollable smile spreading across my face at the thought of being able to kiss her again.

"Good. Let me know if you want to hang out soon, or if both of you do. Friend."

"I will," I reply before he backs out of the driveway.

But first I need to see if she'll even see just *me*.

CHAPTER 28

I WOKE UP THIS MORNING TO TWO TEXTS. ONE WAS AN invitation to Jake's annual post–spaghetti dinner end-of-summer party, and the other was a reply from Nora. No words. Just a red pin, dropped onto Google Maps in the middle of the farm's woods.

I weave through the trees, glancing down at my phone every so often to make sure I'm staying on course. Everything around me is some shade of green, until finally I catch sight of a pop of colors through the trees in the distance. As I step out of the tree line, the colors take shape into the form of wildflowers. Hundreds of them, and in the center is Nora.

The girl who saved my life.

The girl I haven't been able to get out of my head all week long.

The girl who, even if I can't remember how, knows me better than anyone.

She stands up off the ground the second she sees me.

"Hi," I say, noticing the thick patchwork quilt she has laid out on the ground. On top of it is my backpack, unzipped, with the orange shoe box peeking out. The closer I get, the more nervous I can tell she is. "Do you mind if I sit?"

"Okay," she replies.

I walk through the flowers and plop down cross-legged on the edge of the blanket, and after a beat she sits down opposite me.

"I think this is the most beautiful place I've ever seen in my life. So many different flowers all together." I smile, looking around us at the ocean of color.

"We planted all these together in the spring. It was actually your idea," she replies.

"Smart lady." Both of us share a small smile, but then Nora shakes her head.

"Nora." My eyes flick down to the shoe box beside her. "Will you tell me about us?"

"Um." She lets out a deep breath, her head hanging slightly. "Okay." She nods as she sets the box down between us. She seems different, almost . . . hopeless. The back of my neck feels too hot, so I put my hair into a bun with the yellow hair tie off my wrist as she reaches into the box.

The first thing she pulls out is the flattened popcorn bag.

"This is from our first real date. We spent ninety-eight percent of our time right here, but we drove into Pittsburgh a few times so we could, you know, actually do something out in public."

"We really bought our popcorn and stuff there?" I ask, slightly surprised that I would splurge on the movie theater prices.

"Please. We weren't idiots. We swung by Rite Aid on the way and snuck in the rest of our haul under our coats. Like I'm going to pay seven bucks for a pop." She rolls her eyes.

I laugh, nodding in approval.

She holds up a football ticket. "The night we met. You know about that."

Replaying the story in my head, it sounds like so much *more* than a silly meet cute to me now that I know the truth. I can imagine it, the two of us wandering through the halls of Central Catholic. Lying down side by side in the center of our wooden basketball court, her hand sliding into mine and sparking all the way up my arm, just like in the field.

"Why are you smiling?" she asks, pulling my attention back to her hazel eyes.

"You know when you were telling me that story in the meat shop . . . I was kinda jealous," I admit.

"Really?" she asks, and I look away, embarrassed. "Wait, like jealous of what, exactly?"

"I don't know. I guess like, the way you felt about, well, me. I've always wanted that, but it just never . . ." I shrug. "It never felt like something that was going to happen for me."

"This is *so* weird." Nora flops backward on the blanket, looking up at the sky. "You've said that to me before, almost word for word."

Finally, I see a hint of a smile pulling at the corners of her lips.

"Well, at least I'm consistent. What else?" I ask, before I can say what else I'm thinking. That I was also jealous watching *her* talk about her feelings for someone like that, because deep down, even if I couldn't admit it then, I wanted her to be talking about me. I slide the box over to her as she rolls onto her side and props herself up on her elbow.

"Okay, umm." She digs around inside until she comes up with a handful of Polaroids, some of which I still haven't seen. "We decided in the beginning to only take photos of each other this way, so no one could accidentally see them on our phones or something." I expect her to hand them to me, but instead she starts flipping through them. "I actually haven't seen some of these for a long time."

I watch a smile spread across her face, wider and wider with each one. She snorts out a laugh, holding one out for me. "This is one of my favorites."

I squint at it. It's definitely a photo taken here, the crick filling up most of the frame. But other than a whitish blur hovering over the water in the middle ground, there's nothing particularly significant about it. "What is this?"

"You don't recognize yourself?" Nora laughs again, waiting for me to figure it out.

I look again, and—*oh my God.* I can just make out my long brown hair billowing out behind the blur that is me, mixing with the tree trunks. But wait . . . I quickly hold the photo against my chest, my jaw dropping open as I meet Nora's eyes.

"Am I . . ." I lower my voice. "Am I *skinny-dipping*?"

"Yeah, are you scandalized?" she asks, teasing. Flirty.

I grin, my eyes wide. "Kinda! I've never done *anything* like that before."

"That was your idea too," she tells me without looking up from her stack of photos.

"Bullshit."

"You're right. It was mine," she replies, and I Frisbee the photo back at her. She bats it down onto the quilt, laughing.

We spend the next little while passing photos back and forth, Nora telling me about each one. It's so odd, almost unsettling to be looking at all of these memories I feel like I wasn't there for, but if there's one thing I'm sure of . . . it's that I look happy.

"We really had some fun out here, huh?" I ask as she hands over a selfie of me clinging to her back, our smiles blown out by the flash.

"We did," she replies, dropping the stack of photographs back into the box.

"I wish I could remember it all."

"Me too."

"But . . . I'm glad we're here now," I add, meeting her gaze. "Together."

"You are?" she asks, her eyes slightly crinkling at the corners, still cautious.

"I am."

With that, her eyes trace mine in a way that makes my heart race.

She pulls out a couple more things. A novel whose cover features a girl lying on a bale of hay that we supposedly both like a lot, and a winning lottery ticket that we found in a parking lot and never cashed.

"Wait, why didn't we turn it in and get the seventeen dollars?" I ask, inspecting the three matching fried eggs lined up in a row on the grid.

"We decided to wait and do it right before we, uh . . ." My eyes flick up from the lottery ticket to find her looking at me, uncertain again. "Before we left."

I take a deep breath and pull my knees tight into my chest.

"What was I going to tell my parents? My mom?" I ask, a little scared to hear the answer.

"You weren't going to tell them anything," she replies.

"What do you mean? I was just going to disappear?" I ask in disbelief, and she nods. "But it's . . . my *mom*. I wouldn't do that to her."

"I'm sorry, Stevie. It's just . . . what you decided. You wanted to cut off all contact," Nora says.

She'd be sick. I mean . . . she'd *die*.

What was I thinking? I must've really, *really* liked Nora. I must've liked her more than I've even been imagining. More than I even think is possible.

I want to try this. I know I do, but Nora needs to understand that things have to be different this time. I know I've dreamed about maybe going to UCLA someday, but I can't go *now*. I want to take this slow, and slow does not include California.

If we're going to try this, she needs to understand no matter what I decide or when I decide it about coming out, I can't let my relationship with my mom crumble again.

"You—" she starts, but I interrupt her. I've got to get this out.

"Nora, whatever I did or planned, I can't do that again. I can't lose her, okay?" I ask, realizing how desperate my voice sounds. "I mean, she's like . . . my best friend. And we're in such a good place right now. I can't do that to her. I *won't*."

She looks at me for a long moment, biting her lip. "I won't ask you to," she says finally.

"Okay." I take a deep breath and let it out with relief. "Okay."

And then I ask: "Well, what about you? What was your plan?"

"Was I going to tell my mom?" She shrugs, letting out a weak laugh. "You haven't even come close to seeing the worst parts of that lady. No. I never even considered telling her. You weren't the only one who wanted to keep us a secret."

Jeez. I wonder what that means. I've seen the way her mom talks to her. How much worse can it get?

But then my heart sinks as I realize something else. Nora finally had a plan to get out of here and away from her mom and . . . I ruined everything.

"Nora, you could still get out of here. You could still go to California. Without me, I mean."

She lets out a huff, shaking her head like I just said the most ridiculous thing. "You still have no idea what you mean to me. I wouldn't leave without you. I . . . I told you once I want to be with you more than I want to be away from here."

She reaches out, her hand hovering over my leg, maybe to see if I'll pull it away, but I don't. My skin lights up at her touch in a way that I suspect could never get old. As I set my hand on top of hers, her hazel eyes dart up to meet mine, questioning.

I nod and her eyebrows settle back into place as a giant smile finally breaks out on her face.

"Are you serious?" she asks, her eyes welling up.

"Yes. But We. Can't. Tell. *Anyone.* Everyone has to think we're just friends," I say. There's no reason for my friends and family to know, before I even know *myself* if this is what I really want. "And I'm serious about my mom. I'm not letting us grow apart again." I try to keep a straight face to show her how serious I am, but I can't help but crack a smile as she scoots closer to me on the quilt.

"I want to keep this a secret as much as you do. In public we can be friends, strangers, whatever you want, Stevie," she says, slipping her free hand into my hair and tugging my lips toward hers. "But here . . ."

She kisses me, softer this time, like she's still afraid she'll scare me away. Even so, my stomach lifts, giving me that lightness that I felt in the middle of the field the other day. Then she pulls her lips away, leaning her forehead against mine. I open my eyes to find hers still closed.

"I love you," she whispers. The words send a panic up my back, even though they sound so beautiful coming from her.

Less than a second later, her eyes fly open.

"I . . . ," I start, but don't know what to say.

"I'm so sorry. I didn't mean . . . well, I did, but . . ."

"It's fine. Really. I just . . . I'm not—" I feel my face go red.

"No, no, no." She waves her hands in front of her. "I shouldn't have said that. It just kind of slipped out. Please, don't say it until you really mean it. No pressure at all. Even if it's seven years from now."

"Okay," I reply, liking the idea of still being with her seven years from now. She's cute.

She reaches out to take my hand again. My face still feels red-hot, but my stomach is going wild. It's so incredible and so confusing. All of this. She loves me, but I just kissed her for the first time a few days ago. She remembers all this stuff that I don't, an entire relationship that we've had together that for me is only just starting. It must be hard for her to look at me and see the person she loves, but to also have it not really be her . . . me.

"I'm sorry," I tell her, hanging my head as she rubs circles against the back of my hand. "I'm sorry that I forgot us. That I might not ever remember."

"You know what? I'm not." She lifts my chin up with her finger, leaning into me again. "It just means I get to make you fall in love with me all over again."

"You sound pretty confident," I say, pulling my head back just enough to tease her.

"I know." She smiles into my lips as I melt into her.

Something tells me she isn't going to have much trouble with that.

CHAPTER 29

A FEW DAYS OF STOLEN MOMENTS LATER, NORA AND I make plans to go on a date on my day off. Like a *real* date, not just an afternoon of sitting on a blanket in the middle of the woods or walking the back road that cuts through the property where nobody can see us. She wants to take me somewhere that we've been before, someplace where we can get away from the prying eyes of Wyatt for an evening and just feel normal.

As I drive around the last bend of I-279, the city appears out of the rolling hills. Following the directions on my phone resting in the cup holder, I pull off onto our exit and peer past Nora, out the passenger window. The yellow bridges are all lit up and reflecting off the rivers below with the rest of the tall buildings downtown. I've been to Pittsburgh, but I've never driven there and I've never seen it at night like this. I've also never been here without my mom. Every once in a blue moon, we'd venture down to go to the mall or shop around the Strip District with all its crowded specialty grocery stores and street vendors lining the uneven sidewalks. It feels good, though, being here without her. Almost like I'm out by myself for the very first time, like I'm actually eighteen. A little scary, but mostly just . . . freeing. Everything feels so bright and beautiful, too. Perfect.

But maybe that has something to do with the girl sitting next to me.

My eyes fall onto her hand, resting on her thigh. It feels like the opposite of when I was in the car with Ryan. There's no having to convince myself that I like her. And there's no question in my mind about what I want to do. I want to reach across and take her hand, more than anything . . . but my nerves get the better of me. So instead, I focus on the road and try to ignore the way my stomach jumps up into my throat every time I look at her.

We drive through Oakland, into Schenley Park and out the other side, passing rows of houses that only seem to get bigger until finally we come up on a barricade blocking off the road at the intersection. A white banner hanging over it reads SQUIR-REL HILL NIGHT MARKET in big black letters.

After trying to parallel park for about two minutes straight with cars lining up behind me, I finally give in to Nora, who has been whispering, "Usually I park for you. Do you want me to do it?" since my third attempt. I hop out and hurry over to the sidewalk as she climbs over the center console into the driver's seat. *Of course*, she executes a perfect parallel on her first try.

She gets out and drops my keys back into my hand, a cocky grin spread across her face.

"Just come on," I reply, rolling my eyes and knocking my shoulder into hers.

We walk side by side into the river of people flowing up and down Murray Avenue, where lines of tents are set up on either side of the street, each one displaying something different for sale. Handmade pottery, intricate pop-up greeting cards, jam, watercolor paintings, jewelry, and even mounted animal heads made of paper. It's like the Wyatt farmers' market on crack.

"My mom would love this," I say as we pass a fresh-cut-flowers stand.

"Does she know you're here?" Nora asks over the sound of laughter coming from a group of girls tucked into the nook of a closed storefront. One of them sounds so much like Rory that a layer of sweat covers the back of my neck as I turn to look, but of course . . . it's not her.

"I guess I could've just told her I was coming here with you . . . as friends, but it felt too risky. So I told her I went to Rory's house with Savannah," I say. In reality I haven't spoken to either of them since Truck Night, despite their best efforts, but not a single message they've sent has contained any type of apology. I can already feel my blood begin to boil at just the thought of it all. "They actually did text me this morning, asking me to go shopping with them, but I didn't even reply."

"Did you want to? I mean, if we didn't have this planned."

"No. I'm done with them. They freaking lied to me. They took advantage of me and my accident, and it didn't just hurt me, it hurt Ryan, too. *And* you. They're not my friends." I shake my head, curling my hand into a fist. "And you know the worst part? I can't even call them out for it without having to tell them how I know, without telling them about us."

Nora nods. "The Ryan thing is a whole other level, but I remember when the middle of junior year hit, and they started hanging out with a different group of people after Savannah got that new boyfriend. You felt like you guys were drifting apart.

And then Jake said some racist shit to you that made me want to beat his ass, and they just laughed, so . . . you really didn't want anything to do with them after that." She pauses to take a deep breath, calm down. Honestly, though, seeing her all protective is kind of hot. It's kind of eerie the way almost the same thing has happened again. Like the cracks are too deep for any second chance to fix.

"Anyway, you were just kinda hanging out with them enough to get through to the end of summer without raising suspicion. What do you think you're going to do now, though?" she asks.

"Honestly, I don't even want to think about it anymore." I look over at her. "I just want to be here with you."

Nora slides closer to me, her hand beginning to tangle around mine.

I take in a sharp breath of air and reflexively shake her off as if she's a wasp that just landed on me. She snaps her head up, and her eyebrows knit together.

"*Sorry,*" I say immediately, tucking my hand safely into the front pocket of my jeans. "I just . . . what if someone sees?"

"That's why we—" She stops when she sees the panic in my eyes. "Okay. Yeah, you're right. I'm uh . . . I'm going to grab us some food. Stay here, okay?" she asks, already stepping down off the curb toward a group of food trucks parked at the inter-section.

I scan the people around me again but simultaneously kick myself for reacting like that. We just drove all the way into the city for this exact reason, to be able to be together in public. So I can see what it's like for real.

Nobody from Wyatt is here. Nobody knows who we are. Nobody is going to find out.

I remind myself to take a breath and chill, hoping I didn't already ruin the night.

Luckily, when Nora returns, the look on her face tells me that everything is fine. She's got a paper boat of tacos in one hand and some kind of dessert in the other, an excited smile on her face in between the two.

She holds the tacos out to me and I give them a suspicious sniff.

"What kind are they? What's this stuff?" I ask, lifting up the tortilla to reveal a yellowish-green mystery sauce.

"You'll like it. I promise." She reaches out to lift the boat closer to my face, but I don't budge. "Try it!" she insists.

"Okay, okay!" I laugh, before doing as she says, and *Oh man.* She's right. It's some kind of spicy steak with fresh cilantro, pico, guac, shredded cheese, and a tangy lime sauce drizzled on top. "Told you," she says with a satisfied look on her face as she holds out the thing in her left hand. "Here, try this."

I'm not totally sure what it is. Some kind of rolled cinnamon pastry filled with cream. This time, I don't put up a fight, I just trust her and take a bite of the thing.

"Okay. Holy shit, that's the best thing I've ever tasted."

"That's a Steel City Chimney. They were always your favorite. They roast them on this cool wood-fired rotisserie," she replies, her eyes lighting up as she watches me take another bite.

"You know, I don't think it's very fair that you know all this stuff about me but I know basically nothing about you," I tell her over the food in my mouth.

"What do you want to know? Ask me anything."

I swallow the bite of dessert in my mouth and consider the question while I reach in to try the other taco.

"What kind is this one? Those pickled onions look good." I go to pick it up, but Nora smacks my hand away before I can even touch it.

"That one's mine! Jeez, lady," she says as she scoops it out of the boat and takes a bite. "You can ask me anything and that's what you want to know?"

"Fine. How many times have we been here?" I ask, taking another bite of my own taco.

"This is our third time here. They have three or four every summer," Nora replies.

"What's your favorite food?"

"Aw man. *Cheeseburgers,*" she says, her eyes widening with wonder.

"You've got a little drool." I point to my mouth, and we both laugh. "What's your favorite food that you can still eat?"

"Honestly, this freaking veggie taco is bomb." She shoves the rest into her mouth. "I gotta 'ake 'ese at home."

"Looks much more appetizing than your soggy Tofurky."

"Don't knock it. It's actually pretty good," she says, and I give her a look like I don't believe her. "Okay, it's no honey ham." She laughs.

"What's your favorite movie or show?" I ask.

"Oh my *God.* Stevie!" She stops dead in the middle of the sidewalk. "*Dickinson!* You don't remember that, do you?" she asks, her eyes wild with excitement.

"What? Like Charles Dickinson? The *Oliver Twist* guy?" I ask as we start walking again.

"Charles Dickinson!? First of all, I think you mean Charles *Dickens*. And . . . Stevie, please. I'm talking about our queen, Emily Dickinson. They made a TV show about her and it's only the greatest show in television history. See? Something good *has* come out of all this." She pauses to stare at some far-off point in the sky. "What I wouldn't give to relive the Emisue love story all over again for the first time." She grazes my arm with her hand, just barely, but it's enough to give me butterflies. "Okay. Okay. More questions."

"Well, wait. Tell me more about it," I demand, intrigued.

"No. Just move on before I spoil anything, you always get mad at me for doing that. Trust me," she replies, waving her hand at me.

I think for a second. What I *really* want to ask is when *she* knew she liked girls. I haven't stopped wondering about that since we looked through the box, but it feels a little too personal to be asking in such a public space, so I opt for a different question I've been holding on to.

"You told me in your bedroom that you aren't going to college. What were you going to do in California if I was going to UCLA?" I ask, finishing off my taco.

"Oh, umm." I can tell she's surprised at the sudden shift in topic. "There's a farm just outside of LA County that was going to give me a job. It's not like . . . my *ideal* farm, but they're always hiring there. And I figured I can get my feet wet, make some connections with other farms and figure out what I want to do from there. Someday I'd *love* to have my own, grow vegetables sustainably and join a CSA." She takes an excited breath and presses her hands over her chest like she's trying to hold everything in. But it bursts out through her smile anyway.

"I like watching you talk about all that stuff. I can tell how much you love it." It all reminds me of my own future. "I signed into that secret email account of mine that you told me about and read all the stuff from UCLA. I applied undecided. I never really knew what I wanted to be at fifteen, but I thought maybe I'd have my shit together a bit by now, you know?"

"You told me you felt like you needed to get out of Wyatt first, see what's out there before you decide anything else."

"I just . . . wish I had something that I was as passionate about as you are with farming."

"You'll find it, Stevie."

"At Bower?" I ask skeptically.

She shrugs. "I think you can find it wherever you are," she replies optimistically.

But Nora almost had it. And I can't help but wonder what it's been like for her to have had to cancel all of these plans we made together.

"Nora, what would you have done? If I never found that box? If I never found out about us?"

She's quiet for a long moment, thinking. "I wasn't going anywhere. I know that much. I really was going to tell you the truth . . . I just . . . needed some more time to figure out how. All I know is that you and me? We'll always find our way back to each other," she says. The back of her hand brushes against mine, sending an electric pulse up my arm.

I smile and munch on the rest of my cream pastry as we come up on an old movie theater. An older woman is playing the violin under the oversized marquee with all the current movie showings. Her long hair swings back and forth as she sways with the music, her eyes closed. I reach into my pocket and pull out a five-dollar bill to drop into her case.

As the two of us stand there watching her, I feel that magnetic pull tugging me closer to Nora. I take a step sideways until our shoulders are touching, and again, there's a buzzing on the surface of my skin. I wonder if Nora can feel it too.

It's all so different from the dates I went on with Ryan. Everything feels like *more* with her. Like my lungs have felt almost too small all night and I can never quite seem to catch my breath.

With my eyes locked on the violinist, I slip my hand around the inside of Nora's forearm and slide my fingertips down her wrist, over the calluses on her palm, until our fingers intertwine.

We stand there, Nora and I, and this woman who seems to only be playing for us, even as people flow by on either side.

None of them stop to look.

None of them say anything to us.

None of them make me feel like holding her hand is anything but normal.

CHAPTER 30

WITH MY TOTE BAG TUCKED UNDER MY ARM AND a string cheese still in the wrapper dangling from my mouth, I rifle through the pantry for one more snack to eat on the way.

"Hey, don't worry about that." My mom pops her head into the pantry. "Let's go all out at concessions. Oh! Grab the ranch popcorn seasoning. Can't have popcorn without ranch."

I slowly turn to face her as she leans against the doorframe, her purse already slung over her shoulder.

Shit. It's Wednesday. Movie matinee day.

"I totally forgot, Mom. I told Ryan I would come over to go swimming," I tell her, letting the string cheese drop out of my teeth and into my hand.

"Oh, really? But it's our movie day," she says, the sadness clinging to her voice.

"Rain check?" I ask, tossing the snacks into the tote bag on top of my bikini and then checking the time on my phone. The guilt pulls down on my feet, though, making it hard for me to move toward the door.

"Yeah. You know what? With the spaghetti dinner this Friday, I should probably pop over to the hall and get a feel for the kitchen," she says, but her tone is almost too light.

"Maybe if I get back early enough, we can watch a movie together here," I say.

"Okay, sure . . . have fun," she replies quietly from behind me.

"Thanks, Mom. I'll . . . I'll see you later," I tell her as I step out onto the front porch and force my hand to pull the door shut.

But . . . I can't keep doing crap like this. It starts with blowing off our movie date and pretty soon, we'll be right back where we were. And I can't let us get back to that place. I guess I could put tonight off. I turn and grab the handle again. Maybe I should just go see the movie with her, let her know that I'm still here, that things aren't going to change.

But also . . . I haven't missed a single movie with Mom, and Nora's meeting me at Ryan's. Between her job and mine . . . it could be a few days until we can find a moment to see each other if we don't do it now. So I have to see her when we have the chance.

I *want* to see her.

I release my grip on the handle and head for my car, making a mental note to be sure I'm home in time to watch a movie with Mom. It'll be fine. I mean, I'm going to be stuck at Bower for who knows how long, so we have all the time in the world for movies. I'm not going to let it happen again.

Ryan's house is by *far* the nicest place I've ever been to. I didn't even know homes like this existed in Wyatt. I mean, the kitchen alone is about the size of most of the houses near town. It's got two sinks, two ovens, and an entire section dedicated to an espresso maker that reminds me a lot of the one I use at work.

When he asked us to come swimming, I expected to find one of the circular aboveground pools that you see all over here, but no. This one is set right into the dirt, a fancy stone walkway lining the curved edges, all of it surrounded by a tall cedar fence.

"Dude, your house is bananas," I say, scooting my butt off the side and into the shallow end.

"It's all right." He huffs out a laugh as he floats by me on a giant inflatable donut with rainbow sprinkles.

"Are you kidding me? I'd kill to live here!" I reply, shoving his float into the deep end.

"It's more fun with company."

"Where are your parents?" I ask.

"I can't even remember." He shrugs. "Off on a work trip just like they were last week and two weeks before that. They'll actually be gone till the night before I leave for Italy."

"Really? What do you do with this whole place to—" I stop and turn toward the house as the sliding door opens and out walks Nora in a solid-black bikini. I try not to stare too much, but it's hard to ignore the parts of her I've never been able to see before. Her bare thighs and the curve of her waist.

I let my eyes drift down the length of her body and back up again. She sees me looking and stops walking to cock her head at me, smiling in this way that tells me she knows everything I'm thinking. That makes me wish we were alone.

The sound of Ryan splashing in the water reminds me that we are not.

"Nice tan lines," I joke, trying to make it less awkward

before dunking myself underwater to cool off. By the time I resurface, she's running right toward me, launching off the side and into the pool with a cannonball.

After we dump Ryan and his once perfectly dry hair off his donut, the three of us spend the next hour or so playing copycat off the diving board, each of us trying to mimic the leader's movements.

When we're done, we all climb onto separate floats, exhausted, and stare up at the sky from the center of the pool. Ryan on the donut. Me on a flamingo. And Nora on a banana that she just can't seem to stop falling off, which is maybe the most hilarious thing I've ever seen.

"Why didn't we ever hang out in high school?" Nora asks Ryan as I watch some big puffy clouds move across the sun.

"Because I was new and the only Asian kid in the entire school, and everyone thought I was a weirdo," he replies flatly.

"What?" Nora asks, flipping around to try to look at him, but instead she falls off into the deep end again. She coughs some water out when she pops up. "I did *not* think that."

"Maybe *you* didn't, but everyone else at that school did. I don't think a single person talked to me outside of class work. It was like I was invisible."

"Yeah? Well, people called me Beefstick. So . . ." Nora's voice trails off as Ryan spews out a laugh despite clearly trying to hold it back. Nora splashes some water at him, pretending to be offended.

"At least you guys remember high school," I cut in.

"Whoa, that's too dark, Stevie," Nora says.

"Yeah, we were just joking around. Don't bring the mood

down with your amnesia," Ryan says, and all of us bust out laughing.

When Nora goes into the house to pee, Ryan rolls onto his stomach so we can see each other better.

"I know it started out on a weird foot, but I wish we'd started hanging out sooner. Figures I make a good friend right before I leave," Ryan says.

"Well, I'll be here when you get back."

"Will you?"

"Where else would I be?"

"I thought after that conversation we had, you might think about applying to other schools."

"Yeah . . . I decided it would be best to stick to Bower for the first year at least." But even I don't believe me as I say it. "It's too late to apply anywhere else now anyway."

"Well, you *did* get into one other school."

"UCLA?" I laugh. "Yeah, right. *Hey, Mom and Dad, just wanted to let you know I applied to UCLA behind your back months ago and my memory hasn't come back but I'm still gonna go across the country.* They would *never* let me go."

"I mean. You can make your own decisions. We're kind of all adults now," he reminds me from atop his donut floatie like we weren't just playing copycat off the diving board five minutes ago.

I keep forgetting that I *am* eighteen, but even so . . .

I shake my head. "At least now I have Nora here. I want to be with her, but I still have things to fix here."

Right on cue, Nora pops back out of the sliding door holding armfuls of chips and cookies and sodas. Way more than one person should be carrying.

"Yo, Ryan, your parents' kitchen is *stacked*. Did you guys know Oreos are vegan? *Shit*." She drops the package of Oreos on the walkway, and when she bends down to pick them up, she drops two more things. "You are one lucky son of a bitch," she says, even while fumbling with the cans of soda.

"Oh, sure, just help yourself, Nora," Ryan says as I grin, watching her.

"Yeah. I'm definitely not leaving that," I whisper to Ryan.

CHAPTER 31

MY ARMS ARE GOING TO FALL OFF. HERE," I SAY, handing my marshmallow stick over to Nora at the fire pit on my back deck.

My parents both drove over to Tipton with a bunch of the other adult volunteers for the spaghetti dinner to go to some kind of outdoor concert. In other words, they'll be gone until close to eleven tonight. I try not to be frustrated that my dad can make time for that and not for the boat trip we still haven't rescheduled, because at least it means Nora could come over.

"You gotta hit the gym or something, babe," Nora replies, giving me a judgy look as she relieves me of my marshmallow-roasting duties.

"You should've seen all the tables I set up today! They were the heavy metal ones too. Not those plastic ones."

I spent all morning helping get the hall set up for this Friday, on the latest leg of my guilt trip. I completely lost track of time at Ryan's house last week and didn't get home in time to watch a movie with my mom. She said it was no big deal, but she's been a little . . . off since then.

Even today, as I tried to pump her up about how great the dinner is going to be, it was like she always had someone else to talk to. Maybe I'm reading too much into it, though. Maybe she's just been preoccupied with making sure this thing goes off without a hitch. I mean, it was only one night, right?

"I'm just saying . . ." Nora shrugs, pulling me back to the moment.

"I'm strong!" I lift my arm up to flex my bicep in front of her face. She reaches out and clamps her hand around it until I jerk it away from her. "Well, don't *squeeze* it. You'll make it disappear!"

She laughs until her eyes land on my marshmallow, which is now a flaming weapon of destruction. She pulls it out of the flame and frantically blows it out, both of us looking at the little black blob on the end of the stick.

I start to reach for a new marshmallow from the bag when I hear her say, "It's perfect."

I turn and look at her. "Oh, so you're one of those."

"One of who?"

"The people who pretend to like burnt marshmallows, but really they're just lazy roasters."

"Whoa. Whoa. Whoa." She drops her jaw open. "This thing right here is cooked to absolute perfection. Just hand over the graham cracker and chocolate and watch."

I do as she says, then I watch her slide the outer layer of the marshmallow off to create a little cup. Instead of smashing it between the two crackers, she stuffs them inside the marshmallow along with the chocolate chunks.

"Reverse s'more," she says, presenting it to me and watching eagerly as I bite half of it off.

"Tastes like burnt marshmallow, but I'll give you points for creativity."

She mumbles something about my "untrained palate" as she pops the rest of my gooey marshmallow into her mouth straight off the stick.

"I thought you said those weren't vegan!" I yell, my eyes wide.

"Shh. Don't tell anyone," she says with a smirk before getting up to throw two more logs onto the fire. Sparks fly up, drifting into the clear night sky and disappearing into the stars.

She crouches down right next to the pit, rubbing her hands together and then holding them out near the fire, the flames dancing in her pupils. I could get used to nights like this, just Nora and me and something real simple like a cozy campfire.

"Where have you been all my life?" I ask, watching the orange glow dance across her face.

"What do you mean? We've been dating for like two years."

"I mean before that." I shake my head, thinking about all the time I spent wondering if there was someone out there for me. "I mean, like . . . forever."

She comes over and sits down next to me, taking my hand and kissing the back of it.

"I'm here now."

"Can I ask you something?"

"Of course."

"Was there anyone before me?" I ask, nervous to hear the answer.

"Honestly?" She lets out a heavy sigh. "Yes. I did fall for someone once before."

"Really?" I ask, trying to mask my jealousy.

She nods, staring into the fire. "Her name was Miss Gwen and she was my kindergarten art teacher."

"*Nora*. I thought you were serious!" I say, almost shoving her off the wooden bench we're sharing. She laughs as she rights herself, then the two of us get real quiet as she looks at me.

"Nah." She puts her elbow up on the back of the bench and pushes my hair behind my ear, sending a shiver down my neck that makes her laugh. "You're the only girl for me, Stevie Green."

It's music to my ears.

I close my eyes and nuzzle my cheek against her hand that's even warmer than the fire. "I *really* like you," I whisper, wondering if what I'm feeling is actually stronger than that.

"I really like you, too," she replies.

My eyes open for a split second as her lips meet mine, confirming the pine trees surrounding the deck block the view of any neighbors. She kisses me softly, and my hands wrap gently around her neck.

"And I like kissing you," I tell her, taking a breath as my stomach rises into my chest. She smiles and then slides her hand around my waist, pulling me back into her.

I grab onto the front of her sweatshirt and lean backward until my back is flat on the hard wood of the bench. Her left leg plants between both of mine as she lays her body weight down on me, the fire crackling in the background.

My hand trails from her shoulder blade down to her lower back, pressing her closer to me. She pulls my bottom lip down with her thumb, her tongue slipping into my mouth and then back out again. I don't know what two plus two is right now, but I know I want her to do that again. I tilt my head toward her, wanting more, but my hips jerk involuntarily as I do and all at once, we both go tumbling off the bench onto the deck with a thud.

"Oh shit." Nora's groans turn into laughter as I try to push myself up off her. "I wasn't ready for that one."

"Sorry." I laugh, my cheeks warming. "Umm . . . that was fun."

"I'm glad you enjoyed yourself," Nora replies as we both sit up, leaning up against the bottom of the bench. She checks the time on her phone. "I should probably get going. In case your parents get back early. It's almost ten thirty." She drops one side of her mouth into a frown.

"Why don't you stick around and say hi. I mean, I'm allowed to have friends over."

"Did you *tell* them you were having a friend over tonight?"

"Well . . . no, but—"

"So then they'll wonder why you didn't. Look, I haven't seen your parents since the hospital and it's late, I should really . . ." Nora points over her shoulder.

"All the more reason to stay with me, then. What if I hide you in my room? We'll be really quiet and careful, and I'll sneak you out in the morning. Please?" I wrap my hand around the inside of her knee.

"Stevie . . ." She shakes her head. "We can't. I'm sorry."

"But . . . I don't want you to go." I force out a pathetic-sounding laugh, hoping she can't see my glassy eyes. "I hate this."

"Me too. But it's too risky. We'll see each other real soon. Okay?" She puts her arm around me and kisses the side of my head.

"When?" I ask, digging my fingertips into her leg.

"I know you have the spaghetti dinner on Friday, but my mom is heading up north for a farming convention. It's like the only day of the year she isn't at home and she'll be there overnight." She turns my face toward her and catches the tip of my nose with hers until I lift my chin. "Why don't you come over after, and we can pick up where we left off?" she whispers, sending a tingle all through my body.

I walk her out to her farm truck parked in the driveway and open the door for her to climb in.

"Here." She grabs my backpack from the floor in front of the passenger seat and hands it out to me. "I've been thinking and I really can't keep it at my house. I don't have a great hiding place, and if my mom ever found it . . . well . . . it would be really bad. So put it back in your vent. Okay?"

I nod, glad to have it back. I'm having a harder time than usual letting her go. These little secret moments together are starting to feel like not enough. How did we do this for two years? "I wish you didn't have to leave."

"I'll see you Friday night. You better bring me a plate of that spaghetti." She smiles as she manually rolls her window down.

"I will." I shut her door but hop up onto the running board, leaning into the window to kiss her again in the darkness of night. "Oh my gosh, this is so lame. I do *not* want to let you go!" I kiss her again and again. Cheek. Forehead. Nose. Eyelid.

She giggles cutely.

"Good night, Stevie." She grabs my chin and plants one more kiss on my lips before I finally step back and watch her pull away.

I stand there for a long time in the dark, staring at the point where I last saw her taillights, feeling a little like half of my heart just left with her.

Four days. I can make it four days without seeing her, right?

CHAPTER 32

NOTHING SAYS AUTHENTIC LIKE CHEESY ITALIAN music playing out of crackling ancient speakers and red wine served in Styrofoam cups. Fortunately, I don't think any of us here in Wyatt would recognize authentic Italian food if it hit us in the face.

Two of the volunteer servers have already dumped spaghetti sauce down their white button-downs, which Monsignor *insisted* we all wear, as if that's going to make people think we know what we're doing.

"I've got four adults, one with no meatballs, and two kids," I say to Mrs. Dashnaw through the kitchen window as I dab the sweat off my brow. I keep my attention focused on the kitchen as I notice Savannah's red ponytail in my peripheral vision as she takes orders at a nearby table with Rory.

"Make that three kids, Mrs. Dashnaw!" My serving partner, aka Ryan, calls back into the kitchen as he leans on the wall beside me with a bottle of red wine in hand. "The small one rethought her hunger strike," he says to me.

"This serving thing is no joke, and those plates are *heavy*."

"You've gotta hit the gym, Green," he says, shaking his head.

"Why does everyone keep saying that!" I ask. "And also, why am I even serving the food? You're the one with all the experience."

"Because I serve a perfect pour." He straightens up and holds the bottle out like a fancy wine man, and I roll my eyes at him.

Mrs. Dashnaw appears back in her window with a tray of three plates. "I'll be right back with the rest," she says.

"Hey, Stevie, should we be like . . . limiting these people?" Ryan asks while we wait. "Old Big Beard over there just put away his fourth glass."

I open my mouth in disbelief.

"*Ryan.* You're only supposed to pour one glass with each meal!"

"Oh, I have *not* been doing that," he says as my mom approaches us through the window. "Don't tell any—Hi! Mrs. Green. How are you? The meatballs are a huge hit out here."

"As is the wine," I say. Ryan jabs me in the side, out of sight.

"I know!" She leans toward me. "We've raised over six thousand dollars for the mission trip, which means they're going to be able to send even more volunteers over this year, and Monsignor just told me it's the best spaghetti and meatballs he's had since he was assigned here forty years ago. I think he's going to ask me to take over the Lenten fish fry, too!"

"That's awesome, Mom. You deserve it."

"Thanks, sweetie. Just one more hour. We can do this. We can do this." She sounds more frantic than usual. Maybe a little stressed, even though it obviously could not be going any better. Clearly this all means *a lot* to her and now that the fish fry is in sight, the stakes just went up.

She turns to get back to work but then doubles back like she remembered something. "I was thinking after we get cleaned up here, we should do something to celebrate. Ice cream, a movie, anything you want. You deserve a little fun after this."

"Actually, um . . . everyone's hanging out at Jake's after this. Do you mind if I go?" I ask.

She pauses. "I was really hoping that tonight, it could just be you and me. There was that new thriller out you wanted to see . . . ," she says, but this time, underneath the sad tone in her voice, I can feel her claws digging in. I've been trying so hard not to hurt her, but this isn't fair. I've been here with her all day and most of the last four before that, helping get ready for this. I'm seeing Nora tonight. I don't care what it takes.

"Can't we do it tomorrow? I kinda already told Ryan I'd go," I lie, glancing over at him, and he smiles and nods along without even the slightest hesitation.

She lets out a sigh, thinking.

"All right. But not too late and make sure you say hello to Monsignor before you leave tonight, okay?" Even though she's agreed, her face is closed off now. Thankfully I'm saved from a further guilt trip by a loud clatter somewhere in the back and Mom grits her teeth. "I've got to get back in there before Mrs. Tyler overcooks another ten pounds of noodles," she says before disappearing.

Phew.

"You're going to Jake's party with Savannah and Rory?" Ryan whispers, shocked.

"No. I haven't even talked to them since Truck Night. I'm going to Nora's," I whisper back, "but it's the perfect cover."

Mrs. Dashnaw appears with the second tray and before Ryan can take off, I snatch the wine bottle out of his hands.

"You're on spaghetti now," I say, leaving him in the dust.

As Ryan sets a plate down in front of each person, I walk around and pour wine for each adult with a green wristband.

"Don't be shy there, honey," a lady older than spaghetti itself says to me. She uses her crooked finger to tip the bottom of the bottle up until a little wine spills over the brim of her cup. Ryan sends me a smirk from across the table.

What is with these people?

We work our way through the rest of our tables like a well-oiled machine, getting food to the last of our assigned section faster than any other duo. Finally, we make our way to a couple of chairs lined up against the wall in the corner and plop down to watch the rest of them finish up.

"Y'all Catholics can *drink*," he says.

"Well, they start us very young. We get our First Communion gulp in second grade, and it's all downhill from there," I joke.

We watch the tables slowly empty out as people finish eating, almost every single plate licked clean, which is not something I could say for Mrs. O'Doyle's spaghetti dinners. I'd say my mom has this on lock.

"Hey, can I ask you something?" Ryan drops his voice so low that I can barely even hear it. I nod. "Your mom seems like . . . real cool. Like she doesn't seem like the type of person who would have a problem with you and . . . you know. Have you thought about just telling her?"

I let out a big sigh, thinking about her hurt face earlier.

"I have. At first I thought she'd like . . . for sure just flat-out stop talking to me because of all this and the role she wants in the Church . . . but the more I've thought about it, the more I wonder if that's true. The bigger problem is my dad, though. I couldn't ask her to keep that from him, and he's *real* conservative now, like even more than I remember from before. You saw what he was like about just leaving town."

"I guess I hadn't really thought about that. Sorry, Stevie. I probably shouldn't have brought it up. It's not really any of my business," he says.

"It's okay. I'll figure it out. Luckily, I don't have to do it right now," I reply. So far this keeping it a secret thing is working out all right. Although . . . saying goodbye to Nora after our campfire seemed especially hard, and lying to my mom sucks more each time. So maybe . . . *almost* working out all right.

"Well, I think our job here is done. I guess I should head out, but have a good time tonight. Say hi to Nora for me."

We say our goodbyes and after he leaves, I find Monsignor for a quick hello before I head into the kitchen to congratulate my mom.

I have to weave through about twenty people packed into the tight space, but finally I find her sitting up on the counter in the back corner, munching on a piece of bread.

"Mom." I slide up onto the counter beside her and hold my fist out. "You killed it."

"Thanks, baby," she says, sounding completely exhausted. "And thank you for all your help." She leans over and gives me a kiss on the forehead, but it feels a little stiff.

"It was fun, actually, trying the different recipes, serving people here. Mostly just getting to do it all with you, though,"

I reply honestly. Hopefully it also softens the blow of me not wanting to hang with her tonight.

"For me, too." She smiles and something finally loosens. "Maybe we can do it again next summer."

"I'd like that." I look at all the hustle and bustle around us. Basically everyone from our church is here either working or eating. All except one. "I'm sorry Dad didn't come."

"Oh no." She shakes her head. "I knew he wasn't going to be able to make it. Your dad's working hard too . . . for all of us," she tells me. But it still doesn't add up. The Dad I remember would've managed to at least stop by to say hi, offer her some support on her big day.

She flicks her head toward the door, pulling me out of my thoughts. "Go on. Get out of here."

"Are you sure? I could stick around and help clean up," I offer, even though my mind is already racing with thoughts of Nora.

She shakes her head. "I've got plenty of help. Grab a to-go container on your way out if you want. But be home by eleven."

"Midnight?" I try.

She narrows her eyes at me. "Eleven thirty."

"Deal." I grab my to-go container off the counter and head out the door. The wind blows at my ponytail as I head toward the parking lot, storm clouds looming in the distance.

I couldn't care less what the weather does tonight, though, because, finally after these four long days . . . I get to see her again. An entire evening, just me and—

"Stevie! Hey, Stevie!" Rory and Savannah both shout from behind me. I take a deep breath as I stop and turn around to face them.

"Look, we swiped some!" Rory opens her giant purse to reveal three bottles of wine. "Come on. You want to ride with us to Jake's?"

I shake my head. "No thanks."

"Okay, well, when will you be there?" Rory asks, as if I haven't been ghosting them for the last few weeks.

"I'm not going to the party," I tell them.

"Stevie, come *on*. Drink with us. We haven't seen you in literally *weeks* and we're about to leave for college. You're not turning back into old Stevie again, are you?" Savannah asks, making me clench my teeth.

"What Stevie is that? The one that has a *giant* crush on Ryan?" I ask.

"What's that supposed to mean?"

My heart is pounding in my throat, but I have to say this to them. Stand up for myself for once.

"You guys . . . you fucking lied to me. I *never* liked him like that."

"Oh my God. You remember?!" Rory asks, stepping toward me with a smile.

No, but that's all the confirmation I needed that this whole thing was them toying with me.

"I've discovered enough to know that that wasn't even remotely true. And people really got hurt because of it."

Savannah just laughs like this is all so trivial to her. "People? Dramatic much? You don't have to be a bitch about it. We just wanted you to have a little fun for once. Jesus. I remember when you used to know how to take a joke."

"You know what I remember? I remember when you guys

used to treat me like a real friend, like you actually cared about me. I remember when you would've stood up for what's right when some drunk idiot is being a racist asshole."

"Oh my *God*. You're *still* on this?" Rory shouts. "You don't have to take everything so fucking serious, Stevie. We were all just having *fun*."

"Nothing about that situation was *fun* for me or for Ryan! You guys . . . you don't get it. You don't get what it's like to live in this town and not be able to just *blend in* with everyone else. To have some jerk you don't even know point it out in that way. It was embarrassing, *humiliating*."

Savannah puts on a baby voice. *"Oh, poor me. I'm Stevie and I'm so different and everyone is out to get me."* She takes a step forward and drops back to her normal register. "Maybe we just want to enjoy our summer without having to worry about what's going to offend you. Like I'm *sorry* I have a boyfriend now and I'm sorry we've made other friends. What? Do you want me to apologize for growing up or something?"

I take a deep breath, and as hard as it is right now, I force myself to keep my voice calm. Collected.

"It's not about you growing up. It's about who you grew up in*to*, and whether I remember it or not, I don't think you guys have been my friends for a long time," I say, pulling open the door to my Volvo. "Have fun at Jake's," I add before stepping inside.

I can see them out of my peripheral vision, standing in my side mirror, but I don't look back. This is for the best. I should've done it a long time ago.

CHAPTER 33

A N HOUR LATER I LIE AT THE FOOT OF NORA'S BED, watching her eat out of the Styrofoam container as she leans up against her headboard. A sly little grin spreads across her lips as she looks me up and down.

"What?" I ask, glancing down at my white button-down and black dress pants.

"I'm not going to lie. That look is kinda doing it for me."

"Shut up." I laugh, shaking my head.

"No, I'm serious. And it's even hotter when you're bringing me a plate of food like this."

"Isn't that a little sexist?" I ask.

"I don't think so, because I'm a girl too. So I think I'm in the clear?" She shrugs, straightening her leg to slide her foot under my knee. "This is *so* bomb," she says before slurping down another forkful of spaghetti. "I never get to eat home-cooked meals like this."

"Your mom never cooked for you growing up?" I ask as a big bolt of lightning strikes outside the window behind her.

"If she did, it was mostly cheeseburgers and . . . more cheeseburgers. There was one dish she'd make for us on special occasions, though. Stuffed peppers in this sweet tomato sauce with mashed potatoes. *Man* . . . It was so freaking good." She rolls a meatball off to the side of the container. "But it's been years since she's made it. Hell, it's been years since we've sat down to a meal together at all."

I reach out to rub my hand up and down her shin, a few stubby leg hairs that she missed shaving poking at my palm. It breaks my heart when she talks about her mom, but it also makes me feel so thankful for the mom that I have. And even more confused why I was willing to throw her away.

"How long after we started dating did we hatch up the California plan?" I ask.

"We started dreaming about it right from the start, but we didn't get serious until maybe five, six months later. Why?"

"I guess I just wondered what prompted us to actually do it?"

"Do you want any of this?" Nora asks as she holds the container out to me. I shake my head. I think I'm off spaghetti and meatballs for good now. She sets it on her side table and then crawls down to lie sideways across her bed next to me. "We figured out pretty quickly that we couldn't sustain a long-term relationship here, in secret." She shrugs, struggling for the right words. "I mean, at a certain point, this thing between us . . . It was just getting too big to hide."

Somehow, after only dating her for a couple of weeks, I can already understand that feeling.

She brings her hand up and a soft smile spreads across my lips at the feeling of her fingers combing through my hair. I close my eyes and imagine that we're somewhere else. Holding hands as we walk through the grassy park near Wyatt High.

Kissing at the top of the Ferris wheel at the county fair. Or even just being seen together in public without constantly worrying about how people are reading us.

All things that could quite literally never happen.

All things I would give anything to be able to do.

I open my eyes just enough to see her staring back at me, her hand still brushing through my hair, sending a tingle down my body that doesn't seem to fade. Reaching up, I take her hand and kiss each of her knuckles before holding it close to my heart.

"I think I'm falling in love with you," I whisper so quiet that I don't even know if she can hear. I wasn't sure at first, but I know as soon as the words leave my lips how true they are.

Maybe I already *am* in love with her.

Maybe I always have been, even when I didn't remember it.

I peek up to find her pupils engulfing most of the hazel in her eyes.

"Did you hear me?" I ask, a nervous pulse thumping in my throat.

"I heard you," she replies, her eyes shining.

Heavy raindrops pelt loudly against the roof over us.

I'm not sure which of us is leaning in, but I can feel her breath on my face and then I can feel my bottom lip grazing hers. She lets her mouth fall open a little and I press my lips into her. My body ignites, everything burning hotter than I've ever felt before. I kiss her harder each time we readjust. I kiss her so deep that our teeth hit, but still, it's not enough.

I throw my leg over her, and she grabs me around the waist, pulls me on top of her. My attention catches on her biceps, the shadows created by the warm light of the bedside lamp.

I press my hands against the mattress on either side of her head, push myself back an inch, and smirk down at her. "I like your arms."

"You like my arms? Really?" she asks, sounding shy for the first time maybe ever.

"Nicest arms east of the Mississippi." I give them a squeeze and she turns her face into the pillow to stifle a giggle.

I lean right back down to her again and tilt her chin back to me until her mouth reconnects with mine. She unbuttons my pants and runs her hands over the bare skin of my thighs and back up toward my underwear.

A sound escapes my throat that surprises me, makes me pull away an inch, but Nora stretches her neck up to kiss me again.

She slips her thumbs through my side belt loops and tugs me closer, her hips bucking up under me with the same force.

I push myself back, sitting up straight, my chest heaving as I slide my hands under her tank top and over the warm skin of her abdomen.

I need to be closer.

"Nora?" I say, stopping at the bottom of her sports bra.

"Yeah?" she asks, her stomach expanding and contracting under my palms with each heavy breath.

"I, uh . . ." I slide my hands back down and slip my fingertips into the waistband of her shorts. "I don't know how to do this." I laugh, embarrassed and nervous and excited.

"Are you sure you want to?" she asks.

I laugh differently this time. "Yes," I reply. I'm absolutely positive.

"Just do whatever feels right," she tells me, sitting up underneath me and unbuttoning my shirt before slipping it off. She drops it onto the bed and then slides her hands up my back, holding me there up against her.

I don't know much about sex, but I would know what to expect if I was with a guy right now. I mean . . . I wouldn't know what to expect, but I would at least know what goes where. Pretty straightforward. But *this* is different.

"Do whatever you want, Stevie," she adds, maybe sensing the panic on my face.

"I want to kiss you again," I reply, wrapping my hands around her head as she looks down at my bra, making me wish I had worn a nicer one. But then she kisses the bare skin of my chest and I see that she wasn't really looking at it anyway.

She pulls my face down to hers again while we both shuffle under the covers. I motion that I want her to take her bra off, so she does, and she takes mine off too. And the feeling of settling back on top of her is completely dizzying.

She slips her leg in between mine and I press all my weight against her. A loud breath escapes her lips, which only makes me want to do it again.

Layer by layer, we take off the rest of each other's clothes, and she rolls us over so she's on top of me now. I'm glad for it too, because unlike me, she knows what she's doing. Her lips begin moving across my jaw, down my neck, and over my collarbone. Each kiss starts another little fire on my skin as her hand trails down each rib, across my stomach, and then down farther.

And *oh my God.*

A crack of thunder roars all around us.

She leans into the crook of my neck. I can feel her smile against my jaw as every muscle in my body tenses and I squeeze my eyes shut, trying to make this moment last forev—

"What the fuck is going on in here?"

My heart feels like it both stops and beats through my skin all at once as I register the sound of someone else's voice in the room. I pick my head up to see Mrs. Martin standing frozen in the doorway.

Shit. Fuck. *FUCK*.

Nora's hand clamps down on my forearm in a vise grip under the comforter, her fingernails digging into my skin. But I can't bring myself to look at her.

"Put. Your. Clothes. On," Mrs. Martin hisses through her teeth as she looks toward the side wall and then doesn't move a muscle.

"Nora?" I whisper, my eyes coated with tears.

"Stevie, get out of here. Now," Nora says under her breath, but she's still sitting frozen, squeezing my arm.

I wriggle out from her grasp, swallowing the vomit sitting at the top of my throat, then somehow manage to pull my underwear back on and button up my shirt enough to cover myself. Finally Nora snaps back to reality, pulling her sports bra on and her shorts, keeping her eyes locked on her mom the entire time. Maybe I should say something.

"Mrs. Martin, this is all my fault. I—"

Suddenly Mrs. Martin unfreezes and lunges forward. She clamps her hand around Nora's jaw, forcing a high-pitched cry out of her throat.

"I always knew there was something wrong with you." She squeezes even harder.

"Mom . . . ," Nora squeaks out. "Please. I'm sorry." Her face turns beet red as tears roll down her cheeks and over her mom's hand.

Mrs. Martin jerks Nora forward until their noses are practically touching.

"You're dead to me. Do you hear me? You are *dead* to me." She spits into Nora's face and then all at once throws her sideways. Her head crashes into the heavy wooden dresser.

"Nora!" I cry, taking a step back. But as Mrs. Martin moves toward her again, I throw myself forward until I'm right in between them. The edges of my vision turn black as Mrs. Martin catches me by the arm. She drags me up onto my feet and pushes me so that I stumble backward into the bed.

She points her finger at Nora, curled up in a ball, covering herself protectively. "You get your *shit* and you get the fuck out of my house," she says, then storms out of the room.

I hurry over to Nora, but her eyes are looking past me somewhere. I grab her face in my hands. "We have to go," I tell her.

She doesn't say anything, but she gets up onto her feet, her whole body shaking against me. I pull a duffel bag from the top shelf of her closet and set it on the bed in front of her. She stands there, staring at it for a few seconds, before she finally starts darting around her room, grabbing handfuls of clothes and stuffing them inside. The last thing she grabs is a small box from under her bed that she tucks into the bag before zipping it up.

With the rest of my clothes back on, we both head downstairs toward the front door, but Nora stops short.

"Mom?" she says, looking into the living room, but her mom has her back turned to us and she doesn't move a muscle, doesn't say a single word.

"Come on." I take Nora's hand and tug her toward the door.

We step outside into the pouring rain, and both of us are instantly drenched from head to toe. Nora pulls her hand out of mine and I turn around to find her stopped dead on the front walk.

"What am I going to do? What was she even doing home?" she asks over the rain falling around us. "Oh my God. What the fuck just happened?" She crouches down, dropping her head into her hands.

I lean over her, my head still reeling from what I just saw, from seeing the girl I love thrown into a dresser by her own mom.

"Nora, you can stay with me," I tell her.

"And tell your parents what?" she asks, turning to look at me.

The second she turns and her eyes meet mine, I know exactly what I want to do. I know what I *have* to do. I have to protect her. I have to be with her. And I'll do anything to make that happen.

"Listen to me. I've been thinking about it a lot and . . . I'll tell my mom the truth. Okay? She loves me. She'll be okay with it. And my dad is barely around anyway. We'll figure it out."

"Stevie . . ." Nora shakes her head.

"Come on." I pull her up onto her feet and toward my car

as a heavier wave of rain comes down on us. "I'll tell her right now. I'll tell her I'm gay. I'll tell her I'm in *love* with you and that you need our help."

"Stevie, just *stop*!" She rips her hand out of mine.

Why is she being like this?

"It'll be fine. She . . ."

"You already told her!" she yells, then looks down at my feet.

"What?" I ask, confused. "I don't understand. What do you mean?"

"Stevie . . ." She meets my eyes again. "You already came out to her." Her voice is softer now, barely audible over the rain. I shake my head.

I . . . what?

She takes a few steps closer and wraps her arms around my elbows, the rain running down her face.

"I'm sorry it's another thing I didn't tell you. It's just . . . things were so good between you guys and you were so set on keeping it that way. When you told me not to make you choose, it didn't feel fair to tell you. I didn't want to ruin that for you."

I shake my head at her. "No. No, if she knew she would've told me. She would have." Unless . . .

"It didn't go well. It was a few months after we started dating and you tried to come out to her, but she basically denied it. Said there's no way you could know that at your age. She thought you just hadn't met the right boy yet, and something about how labeling yourself like that could ruin your life before it even got started. But you always thought with the Church and everything, she was worried about how it would make you look, how it would make your family look. So you never told her about me. That's why your relationship fell apart. You didn't just drift apart, Stevie. She couldn't accept you."

Tears roll down my cheeks, mixing with the rain as I think about every time I've felt guilty the past two months about how things went down between me and my mom. Every time I thought it was all my fault . . . because she *let* me think that. How could she let me think that? It's like Savannah and Rory all over again but a million times worse.

I can feel the pieces of me that want to fall apart, but I take a deep breath. As pissed as I am at my mom right now . . . I need to focus on Nora. Nora, who no longer has a mom at all. She needs somewhere to stay tonight. She needs me to hold it together.

I reach out and hold her head in my hands and she presses her forehead into mine.

"I know where you can go."

CHAPTER 34

BY THE TIME WE GET TO RYAN'S HOUSE, IT'S ALMOST 10:45, which means that I only have about half an hour before I have to leave for home if I'm going to make curfew. Nora changes into some of Ryan's clean clothes since even her duffel bag is completely soaked through, and I towel off my spaghetti dinner uniform as best I can.

She climbs onto the queen-sized bed in the guest room and I kneel on the area rug right next to her.

"You could've told me," I whisper as I rub my thumb gently over her forehead, where the skin is beginning to turn shades of blue and purple.

"I never wanted you to know," she replies, looking away from me.

"You mean, you never told me? Even before?"

She shakes her head and closes her eyes, tears rolling sideways across the bridge of her nose.

Even though I'm still a little damp, I climb up onto the bed behind her and wrap all my limbs around her, my entire body engulfing her as she sinks back into me.

Sobs begin to rack her body and I hold her tighter, burying

my face in her neck. My chest is aching for some sort of release, but I don't let myself cry.

"It's going to be okay. I've got you. You're okay. I love you. I love you. I love you . . ." I whisper it over and over into her ear. I don't know how long we lie there for, but I hold her until she stops crying, until her breathing deepens and I'm sure she's asleep.

These last few weeks she's felt so strong to me, like my safe place, but right now it feels like without me, she might just crumble away into nothing. So even though my curfew must be approaching or even past, I stay awhile longer.

Eventually I carefully slip my arm out from under her and manage to climb back onto the floor without stirring her awake. I pull the quilt up over her shoulders and give her one last gentle kiss on her forehead before heading out into the hall.

Ryan is sitting at the kitchen counter when I get downstairs, like he's just been waiting to make sure everything is all right.

"Thanks for letting her crash here," I tell him, leaning my elbows on the granite.

"Stevie, what happened?" he asks, concern painted across his face.

I let out a sigh.

"Is it okay if I let her tell you herself tomorrow?" I ask, unsure of what exactly she'd want me to tell or keep under wraps.

"Sure, but . . ." He walks around the counter to stand beside me. "Are *you* okay?"

"Yeah, I'm fine," I reply quickly, but the second I look over at him, tears that I've been holding back all evening finally spill over. He pulls me into a hug as I cry into his shirt.

How many times has her mom hurt her?

I think back to my first time meeting Nora at the farm, the bruises on her arm that she brushed off as if they were nothing.

She wasn't *just* getting out of Wyatt to be with me. She was getting away from her mom at the same time . . . and *I* kept her here.

"Just take care of her, okay?" I ask as I finally pull away, my voice still throaty with tears.

"I will. I promise." Ryan steps back too, his shirt damp now. "But I have to be at work tomorrow at eleven."

"Okay. I'll be here by then," I tell him.

He opens the front door for me, but it's still raining cats and dogs.

"Hang on." He quickly slips on a pair of slides and grabs an umbrella from a tall vase on the floor. "Okay, come on," he says, putting his arm around me and walking me all the way out to my car.

I don't stop crying the whole way home. Between the storm and my tears clouding my vision, I'm beyond lucky there are virtually no other vehicles on the roads right now.

I sit in my car out in the driveway for a few minutes, forcing myself to slow my breathing as I wipe my face and blow my nose using a stack of napkins from the glove box. After I get myself together enough, I head inside, the rain soaking clean through me once again.

"It's a little late there, kiddo." My mom's voice startles me as I head in through the door.

"Sorry," I say as I step to the edge of the entryway. She's sitting on the couch in the family room reading another romance novel.

"It's almost midnight. Curfew was at eleven thirty." She makes a big show of checking her watch.

Could there *be* anything more trivial right now? Nora just got the shit beat out of her by her own mom, and kicked out of her home forever with no place to go, and my mom is worried about my *curfew*? But of course I can't say any of that.

"I lost track of time. Won't happen again."

"If I'm going to trust you to be out late with your friends, you need to respect the rules."

Trust.

Kind of like how I trusted her when she told me she had no idea what happened between us? Kind of like how I trusted her when she let me believe it was all my fault? When she made me feel *sorry* for her?

As much as I'm *dying* to call her out on her bullshit, I bite my tongue. I need to get my head on straight and figure this out with Nora. The last thing I need right now is to risk being kicked out too. I can't believe just over an hour ago I was *actually* going to trust her, to ask her to help me.

"Sorry, Mom," I repeat, then clench my jaw shut.

"Oh my God, you're dripping wet, sweetie," she replies as she gets up off the couch and comes closer to me. "Go on. Get dried off and get to bed," she says.

I try my best not to lean away from her as she plants a kiss on my cheek, but honestly, I can barely bring myself to look at her right now.

"You okay?" she asks, planting her hands on my arms and holding me out to look at.

"Just tired and cold," I reply, shivering under her grip.

"Okay, well, let's both head up."

I follow her upstairs and watch her blow me a kiss from her bedroom before closing her door behind her.

I lock mine behind me and let my wet clothes fall onto the wood. Then I pull on a clean pair of sweat pants and a soccer hoodie from my closet before collapsing facedown onto my bed.

I turn my head to the side to look at the heap of clothes on the floor, and despite all the terrible shit that happened today, for just a moment, I relive the earlier part of our night, together in Nora's bed.

The feeling of her body underneath mine as she unbuttoned my white shirt. Her hands sliding over the backs of my thighs. Her adorable little embarrassed giggle when I complimented her arms.

I look down and realize I've been playing with the yellow hair tie on my wrist. The one that Nora told me she gave me the first time we had sex, and I remember that I have the shoe box back in my vent now. I don't have to sit here and imagine things. I can actually look through all our old memories, all our photographs.

I hop out of bed to retrieve it from the vent and flip it open on my bed. I haven't looked at any of this since we went through it together in the woods, but when I dump it out, I realize there are a couple of new items. The first is the California travel guide with all its Post-it Notes, and the second is a small black-and-white composition notebook.

I pick it up and sit back against my headboard as I open up the cover to the first page.

June 18

Dear Stevie,

I don't know if this journal is going to make me feel any better, but I have to talk to someone and the only person I can talk to is you, even if you can't hear me. I just got back from the hospital. It's been six days since the accident and they still have you in an induced coma. I met your parents. It was weird. It IS weird. That they know I even exist at all. But even more that they don't know that you're everything to me. Your mom seems really nice. I see why it'd be hard to think about letting her go. Despite everything, I can tell she really loves you.

Sometimes when they both leave, I sneak into your room for a couple of minutes to hold your hand. I know you'd probably give me shit for being too risky, but you don't know what it's like to be here with you . . . without you.

I so wish it was me in that bed, because it should be. This is all my fault. You didn't want to do it. You told me you didn't want to do it. I am so fucking sorry. I'm sorry, Stevie. Please wake up.

I love you,

Nora

I flip to the next page.

June 23

Dear Stevie,

It's been eleven days. I overheard the doctor today and she said they're waiting for you to wake up now. I really need . . .

I stop reading and fan through the pages, each one dated a day after the last. A handwritten letter for every single day of the summer up until that afternoon I went to meet her in the woods, when she told me about each item in the box. She must have put this in there before she gave it back to me after our campfire.

I flip back to the beginning and read the entire thing, page by page, the words blurring as I constantly have to dry my eyes. Each letter helps me understand exactly what it all felt like for her, especially with everything she was going through at home. Each one breaks my heart a little more.

After the final letter, I turn the page to find a quote that she cut out and taped into the middle of the lined paper.

If you remember me, then I don't care if everyone else forgets.
—Haruki Murakami

I take a deep breath so I don't *really* cry, so my parents don't hear me, and I hug the notebook against my chest.

I try not to think about the look on Nora's face when her mom walked in, the way her hand clenched onto my arm, because she was completely terrified. I try not to think about the way her mom grabbed her around the jaw and threw her like a rag doll into the dresser.

I try not to think about how at some point tonight or maybe in the morning, she's going to wake up, and I won't be there next to her anymore. She'll be all alone.

We shouldn't have to live like this. I don't *want* to live like this. And Nora . . . she can't stay here at all. Not now. In a little over a week Ryan's parents will be back and he'll be gone and she'll have absolutely nowhere to live. And what am I going to do now that I know the truth about my mom? Now that I know she doesn't love me as much as I thought she always did. As unconditionally. Am I just supposed to go to Bower and pretend it's what I want because it's really what she wants? Should I sacrifice my dreams and my happiness to fix something I didn't even break?

That's no way to live my life, and I want to *live*.

I want to live my life with Nora.

My eyes fall onto the rest of our things on my bed. The stack of Polaroids taken in the woods. My acceptance letter from UCLA. The California travel guide . . .

I sit bolt upright and gasp in a breath as an idea forms.

A *crazy* idea.

It percolates in my brain for a few minutes as I sit there, connecting all the dots.

Huh.

A month ago I thought it would be so far out of the realm of possibility, but now . . . maybe not so much.

There aren't many certainties in my life right now.

But Nora? I am certain about Nora. I will always be certain about Nora.

Nora can't stay here and I can't stay here without Nora.

But also . . . *I* don't want to stay here.

And maybe I don't have to.

CHAPTER 35

THE SECOND I WAKE UP IN THE MORNING, I HOP OUT of bed and throw my tangled hair into a messy bun. Then grab the shoe box out of the air duct and dig out our winning lottery ticket. I tuck it into my backpack as I head downstairs to carefully slip out the front door while my mom is watering plants on the back deck. I drive straight to the corner market just down the street.

You still at home? I text Ryan as I wait for the cashier to count out my seventeen dollars of winnings.

Just about to head out, he replies.

Can you leave your front door open? I'm on my way, I text back.

The cashier hands over the money and I head out the glass door, then slide into my car. I try my best to keep my speed somewhere close to the limit, but it's almost impossible at this point. I finally throw my car into park when I arrive in Ryan's driveway, then hurry in through the front door. Nora jumps slightly at the kitchen island, where she's eating a bowl of Rice Krispies.

"Sorry," I say, dragging my hand along her shoulders as I step behind her and sit up on one of the barstools.

She turns to face me and I'm surprised to see that the bruise is all gone. "Your face. It's . . ." When I look closer, I notice a layer of something covering it. It's down on her jaw, too, where her mom was holding her.

"Ryan gave me some of his mom's cover-up," she says, her voice a little hoarse. "I know it still probably looks like shit and my eyes are all puffy—"

"Stop," I tell her, planting a kiss on each one. "You look beautiful."

"Liar," she replies.

Both of us are quiet as I watch her eat spoonful after spoonful of cereal until all that's left is almond milk.

"I thought maybe she'd call, but . . ." Nora shrugs and shakes her head.

"Would you really go back there even if she had?" I ask, surprised but trying not to sound insensitive.

"I don't know. I don't know what I'm supposed to do now," she replies.

"About that . . . I've got something for you," I reply, reaching into my pocket and then holding out the small wad of cash.

"What's that for?" she asks, furrowing her brow at me.

"Just take it. It's for both of us."

"Gee, thanks," she says sarcastically as she slips it out of my fingers.

I lean forward as I watch her unfold it and fan out the bills, a ten, a five, and two ones. "I'll try not to spend it all in one—" She stops, her eyes widening as she shuffles through the bills again . . . and again . . .

Finally, she looks up at me, and an uncontrollable grin covers my entire face as I watch her realize what I'm telling her.

"No. W-we can't. You don't even remember—" Her voice trails off.

"Look. I know I can't remember our relationship. I don't remember meeting you or going on our first date or our first kiss or our thousandth. I don't remember anything from that time and I might not ever, but . . . Somehow, when I'm with you some deep-down part of me remembers and tells me that you're right, that we are everything. It's hard to explain. I don't know how this is possible, but I don't think I ever really stopped loving you, Nora." I twist her barstool toward me, taking her face in my hands.

She rubs her cheek against my palm, and I can almost feel her holding her breath.

"I want to be with you now. For real. Out in the world, not hiding away in the woods, not hiding away *anywhere* or from any*one*. I want to drink coffee with you before I go to my classes at UCLA. I want to stay up too late watching whatever the hell *Dickinson* is. I want to make friends with people who are the same as us, and different, too. I want to do it all with you."

I already see her eyes well up but I keep going.

"And who knows, maybe it won't work out. Maybe I'll hate your gross vegan cooking and you'll hate that I never throw my dirty clothes into the hamper, but . . . we deserve a shot, Nora," I tell her as both of us are smiling and crying and maybe thinking about all the things that could one day become mundane.

She finally releases whatever she's been holding in and it comes out as some combination of a laugh/cry/snort.

"We're going to need a lot more than this," she says, tossing the money down beside us.

"You're in?" I ask, throwing my arms around her and pulling her in as close as I can.

"I've always been in," she whispers.

The next day we sit on the floor of Ryan's guest bedroom with a notebook and pen, ready to get this plan in motion. I have no idea where to start, but we had all this figured out once, so hopefully Nora can steer the ship.

"Ryan's parents will be back on August twenty-fourth so I have to be out by then. But if we leave the next day, I could spend the last night in Wyatt at Griffin's Motel, then we could ride to the airport with Ryan that morning," Nora suggests, writing the date down in front of us. I stare at it, doing the math in my head, and then let out a sigh.

"That's in nine days," I reply. We have nine days to pick up *everything* and move across the country, just the two of us. Only nine days left to live the only life I've ever known.

"Is it too crazy?" she asks. But I look at Nora and remember that I'm leaving it behind for a better one. As scary as it might be, it's even more exhilarating. And finally my future feels right.

"No. No, let's make it happen. So, the first thing I guess is figuring out our budget?" I open up the banking app on my phone and flip it around to show Nora: $2,237.15. "Do you think this'll be enough to get us out there?" I ask, already cringing.

"Uh . . . no." She laughs and then gets up to retrieve me the box from beside her duffel bag. "But this should be." She hands it to me and when I open it up, my jaw drops open. I have never seen this much cash in my life.

"Oh my God, Nora, did you rob a bank?" I ask, fanning through a pile of twenties, fifties, and hundreds.

"I've been saving for a rainy day."

"This is all from the farm?" I ask, my gaping mouth turning up into a smile. "Jeez, you must've worked *a lot*. How much money is this?"

She reaches into the box and pulls out a tiny notepad, reading off the last line. "Fifteen thousand, four hundred and twenty dollars."

"Oh *SHIT*. We're moving to Beverly Hills!" I shout, and Nora laughs.

"Slow down, Mike Tyson. See, this is exactly why *I* will be in charge of our finances." She puts the lid back over the money and slides it away from me.

"Says the girl with a giant pile of money in a box?" I ask.

"Key words being *giant* and *pile*." She begins scribbling words down in the notebook as she goes on. "And we'll be lucky to get back into a studio apartment in the building we found in Palms. Then we have to pay first month's rent and security deposit, get our bus passes, at least get, like . . . a mattress to sleep on. Then there are pots, pans, linens, utilities, *food*."

"Okay, yeah. We have *a lot* to do. I sent a few emails to different people in admissions this morning to explain why I haven't been in contact and hopefully get signed up for some classes."

"We've gotta buy all your textbooks, too," she adds. "And get your financial aid sorted."

I excitedly reach across to grab her hand before we get overwhelmed. "Nora. I'm going to be a freaking *Bruin*! Me!"

"I *know*." She smiles. "I can't wait for you to show me around campus. When does semester start again?"

"September eighteenth, but I think it'll be good to get there with plenty of time to get settled, you know? Maybe I can even find a campus job or something before then."

"That's true."

"Do you think we'll be able to find an apartment on such short notice if we can't get into that building?" I ask.

"I don't know, but I'm going to spend the rest of the day calling around until I get it figured out." She pulls Safari up on her phone and starts typing. "I'm going to give you some of this cash to deposit into your account, so you can wire the money for rent when I do find one, and buy our plane tickets and stuff."

"Oh, so you *do* trust me with the money?" I ask, smirking.

"Just don't spend it all on a cow. Okay?" she jokes, and I roll my eyes at her.

She sets her phone and pen down for a second, and the two of us look at each other. All of this feels sort of like a dream. Like I'm going to wake up and laugh that I thought I would *actually* move across the country with Nora.

"Are you good?" she asks.

"I think so." I nod, taking a deep breath in.

"Hey, Stevie?" Nora says, moving the notebook aside so she can scoot her knees up against mine. She holds my eyes and takes both of my nervous hands securely in hers. "We're going to be okay."

And I think she's saying it for herself as much as she's saying it for me.

CHAPTER 36

NORA AND I SPEND THE NEXT WEEK GETTING ALL of our plans into place. Together, we find and get a deposit down on an apartment we hope is livable, book our plane tickets out of Pittsburgh, and set up our bus passes.

When I told Kendra I needed to talk to her the other day, she thought I was going to ask for more hours permanently. She looked more than a little disappointed when I gave her my notice, but I just told her I wanted to focus on my studies this upcoming year. And she seemed to accept that.

Then I finally got a reply from the UCLA admissions office and they were more than understanding about why I haven't been in contact all summer. After they set me up with an advisor, the two of us hopped on a Zoom call to figure out my class schedule. We decided to take it slow with a semester of the most basic gen-eds in five different areas, since I might need to play some catchup anyway. And that's actually perfect, because I still have no idea what I want to major in.

In between, it's hard for me to interact normally with my mom at first, but every day when I say good night to her, I'm a little less angry. And by the last day before we leave, the only thing I really feel when I look at her is, well . . . sad. When I look at *both* of my parents, really.

"Hey, guys," I say to them early that evening. My dad is actually home before it's pitch-black out for once. He's sitting on the couch watching Fox News and flipping through a hunting magazine, and my mom is emptying the dishwasher in the kitchen.

"Hey, kid, what's up?" Dad asks, sitting up a little.

"You two want to go out to eat tonight? My treat," I offer.

"Oh, you don't have to pay, sweetie. You thinking Lola's or . . . ?"

"I want to. Actually, I was thinking we could go to Valley Grille over in Tipton," I suggest.

"What's the occasion?" my mom asks, holding a stack of clean plates.

I shrug. "Just thought it'd be nice to go somewhere different, spend some time together."

. . . *Before I leave forever.*

The Valley Grille is packed to the gills tonight, every table full. We haven't been over here since we celebrated my mom's fortieth birthday when I was in fifth grade. It's nothing fancy. I mean, it's not earning any Michelin stars in its lifetime, but I think it's the nicest place we have within thirty miles and that feels right for tonight.

The host walks us through the tables and seats us at a booth against the wall.

The only thing louder than the group of men watching the

Pirates game at the bar is the group of old ladies in the corner playing cards for nickels. On top of that, one of the kids from the family of six next to us has spilled his milk not once, not twice, but *three* times, and his mom is still insisting that he's too old for a sippy cup.

Okay. Maybe it's not quite as nice as I remember, but it doesn't matter. I'm still going to make the most of it.

The waitress brings the little boy another glass of milk and then plasters on a smile to introduce herself to us and take our orders.

"My daughter's paying so I'll take the biggest steak you've got," my dad says, with a mischievous grin that I haven't seen much of all summer.

I laugh and shake my head at him, because I know he's waiting to get a rise out of me, and this poor waitress is just trying to get through her shift.

"Just kidding. Give me a Bud and the house burger, medium rare, with fries," he says, closing his menu.

"You're in a good mood," my mom says to him after the waitress leaves to put our orders in.

He sits back in his chair and lets out a breath of relief. "It's nice to be done at the garage a little earlier today, and out to eat with my family."

I agree. I'm glad to be hanging out with Dad from before, the one who isn't constantly saying something offensive or thoughtless. But it also frustrates the hell out of me too. He really couldn't have been home earlier any other days this summer? He waits until *now*, the night before I leave, to find some time in his busy schedule to spend a couple of good hours with me?

My mom looks at him pointedly, like she wants him to say something, and he seems to take the hint.

"Stevie, I—well . . . ," he starts, his face turning down toward the table. "I just want to say that I'm sorry I haven't been around more all summer with you and your mom." He looks right at me. "I've, umm . . . just been trying to get ahead of all these medical bills we've been getting."

Oh.

"Is it really bad?" I ask, cringing. Guilt bubbles up inside of me, thinking about the envelope from early summer I'd forgotten about. The reason he isn't around more is *because* of me, but not because he didn't want to be spending time with me. I wish he'd told me sooner, instead of it being another secret getting between us.

"Ah." He waves his hand away like it's nothing. "That's not for you to worry about, kiddo. Your dad's got it covered." He winks and puts on a face that makes me feel like everything is genuinely okay, even though it really might not be. But I also have to remind myself that he's said some pretty awful things this summer that have driven a wedge between us. So it isn't all my fault, and it isn't *just* because of the bills.

My mom must've never told him that I tried to come out to her. He wouldn't be able to hide his feelings about it as well as she does.

I wonder what would happen if I did tell him. If I told him right now.

Each time I play through the scenario in my head, the outcome just gets worse as my brain comes up with new and terrible ways he could react. The last one I let myself imagine is him flipping the table over, the Sierra Mist and chicken sandwich I ordered flying across the milk-saturated carpet.

"Earth to Stevie," my mom says, and my vision refocuses as she waves her hand in front of my face. I realize I've just been staring at the two of them for the past minute or so.

"Sorry, I'm back. I'm here." I shake the thoughts away as the waitress drops off our drinks.

"I was saying I'm volunteering to work the farmers' market tomorrow if you want to come with me. I'm sure they could use the extra hands. It goes until four thirty," she says to me.

"Oh." Ryan and Nora are picking me up for the airport at 4:15 tomorrow. "I think I'll stay home, actually, gotta catch up on sleep before school starts," I reply.

We make some small talk over the next twenty minutes or so, until our food comes. It's been so long since we've all had a sit-down meal together that I think we all need a little warm-up time. But after our food comes and we all dig in, everything starts to feel much more natural. Closer to how things used to be.

"You know, this place used to be a real dive," my dad says, washing his burger down with a swig of beer. Then he gets on a roll of telling stories from when he was in college and used to come here with his buddies. I've heard most of them before, but he never manages to tell exactly the same story twice and his delivery makes me laugh.

He continues, ". . . so I get up on that bar, get a running start, and body-slide the whole way down the thirty-foot bar. People's beers and empty glasses went flying everywhere!"

"Last time you told that story the bar was only twenty-five feet long."

"Bullshit." He smiles, shaking his head at Mom.

"No, she's right, Dad. I think you add a few more feet every time you tell it," I add.

"Ah, what do you guys know," he replies. He tries to hide his guilty smile behind his beer as he swallows the last gulp.

"Should we swing through Dairy Queen on the way home like old times?" my mom asks as I take my debit card back out of the check holder. "I know it's been a while, but—"

"That'd be great," I reply before she can even finish.

Later we pull out of the Dairy Queen parking lot, my dad digging into his hot fudge sundae stacked miles high in a plastic cup as my mom and I try to keep our twists with rainbow sprinkles from dripping over the sides of our cones.

"It's been a *long* time since we've done this as a family, hasn't it? What, five, six years?" Dad asks. He's not wrong. We used to come at least once per week over the summers when I was a kid. Then we started coming less and less each year, until finally a whole summer had passed and we hadn't gone a single time. I'm not even really sure why. I've been thinking things changed so much these past two years I can't remember, but maybe things were changing well before that.

"At least. I miss doing this kind of stuff with *both* of you. We should make time to do it more often," my mom says, glancing back at me as she pulls up to a red light.

I smile and nod and try to keep myself right here in the car with them, instead of thinking about what's changed and what will change tomorrow. My mom swipes my dad's red spoon out of the side of his sundae and steals a bite out of the bottom.

"'Ey!" he says, turning away from her. "Don't be taking all the good stuff!"

"I want some peanuts!"

"Then you should've ordered some," he replies with a laugh.

I smile, watching them fight over the spoon like kids until my dad gives in and lets her have one more scoop just before the light turns green.

As we drive back toward Wyatt, I open the window and breathe in the grass and the goldenrod, and the occasional whiff of cow manure.

A few minutes later my mom peels the paper off her cone and chucks the rest out the window just like she always used to. I've never been sure if it's considered littering or not, but I've always found it pretty entertaining. Especially when she doesn't throw it hard enough and it sticks to the side of her car like a badge of shame.

"Mom, you want to take Methodist Road? Take the long way home?" I ask, like that will make this night last forever.

"Let's do it." She turns off the main road and onto a smaller one with no lines and tall grass hanging over the edges, the music quietly humming in the background as the bright-orange sun sets below the pink-and-blue cotton-candy sky.

This is the type of night I was hoping for when my dad was going to rent the boat. This is what I've been longing for all summer. A day that feels like old times, like things are *normal* between us. And finally, *finally* I get it . . . right before I'm about to leave forever. Our last night together. It's almost unfair.

And on top of it all, "So Far Away" by Carole King starts playing over the radio.

"Hey, it's our song, guys!" my mom says.

"Gosh, I haven't heard this in years," Dad says. The moment he turns up the volume, I'm transported back to my childhood, when I used to make them play it on a loop and we'd all sing along together.

I try to join in with them without my voice cracking, but it's no use and I resign myself to biting the inside of my cheek for the rest of the ride home, thankful for the cover of darkness setting in.

I close my eyes and listen to the two of them, my mom slightly off-key but giving it her all and my dad jumping back and forth between singing and whistling.

I shouldn't have to lose all this just for being who I am, but that's exactly what's going to happen after they read my letter tomorrow.

Still, if I'm only going to get a few more moments with them . . . I'm glad they can be exactly like this.

CHAPTER 37

A S I STAND AT THE BOTTOM OF THE STAIRS WATCH-ing my parents move around the kitchen the next morning, I try to remember all the little details that I've never taken the time to notice before.

The way my dad leaves the sugar canister open for my mom when he's done and shuts every cabinet door behind her. The way my mom closes her eyes and hovers over her WORLD'S BEST MOM mug before she takes a sip of her steaming coffee. The way they move around each other, hands dragging across each other's arms and backs so they orbit and never fully collide. I don't ever want to forget that.

"Oh shit," my mom curses as she bangs her mug on the corner of the countertop. Another green-and-white ceramic chip breaks off and falls to the floor.

"I think it might be time for a new one anyway, Mom," I tell her, making my presence known as I walk into the kitchen.

She drops her jaw dramatically.

"You wash your mouth out with soap! This is the perfect mug," she replies, clutching it tight to her chest like it's really something that was worth holding on to for all these years.

"If you say so," I say as I force a smile and swallow the

tears that have been scratching behind my eyes all morning.

"I'm headin' out," my dad announces, slipping on his boots behind me.

I'm not sure that I've even hugged him once since I woke up in the hospital, but before he has the chance to turn and leave through the front door, I run over and throw my arms around him.

"I love you, Dad," I whisper.

He tenses up at first, surprised I'm sure, but then his strong arms settle around me as I turn my face into his coveralls. I've never liked the way the smell of the garage follows him everywhere he goes, but this morning I find some sort of comfort in it as my fingers rub against the peeling vinyl letters across his back, spelling out GREEN'S AUTO REPAIR.

"All right. I'll see you tonight, kiddo." He kisses the top of my head.

An *I love you too* would've been nice, but my dad's never been particularly great when it comes to feelings. It doesn't mean he doesn't love me. I know he does . . . well, for now, at least. After he reads my letter tonight, he might feel a little different, so maybe it's best that I don't have to hear it from him now and imagine him regretting it.

He lets me go and turns for the door at the same time.

I blink the tears out of my eyes, doing simple math problems in my head to think about anything other than *this*. To force my emotions down somewhere deep.

"Here's your coffee, Stevie. I'll see you tonight," my mom says from behind me as I watch my dad climb into his truck out the front window.

Wait. She wasn't supposed to leave so early. We were supposed to have more time.

I try to calm my breathing.

$21 \times 3 = 63$

$128 \div 2 = 64$

$7 + 5 = 12$

"Where are you going? The farmers' market doesn't open until nine. I was thinking we could have breakfast before you go," I say, keeping my back to her, knowing what will happen if I have to look at her.

"Anne wants me there at eight to help set up," she says.

A tear rolls down my cheek.

$32 \times 6 = 192$

$47 - 28 = 19$

Her hand settles on my back and my dad's truck is nothing but a blur as it disappears around the oak tree that the three of us planted together when I was a kid.

$74 \div 3 = two, carry the one \ldots shit.$

"Stevie, what's wrong?" my mom asks. Concern fills her voice as she spins me around, her dark-brown eyes meeting mine.

"I'm just . . ." I could tell her. Right here. I could tell her everything and hope that things would go differently this time. ". . . I wish every night could be like last night," I finish lamely, the rest of it getting stuck in my throat.

"Oh, sweetie." She wipes the tear off my cheek and sets the coffee she poured for me on the kitchen island behind her. "We'll have more. Okay? I promise."

I nod even though I know how wrong she is.

"Maybe we can watch a movie or start a campfire when I get back." She offers me an encouraging smile.

I don't answer her. Instead, I avoid her eyes as she pulls me into a hug. Just as she starts to let me go, I pick my arms up from where they were dangling at my sides and wrap them tightly around her, making her stay a little longer.

"I can cancel today if you want?" she asks.

"No. No. You should go," I tell her, knowing I can't have her here today for several reasons. I still have a lot of packing to do, and if she stays, it'll be that much harder for me to leave. I'm starting to fully understand why I made the decisions I made the first time around, the reason I put distance between the two of us. It wasn't just because of the way she reacted to my coming out, it was to make things easier on myself, too.

"Okay, well, text me if you need anything. I'll see you tonight," she says, giving my hand one last squeeze.

And then just like that, she's walking out the front door as if this is any other day of the week. As if I'm not moving across the country tonight. As if this isn't the last time we might see each other.

After she's gone, I reach into my back pocket and give my letter one final read before leaving it on the kitchen counter for them to find when they get home tonight. One way or another this letter is going to change everything.

Mom and Dad,

Hi. I'm sorry I have to tell you like this, but it seemed like the only way. Plus, I thought it might be a little easier to get all my thoughts out on paper.

~~I'm g~~ I'm not straight. It's still hard for me to say, but I know it's true. I found out that Nora Martin and I have been dating in secret for the last two years. That's why I was in the woods on the Martin farm that day. And I know why things fell apart between us, Mom. She told me everything that you didn't. She told me how you reacted when I tried coming out to you before. I wasn't the one who shut you out—you shut me out, the real me.

And the other part of the truth is, I was never going to stay in Wyatt. I was never going to attend Bower. I got into UCLA. Nora and I had plans to disappear to California at the end of summer, but then the accident happened and I couldn't remember any of it. I still don't, but we somehow found our way back to each other and . . . it feels an awful lot like fate.

It's how I know I love her. I really really love her.

I also really really love you. I wanted to make things different this time, but I've realized, no matter how hard I try, we can't stay here in Wyatt and be together, and I can't pretend to be someone I'm not, even if you would prefer that. I know that might be hard for you guys to accept, but it's how I feel and who I am. If there's one thing I've learned since my accident, it's that good things happen when I follow my heart, even when it's hard, even when it feels impossible.

I know you're going to be mad or disappointed in me or whatever. I know you probably hate me now. Nora's mom kicked her out, and if you feel similarly, I'll try to understand. ~~I don't~~ I won't come back, even though I'll always miss you. By the time you read this, I'll already be on my way to the airport. Please don't try to stop me, but if you want to talk, I'd be happy to talk over the phone once I get to California.

I'll be okay. I hope you will be too.

I love you,

Stevie

CHAPTER 38

AS WE WALK INTO THE AIRPORT, THE SOUND OF MY suitcase wheels rolling across the tile covers up the pounding of my heart. I check the time on my phone. My parents should be getting back home about now, so I put it into airplane mode.

Soon they'll be hunched over the kitchen island reading my note. I'm sure there will be a text waiting for me when I arrive, telling me that I'm not who they raised and that I should never come home. Or worse, nothing at all. Ever again. But I don't want to know until I'm there.

"Stevie?" Ryan asks, waving his hand in front of my face until my vision focuses on him. "Did you hear me? I'm this way." He points over his shoulder to the opposite end of the airport from where we're headed.

"Oh, okay . . ."

It surprises me that a lump rises in my throat as I look at him. He's become a really good friend this summer and I'm going to miss him. I'm so tired of saying goodbye.

"Send me a postcard," I tell him, trying to keep it light as he gives me a hug.

"Don't let those Angelenos turn you into one of *them*," he says, making me laugh.

"What does that even mean?" I ask.

"Oh, you'll see." He adjusts the strap on his bag. "See you, Nora. I know you won't turn into an Angeleno," he says, giving her a one-armed hug.

"What. Does. That. *Mean?*" I press, and both of them start laughing at my expense.

"Okay, see you guys," he says, turning away from us.

"Oh, Ryan! Wait." I jog a few steps to catch up to him, digging around in my front pocket until I pull out the pocketknife he won me at the fair.

I turn it around in my hand, running my thumb over the wood. Something that will always remind me of the person I was so desperately forcing myself to be. Once I give him this, I'll finally be free. I'll be stepping into my new chapter, my new life.

"I want you to have this," I tell him, dropping it into his hand.

"Oh my God," he says in a hushed tone, closing his hand around it as quickly as humanly possible. "Probably not the best thing to be waving around at an airport, Stevie."

Oh, right.

"Well, just put it in your checked bag," I say.

"You sure?" he asks, holding his fist up to me.

"Yeah, something to remember this place when you're eating authentic spaghetti and sweeping girls off their feet at the Spanish Steps," I tell him.

He smiles at that and tucks it into his suitcase.

"Wyatt's a pretty hard place to forget, but . . . thanks, Stevie."

I wave as we go our separate ways, but this time the sadness in my chest feels manageable, because I know this won't be the last time we see each other.

As Nora and I check our suitcases and head for the TSA line, I wonder why it feels like I'm still holding a weight on my shoulders. I thought once I got here, I would feel some sort of relief. I mean . . . I did it. I'm getting out. I *want* to go to UCLA. I want to move to California and find my place in the world. And most of all, I want to do it with Nora. I want it more than anything. But I can't shake the feeling that something is off.

"What's wrong?" she asks as we're making our way toward the front of the line.

"Nothing," I reply, thinking about checking my texts.

"Stevie, we do not have to go." She takes my hand and turns me to face her. "We can figure something else out. We can even stay in Wyatt if that's what you want."

"No. I want to go. I never wanted to stay in Wyatt, even before we met. It's just . . ." I can feel a pressure building in my chest as we move through the line. "I didn't know it would feel like this. I've wanted out of Wyatt for as long as I can remember, but now that it's actually happening the way it's happening . . . I don't know . . . It hurts."

She steps closer, cupping my cheek in her hand.

"I'm okay," I tell her, trying to convince myself of it. Trying to convince myself that I'm okay leaving, that I don't need anything from Wyatt, or *anyone*. "I'm okay," I repeat, the weight of my phone screaming at me from my pocket, telling me to check my texts *just in case*.

But I ignore it.

"Let's go. I'm ready," I tell her, grabbing the handle of my duffel bag and closing the space between us and the lady ahead of us as she steps up to the very front of the line.

Nora doesn't say anything. I'm not sure there's anything to say. She just steps up beside me, her arm pressing up against mine to let me know she's here.

"Next," the TSA agent sitting on the stool at the podium says.

That's me. I guess this is it.

As I take a step forward, I hear something way off in the distance.

My name.

It's quiet. Barely even loud enough to be heard. But I do hear it.

"Stevie!" the voice calls out again, this time slightly louder. Closer.

I hold in my breath and close my eyes as I turn, ignoring the TSA agent, who's growing impatient with me. I wait until I hear my name called a third time before I allow myself to open my eyes . . .

There on the other side of the river of people flowing past . . .

Mom and Dad.

I let my breath out in a gasp as they sprint across the tan tile.

"Ma'am, next!" the TSA agent yells, but I don't even look at her. Instead, I duck under the tape and out of line to meet them, Nora close behind me.

"Stevie!" my dad calls out, his breathing heavy and dragging, his coveralls coated in car oil and gasoline and who knows what else. My mom comes up right behind him as I step up to meet them both, all of us trying to catch our breath.

I don't know what to say. Even if I did, I'm not sure I could actually get anything out right now.

What are they doing here? Are they just here to stop me?

"Dad?" I croak out, and he immediately pulls me into him hard, almost violently, wrapping his arms around me so tight that I think he might not ever let go. But eventually he does, and as I step back, he holds up a piece of paper. My letter.

"This is . . ." He keeps his head down as he closes his big hand around my letter, crumpling it into a ball and dropping it onto the floor at our feet. "I don't care about this. I *love* you. I'm sorry if I've said things in the past to make you think that I . . . that I would ever in a million years not love you. That I would ever not want to see you again."

He still loves me.

When he picks his head up to look at me, tears spill over his cheeks, making gray lines down his face. "Look. I don't really understand all of this." He motions between me and Nora. "Okay? I don't, but . . . I *know* I don't want to lose you. Please. *Please* don't leave because of me . . ."

"Dad, you don't know what that means to me. But I'm not leaving because of you. I'm leaving because of *me*. Okay? I just . . . I know you love this town, but it'll never accept us. I can't stay in Wyatt. *We* can't." I look over my shoulder at Nora standing just behind me with our bags.

My mom steps in front of me but keeps her eyes locked on her feet. "I'm not really sure what to say. I know what I did was . . ." She shakes her head and takes a deep breath, steadying her voice. "With the Church and everyone . . . I just didn't want your life to be harder than it's already going to be . . . or maybe that's just what I told myself to feel less shitty about how I reacted that day. And then when you didn't remember, I just thought it was the second chance I'd never get otherwise. I thought things could go back to the way I so desperately wanted them to be again. But the truth is I didn't erase it. I hurt you then and again now, instead of shielding you from hurt like I wanted to, like a mom is supposed to." She finally meets my eyes. "I know I don't deserve it, but . . . if you could *ever* forgive me, Stevie, I—I . . ." She breaks down in silent tears and I pull her into my chest, the two of us clutching each other.

"I forgive you. Of course I forgive you," I tell her, and I can feel her shoulders relax around me.

"Thank you," she whispers, pulling my head down into her sweater now. "I want you to know if I could go back . . . I would tell you that it's *okay*. I would tell you that I love you, that I will always love you no matter who you fall in love with, and no matter what the Church or anyone else says. That I'll be there for you when it gets hard, not that you should avoid the hard times. I would tell you that I'm so happy you found someone to share yourself with, and I'd really want to spend time with her so I could see all the things that you see in her."

"Hi, sweetie," I hear her whisper over my shoulder to Nora, and my heart swells as I sob into her chest.

She steps back and holds me out in front of her, a big smile spread across her face. "And you got into UCLA. Oh my gosh, Stevie, I am *so* proud of you."

She's proud of me.

She takes my face in her hands, holding me so close that I can see my reflection in her pupils. I wait for her to ask me to come back home, to tell me that I don't need to rush into going.

"Now . . . You two take care of each other. Call us *anytime* from *anywhere*. I don't care how late it is or what kind of trouble you're in. You *call* us. Even if you just forgot something and need us to send it."

Wait . . . what?

I lean away from her, squinting in disbelief.

"You're going to let me go?" I ask.

My dad opens his mouth, but she takes his hand, gives it a squeeze, and throws him a look that says not to test her. And he listens.

"I know what happens if I convince you to stay, and I don't ever want to lose you the way we almost did," she says, her voice warbling near the end.

She takes a deep breath and swallows hard.

"So I'll let you go for now." She pulls me into her again, squeezing me as tightly as she can. I wrap my arms around her and dig my face into the crook of her neck, taking in the smell of her perfume.

"But it's not forever. You come back, okay? Fall break, Thanksgiving, anytime at all. Just come back. We will always be here waiting for you . . ." She steps away and extends her arms past me to the side. To Nora. "Both of you," she adds, pulling Nora into a tight hug too, making my heart practically burst.

"Thank you," Nora says, her voice a little quivery.

"I love you guys," I tell them, giving my dad another hug.

We all step back, clearing our throats and trying to get our shit together, but no matter how many times I wipe them away, tears continue to leak out of the corners of my eyes.

"We'll see you," my dad says to Nora, giving her a closed-mouth nod. He extends his hand to her and Nora shakes it.

"You two better get going or you're going to miss your flight," my mom says, sadly, but still with a reassuring smile.

"Yeah, we should go," I agree, looking between the two of them. "Well, I guess this is it."

"I guess so," she says. "Call me when you get in."

"I will." My lungs ache as they rip the Band-Aid off for all of us and begin walking toward the exit, my dad putting his arm over my mom's shoulder and holding her close.

It takes every ounce of strength I have in me to tear my gaze away from them, but as soon as I do, I'm met with Nora's hazel eyes.

And I'm hit with a surge of all kinds of emotions.

Sorrow for everything I'm leaving behind. For my parents. For mine and Nora's little secret patch of woods where we fell in love, where we lost each other, and found our way back. For Wyatt and all it once meant—the good and the bad.

Relief that I'm getting out of here, but even more that I can come back. That my parents showed up for me. That I don't have to leave my life here behind forever in order to move forward.

Hope for our future. For finding out who I want to be at UCLA, and waking up next to Nora every morning and all that we'll tackle together.

But most of all, I feel love. Real love, knowing that wherever I go, no matter what my brain forgets, I will always have

Nora looking right back at me to help me remember.

She smiles, revealing the tiny cute gap between her front teeth, and I have never been more sure of anything in my life.

I love her.

Oh my God, do I love her.

I slide my hands up her arms that I could never in a million years get tired of touching, and onto her neck, my fingers twisting around the tiny ponytail at the back of her head.

I pull her into me, and I kiss her. In public. For the first time ever.

Her lips twist around mine, and for once, I don't care who sees. I don't care if my parents turn around or if the TSA agent is looking or if the entire world has stopped to watch.

Because even though I still feel that pinch of shame, I remind myself that one day . . .

One day I won't.

Maybe sometimes, there's a beauty in forgetting.

ACKNOWLEDGMENTS

First, I'd like to give a HUGE thank-you to my editor, Alexa Pastor, for all the hours you poured into every single draft of this book. It can be really hard for me to figure out what needs to change in order to make my stories better, and you're always SO good at steering the ship and making sure I don't get lost in it all. It always amazes me. And thank you to the rest of the crew at Simon & Schuster for all the work you do.

To my agent, Emily Van Beek, thanks for believing in this book from the very beginning and for always being my biggest champion.

Thank you to Elissa Alves, for designing that amazing submission package that I still totally stare at once in a while. And thanks to Sydney Meve.

To Mom, Dad, Mike, Luke, and Aimee, thank you for all the love and support last year. The phone calls, FaceTimes, family dinners, and game nights. I really needed all of it. I love you guys.

And lastly, thank you to my wife, Rachael, for helping me keep my head screwed on straight through all of this. 2022 would've been especially rough without you by my side, and I'm really not sure how I would've gotten through it. Thank you for reading my drafts and encouraging me to keep pushing in work and in life, and for holding my hand when that's all I needed. Growing up in Greenville, I always hoped there was someone out there for me. I just never could've dreamt up you.

ABOUT THE AUTHOR

Alyson Derrick is the coauthor of *New York Times* bestseller *She Gets the Girl*. She was born and raised in Greenville, Pennsylvania, a town where burn barrels take the place of recycling bins. After making her great escape to Pittsburgh, where she earned her bachelor's in English writing, Alyson started her own food truck, but soon realized she much prefers telling stories over slinging cheesesteaks. Alyson currently resides in Pennsylvania with her wife and their dog, Hank.

READ A GORGEOUS HATE-TO-LOVE ROMANCE
FROM ALYSON DERRICK, CO-AUTHORED
WITH RACHAEL LIPPINCOTT

FALLING IN LOVE IS AS EASY AS
A FIVE-STEP PLAN . . .